MURDER AT THE LOCH

A Selection of Further Titles by Eric Brown

The Langham and Dupré Mysteries
MURDER BY THE BOOK *
MURDER AT THE CHASE *
MURDER AT THE LOCH *

Other Titles
DEVIL'S NEBULA
HELIX WARS
THE KINGS OF ETERNITY
NECROPATH
STARSHIP SUMMER
THRESHOLD SHIFT

* *available from Severn House*

MURDER AT THE LOCH

A Langham and Dupré mystery

Eric Brown

Severn House Large Print
London & New York

This first large print edition published 2016
in Great Britain and the USA by
SEVERN HOUSE PUBLISHERS LTD of
19 Cedar Road, Sutton, Surrey, England, SM2 5DA.
First world regular print edition published 2016 by
Severn House Publishers Ltd.

British Library Cataloguing in Publication Data
A CIP catalogue record for this title is available from the British Library.

ISBN-13: 9780727894946

Severn House Publishers support the Forest Stewardship Council™
[FSC™], the leading international forest certification organisation. All
our titles that are printed on FSC certified paper carry the FSC logo.

MIX
Paper from
responsible sources
FSC® C013056

Typeset by Palimpsest Book Production Ltd,
Falkirk, Stirlingshire, Scotland.
Printed and bound in Great Britain by
T J International, Padstow, Cornwall.

Dedicated to the memory of
Marie Carson

One

'And this will be your study,' Maria said, opening the door and standing aside.

Langham entered the room and looked around in wonder. 'My word, it's huge.'

'There will be room for *all* your books, Donald, even the ones you have boxed up at the moment.'

'Luxury,' he said, staring through the window at the quiet Kensington street and the snow-covered park beyond. 'And it's warm,' he went on, already planning where he'd position his writing desk.

'It's centrally heated, unlike the icebox of your flat. I don't know how you work in such conditions.'

'Wearing a coat and a balaclava, and with a thick blanket on my lap.'

She stared at him. 'Honestly? You wear a bala-clava?' She raised a hand to her mouth. 'Oh! But you must look so funny sitting there in your balaclava with your pipe sticking out!'

Langham pulled her to him and they kissed. He gestured around the empty room. 'Don't you use this for anything at the moment?'

'The apartment is really too big for one person. I told my father this when he found it for me and he said he'd pay the rent. But he insisted I take it.'

1

'The best for his only daughter,' he said. 'But hang it all, I can't have him paying the rent once we're married. It wouldn't be right.'

It felt strange, saying the words 'once we're married'. The notion filled him with a rosy glow.

Maria strolled to the window, leaned against the sill and stared out. She wore a green trouser suit and a white blouse and looked so wonderful Langham could have wept at his good fortune. He crossed the room and slipped an arm around her waist.

'Do you know something?' she asked, turning to him. 'I think my father will insist on continuing to pay the rent. He will call it his "little present" to us.'

'We'll see. We could easily afford it, on your wage from the agency and what I earn from the books. But . . .'

'Yes?'

'Of course, I've yet to ask his permission to marry you.'

'He is no fool, Donald. He knows how I feel about you, and anyway, he likes you. He's told me so. He enjoys talking about books with you.'

Langham shrugged uncomfortably. Maria's father was the French cultural attaché to Great Britain, and Langham could not help but feel intellectually inferior to the great man whenever they met. He'd never told Maria this – she assumed his awkwardness was due to social stigma on Langham's part. 'Oh, you English and your preoccupation with class!' she'd chided him more than once.

They returned to the sitting room, and Maria

went into the kitchen and made a pot of tea. Langham wallowed on the sofa and picked up an old issue of *The Sketch* from the side table, turning to Rupert Croft-Cooke's novel reviews.

Earlier that afternoon Maria had phoned Langham to say she was finishing work at the agency and would he care to join her for tea? He'd finished the third draft of his latest thriller a week ago and was at the stage of post-novel satisfaction when he took every opportunity to set aside whatever he was working on – reading for review, in this case – and indulge himself. He'd even suggested they dine out that evening at the Moulin Bleu in Highgate.

Maria returned with the tea tray and poured two cups of Earl Grey. 'We need to decide what we are going to do on Tuesday when Charles is released,' she said, sitting beside him on the sofa and raising the bone china to her rouged lips.

'Didn't I suggest dinner at Claridge's?' he said. 'We could invite a few friends.'

'I wonder if Charles will feel like socializing so soon after gaining his freedom?'

Her boss, and Langham's literary agent, Charles Elder, was coming to the end of a sentence on a charge of gross indecency in a public bathhouse – a conviction which Langham considered a travesty of justice. He'd served four months and was due for release on Tuesday.

'They're letting me out early on account of my good behaviour!' Charles had carolled when Langham and Maria had last visited him at Wormwood Scrubs. 'I've been a paragon, my

3

dears! I must say, I've rather taken to working in the library, and some of my colleagues are delightful fellows!'

Langham had feared that a spell at Her Majesty's pleasure would bode ill for Charles's finer sensibilities, but the gargantuan epicurean had shown a resolve and fortitude that Langham never knew he possessed.

'We could always have a little gathering here, then?' Langham said. 'It'd be nice to mark the occasion in some way.'

'And I could cook one of Charles's favourites – beef Wellington, perhaps – and buy a few bottles of Beaujolais. We could ask Caroline if she'd care to come along, and how about Alasdair?'

Caroline de Quincy was a retired American actress they'd met that summer and seen frequently since, a lovely woman with a droll sense of humour; Alasdair Endicott was a young novelist, shy and retiring but 'sound' in Langham's opinion.

'Let's do that,' he said. 'A small gathering will make Charles less likely to feel that he needs to perform.'

'Oh,' Maria laughed. 'But you know Charles – of course he'll need to put on a show. He'll regale the party with his many exploits behind the grey walls of the Scrubs.'

'It'll be good to have him back,' Langham said. 'I still feel bitter about the sentence. Bitter and impotent.'

He was saved from reflecting further on the injustice by the shrilling of the telephone bell across the room. Maria rose to answer the call.

4

'Hello?' she said. 'Oh, yes. Donald is here. I'll hand you over.'

Langham crossed to the bureau and sat down. 'Ralph Ryland,' Maria said, handing him the receiver.

She resumed her seat on the sofa, watching him as he said, 'Ralph, how did you know I was here?'

'Tried your place,' the private detective said. 'No answer. So I put me deerstalker on.'

'I might have guessed. How are things at the agency? Busy?'

'Busy? I'm rushed off me ruddy feet, if you want the truth.'

'That's good, isn't it?'

'Sometimes I bloody well wonder,' the cockney said. 'Look, something's come up.'

'I'm not sure I like the sound of that.' Langham looked across at Maria, who was frowning in enquiry.

'You recall Major Gordon?' Ryland asked.

'How could I forget him!' Gordon had been their commanding officer in Madagascar and India, an optimistic, fair-minded Scot who'd always had the welfare of his men at heart. Langham had served under him for five years in Field Security, and cherished fond memories of the diminutive, moustachioed major. 'Nothing wrong with him, is there?'

'Not as such – at the moment.'

'What do you mean, "at the moment"?'

'I've just had a call from him,' Ryland said. 'He's always kept in touch.'

'Yes, he drops me a note from time to time

5

when he's read one of my books. What did he want?'

'Well, to cut a long story short, Don, he thinks someone wants to kill him.'

'Kill him?' He stared across at a startled Maria. 'But who on earth would want to kill the major?'

'The thing is he didn't sound sure that he *was* the intended target. He said that "they" might have been after someone else. I asked for details, of course, but the old boy was cagey. He said he didn't want to say too much over the blower, just said something about a shooting incident. He wants me to go up there and do a bit of snooping around.'

'And you intend to, of course?'

'Of course. I'd do it for free, for the old boy – but Gordon said he'd pay the going rate. I'm heading up there tomorrow.'

'Doesn't he live somewhere in the Highlands?'

'That's right. Five hundred bloody miles away. He owns an old castle in the back of beyond, bought for a song just after the war. It was a pile of ruins, but he's done it up over the years and opened it in 'fifty-two as a hotel. He's invited me to stay for a few days, meet the guests and try to find out what's going on.'

'Right-o,' Langham said, wondering at the reason for Ryland's call and fearing the answer. 'But I don't quite see . . .'

Across the room, Maria was miming, *What is it, Donald?*

'Well, y'see . . . I was wondering – seeing as how you and the major were pretty close during the war, and on account of the fact that some of

6

his guests sound a bit lah-di-dah for my taste . . . I was wondering if you'd care to come along as back-up? Moral support, like. They say two minds are better than one. And also – on the way – I have a proposition to put to you.'

Langham frowned. 'A proposition?'

'I'll tell you on the train. How about it?'

'Well . . . Look, Ralph, I need to think about this. When did you say you're setting off?'

'Catching the six thirty a.m. from King's Cross, changing at Edinburgh and arriving at Inverness around three. I've hired a car from a local garage and I hope to reach the castle in time for dinner.'

'The thing is when are you planning to come back? I have something happening on Tuesday.'

'There's a direct sleeper from Inverness to London at six o'clock on Monday evening. Plan is go up there tomorrow, take a shufti on Sunday and most of Monday, and head back on the sleeper. You'd be back in the Smoke early Tuesday morning.'

'Well . . .' Langham dithered.

'Not got the frighteners on account of the Barnes crash, Don?'

'Of course not,' he said truthfully. Ryland was referring to the signal failure at Barnes a week earlier which had resulted in the deaths of thirteen passengers.

'Ah!' Ryland said with sudden illumination. 'Your little lovebird. You don't want to be parted from the missus-to-be, eh?'

'That's more like it,' Langham admitted. 'Look, Ralph, I'll talk it over with Maria right away and call you back.'

7

'I'm at the office till six,' Ryland said, and rang off.

'Well,' Maria said as he joined her on the sofa, 'what was that all about?'

He poured himself a second cup of tea and recounted what Ryland had said.

'Strange,' Maria said when he'd finished. 'And I wonder what that "proposition" might be?'

Langham shook his head. 'I can't begin to imagine.'

'Well, do you intend to go?'

He looked out of the window. A new flurry of snow was obliterating the view of the park. 'I must admit the thought of the Highlands in the middle of winter when I could be snugly at home with you . . . The thing is—'

'Mmm?'

'I have a soft spot for the old major. He's a good sort. I hate to think that he feels he's under some kind of threat. There's obviously something going on.'

'Then you must go. And as Ralph said, there's a train back on Monday evening. You'll be here in time for Charles's release.'

He thought about it. 'Tell you what, how about you come along too? I'm sure Ralph wouldn't mind, and the major would be overjoyed to meet you.'

Maria was shaking her head. 'Oh, I would love to, Donald. But I cannot, remember? That meeting with Travers from Gollancz tomorrow? I've put it off once already.'

'Dash it, Maria. I'll miss you like crazy.'

'It is only for three days, and then you'll be

8

back in my arms. I think you must do it, for both Ralph and the major.'

Langham nodded. 'Very well, I'll ring Ralph now.'

'And I shall dress for dinner, *mon cher*,' Maria said, and swept into the adjoining bedroom.

Langham crossed to the bureau and picked up the phone, hesitated at the thought of what he might be letting himself in for, then dialled Wandsworth 4545.

Two

The train tore through the snow-covered Yorkshire countryside.

Langham had awoken at the ungodly hour of five thirty a.m. in order to catch a taxi to take him to King's Cross in time for the six thirty a.m. express to Edinburgh. He'd spent the night at Maria's, and it had taken a supreme effort of will to ease himself from her embrace and dress, despite the balm of central heating.

He'd slept for the first few hours of the journey and had only awoken ten minutes ago to find the grey, mean streets of north London far behind him. The rolling dales of north Yorkshire met his waking gaze, the undulating snow interrupted only by the stark lines of dry-stone walls, scattered sheep and the occasional lonely farmhouse.

In the seat opposite, Ralph Ryland pulled a

9

thermos flask from his travelling bag and poured two mugs of tea. The private detective was dressed, bizarrely, in herringbone tweeds and a flat cap, the apparel sitting uneasily on his slight frame and weasel-thin head. He usually affected a frayed rayon suit and a bootlace tie like some shady East End spiv.

Langham accepted a mug of sweet, milky tea, took a sip and tried not to pull a disgusted face. He preferred his brew black, without sugar.

'I was meaning to ask at King's Cross,' Langham said, indicating Ryland's tweeds, 'why the get-up?'

Ryland shot his sleeves proudly. 'Used to be my brother's, but I inherited it when the Jerries did for him at Dunkirk. First time I've worn it. I thought, seeing as how I'll be in the Highlands, it'd be fitting to wear Doug's old tweeds. And Major Gordon said he'd take us shooting.'

'I think I'll remain before the roaring fire, sampling his whisky,' Langham said.

Ryland raised his mug. 'What do you think of the brew?'

Langham smiled. 'It brings back memories,' he said. It did – unpleasant ones – of the noxious, sickly sweet concoctions served by the NAAFI during the war.

'Here, you remember the chai those wallahs made in India, Don? They brewed it in a kettle: tea leaves, condensed milk, sugar and all.' Ryland gazed through the window at the passing winter landscape. 'You ever miss those days?'

'Madagascar and India? No, I don't really. To be honest, they seem such a long time ago

– events that belonged to the life of another person. Don't get me wrong, I had some good times back then. I suppose I feel a bit guilty saying I didn't have a bad war, but it's true.' He shrugged. 'But no, I can't say that I miss them. You?'

'Now and again I do, when I've been doing nothing but routine cases for weeks and weeks and think I could do with a bit of action. I think back to Diego-Suarez, and then that mission in Goa looking for them Italian spies . . . and I wish I were back there. But then an interesting case comes up and I forget all about the war.'

'I suppose I live vicariously through my books,' Langham admitted. 'I send Sam Brooke out on a case and let him do all the running about for me. I've always wanted to write for a living, and I'm happy.'

Ryland stroked his thin ginger moustache which curved lugubriously around his small mouth. He was watching Langham with a calculating expression.

'What?' Langham asked.

'That proposition I mentioned over the blower . . .'

Langham had wondered about Ryland's 'proposition' when he'd awoken in the early hours, Maria warmly asleep beside him. He thought he knew what the detective was about to say.

'I was thinking recently,' Ryland said. 'Things are getting busy at the agency. Sometimes I have to turn away work. Not that I'm complaining – it means I can pick and choose what I do, you see. But it seems a crying shame, turning away potentially lucrative cases.' He shrugged his bottle-slim shoulders. 'I'm a one-man band, Don, and I can only take on so much.'

Langham smiled. 'Is all this a circumlocutory preamble to asking me if I'd care to come and work at the agency again?'

'I don't know about a circular perambulator, Don, but you've hit the nail on the head. I was thinking it'd be like old times. You could work for the agency two or three days a week, just like you did after the war. You could even pick your own cases. And you'd win both ways, see? You'd be well paid for your work and you could put it all down as research for your books.'

Langham considered the time he'd worked two days a week at Ryland's agency and how the experience had indeed fed into his books. He'd found the various cases interesting, if occasionally dangerous – the perfect accompaniment to the sedentary life of a desk-bound writer.

The odd thing was that in the early hours of that morning, when he'd guessed what Ryland wanted, he hadn't dismissed the notion out of hand. His books brought in enough to keep him in the frugal bachelor lifestyle to which he'd become accustomed, but things would change when he married Maria. She had rather expensive tastes, and as he had no intention of accepting her father's largesse in paying the rent on the Kensington apartment, he'd need a little extra income.

If he worked at the agency two days a week and wrote for three or four, he could still turn out two novels a year as he was doing at the moment.

Ryland was watching him. 'Well, Don?'

'It's tempting, Ralph. I'll tell you what, I'll think about it, OK? When I get back to London I'll talk it over with Maria.'

Ryland nodded. 'Fair enough. The offer's on the table. And remember, you can pick your own cases.'

Langham sipped his disgusting tea and watched the snow-encumbered countryside slip by. The train passed over a viaduct and far below a wide river scintillated in the brilliant winter sunlight.

A little later Ryland asked, 'And how's it going with the most beautiful popsie in Kensington? Everything still strawberries and cream?'

Langham tilted his head and regarded his friend. 'Spoken with the barely suppressed cynicism of someone married for over twenty years.'

Ryland smiled. 'What did Wilde say? "Bigamy is having one too many wives, and so is monogamy"?'

'I didn't know you read Wilde, Ralph. And anyway, I thought you and Annie . . .'

Ryland's wife was a dumpy, pretty woman in her early forties whose maternal officiousness disguised a love and respect for the detective. They had teenage twin girls and lived in a neat semi-detached bungalow on a new estate in Lewisham.

'Oh, Annie's a good sort, only . . .' Ryland shrugged. 'Marriage has its moments, I suppose. But those moments become rarer and rarer the longer you're married. As you'll see for yourself, Don.'

'Well, I'll take each day as it comes and enjoy

13

things without looking too far ahead. That's my motto in life.'

Ryland finished his tea. 'Anyway, when's the wedding bells?'

'One Saturday in late May, yet to be finalized. I meant to tell you. I was wondering . . .'

'Of course you can ask me for any wedding-night tips, Don.'

'Thanks for that, but I think I'll manage. No, I was wondering if you'd care to be my best man?'

Ryland sat up in his seat; in his tweed suit with his back ramrod straight and his mouth half-open he resembled a ventriloquist's dummy whose operator had been rendered temporarily speechless.

'Gawd 'elp me, Don. You know I ain't one for giving big speeches, but I'd be honoured.'

'Excellent. I'm not into speechifying either, so we'll keep it down to just a few words, OK?'

'Suits me fine. Well, I'm flattered. Never been a best man before. Annie'll be made up, too. I'll have to hire a suit, of course.'

Langham laughed. 'Well, as long as you don't come in those tweeds.'

Ryland shot his cuffs again. 'What's wrong with it? I think I look a positive gentleman, I do.'

The detective eased himself back into his seat, closed his eyes and five minutes later was snoring soundly. Langham dug out a book he was reading for review – a gripping adventure *à la* John Buchan, appropriately enough set in the Highlands – and settled down to read.

Three

A couple of hours later the train steamed into Edinburgh Waverley station.

Langham gathered his travelling bags, nudged Ryland awake and climbed down on to the platform. They had forty minutes to wait until their connection to Inverness, and Langham suggested they have a bite to eat at the station café.

They settled themselves in the polished wooden booths beside a plate-glass window looking out over the busy platform. Travellers scurried back and forth like disturbed termites, and he wondered why people travelling by rail invariably appeared harassed, as if beset by the mortal fear of missing their train. A pall of steam hung under the high glass canopy and a prevailing air of gloom haunted the station. Or was it, Langham wondered, merely that the station harboured bad memories for him?

He stirred his tea morosely and contemplated the forlorn aspect of his desiccated-looking ham sandwich. Ryland said, 'A penny for them, Don.'

Langham looked around the café, its municipal décor and green-painted walls unchanged since that day back in 'forty-one.

'I was in Fife, on basic training with Field Security. I was in a freezing Nissan hut doing some godawful exam when a corporal came in with the telegram.'

15

'Your wife . . .' Ryland said.

'I must have told you this before.' He took a bite of his sandwich, and it tasted as insipid as it looked.

Ryland smiled. 'You were laid low with fever in Madagascar, remember? When you were lucid you ranted about Susan and what had happened.'

Langham stared at his tea and sighed. 'Cerebral haemorrhage. She was at work in a sorting office in London. Died instantly. I remember waiting here for the connection to King's Cross. I had an hour to kill but I swear, Ralph, it seemed more like three bloody hours I was here, drinking bad wartime coffee and trying to work out what I was feeling.'

'Wasn't exactly a successful marriage, was it?'

'We rushed into it without thinking and grew to regret it. We were soon strangers to each other and each resented the other as a kind of jailer. Then war came along, and I felt as if I were escaping when I joined up.'

He shook his head. 'And do you know what, Ralph? The sense of liberation when I heard that she'd passed away . . . soon followed by a crushing guilt. Only later, at the funeral, did it really hit me that Susan was dead.'

Ryland stared through the window at the hurrying travellers. 'I can see why this place gives you the blues.'

Mangy pigeons hopped amongst the crowds, pecking minuscule titbits from the concrete. Langham wondered how many thousands of pecks it took to constitute a decent meal. He

16

recalled suddenly that Susan had harboured an irrational fear of the creatures.

'All in the past, now,' he said. 'But do you understand why I consider myself so lucky to have Maria? There I was, forty and little expecting ever to find anyone again. And then Maria walks into my life like some kind of miracle. I swear I'm the luckiest man alive.'

Ryland reached across the table and tapped Langham's hand. 'And you deserve it, pal. You deserve it.'

They drained their tea, finished their sandwiches, then made their way to platform six and boarded the mail train to Inverness.

They had a compartment to themselves, for which Langham was grateful. He wondered how Maria's meeting with the editor from Gollancz was going. As the train slipped out of the station and began the slow journey north, he thought back to the early hours of that morning, with London asleep in the grip of snow and the woman he loved warm in his embrace.

'About Major Gordon,' he said a little later. 'When did he contact you?'

'Late Thursday afternoon, just as I was about to shut up shop. He was on the blower for about fifteen minutes.'

'But you said he didn't want to go into details?'

'That's right. I think he feared he might be overheard.'

'Which might indicate he thought the perpetrator was someone resident in the castle, do you think?'

'That's what occurred to me,' Ryland said. 'And

17

all he said about the incident was that it involved a shooting on a pontoon—'

Langham stopped him. 'A pontoon?'

'The castle sits on the edge of Loch Corraig. Perhaps it's something to do with salmon fishing?'

Langham was dubious. 'I might be wrong but I thought you fished for salmon in rivers, as they returned home to spawn? But a pontoon might have something to do with fishing, nevertheless.' He shrugged. 'And how did the major sound? Overly nervous? Scared?' He tried to imagine the bluff, no-nonsense major evincing any sign of trepidation, but failed.

'He seemed to be taking it in his stride, or perhaps he was putting a brave face on it.'

'And yet he had the wind up enough to ask if you'd come up and investigate.' He thought back to his conversation with Ryland yesterday. 'You mentioned the lah-di-dah guests. What did the major say about them?'

'Not a lot. Just mentioned a few names before he was interrupted.'

'Interrupted?'

'I got the impression that someone had entered the room. He wound it up pretty sharpish and rang off.'

'So, these guests?'

'He said he had a few people staying with him at the moment, but he didn't get round to listing all of them. There was a Dutch fellow, some kind of engineer, who was working over here, and a woman – he gave her name, but I can't recall it – who was a Hungarian princess or something.'

18

'Hungarian royalty?' Langham said. 'Not the kind of guest you'd expect at a Highland castle in the middle of winter. Who else?'

'The last person he mentioned was a retired professor from St Andrews.' Ryland turned his head and regarded Langham slantwise, like a fox. 'The prof was there to conduct an investigation into reported "paranormal activity". Ghosts.'

'Ghosts?' Langham rolled his eyes. 'Saints preserve me! I had enough of spooks and such nonsense at Humble Barton this summer.'

'I thought that'd get you going, Don. Meself, I don't see what's wrong with a ghost story now and then. And the thought of a spook in an ancient Scottish castle . . .'

'I don't mind the odd story,' Langham said, 'as long as that's *all* it is, a fictional story. It's when people start believing in these things as established fact that I get a little hot under the collar. The thing is,' he went on, 'I can't for the life of me believe that the major would have any truck with peddlers of such nonsense. Did he say why he'd invited this professor to the castle?'

Ryland shook his head. 'No, just that the prof had been there for quite a while.'

'And when did the incident on the pontoon occur?'

'A few days ago, on Wednesday.'

'When all the guests you mentioned were at the castle?'

'That's right.'

'And there were other guests, you said?'

'Yes, but the major didn't get round to telling me who they were.'

19

Langham nodded and stared out of the window. He had expected Scotland to be blanketed under the same fall of snow that covered much of England, but the vagaries of the British weather had spared this area of the isles. Instead a thin drizzle, more like a mist, drifted in from the north and obscured the rolling green farmland.

For the remainder of the journey to Inverness he read his book and occasionally stared out at the passing countryside. As they chugged north the rain intensified, turning from drizzle to a driving, torrential downpour. Langham was not much looking forward to the last leg of the journey, a fifty-mile drive down minor roads in descending darkness. And no doubt the hired car would be draughty and lacking such luxuries as heating.

Ryland read the *Daily Mirror* from back to front, poring with particular intensity over the sports pages and commenting on Millwall's poor showing in the league.

Twilight was already falling when the train panted into Inverness station at three twenty, fifteen minutes late. Not much could be seen of the little town, other than huddled, lighted houses and distant pine-clad hillsides. At least the rain had abated as Langham gathered his luggage, buttoned his overcoat and stepped on to the quiet platform.

A short walk through darkening streets brought them to a tiny garage. Ryland found the owner, filled in a form and handed over a guinea, and minutes later they were accelerating along the rain-slick road out of town. Langham was correct about the hired car, a battered Ford Popular – it was draughty and possessed no heating. He kept his overcoat snugly fastened and was thankful that Maria had insisted he bring his scarf.

They took the main road west and were soon heading into bleak, forested countryside. The rain started up again, drumming on the car's thin coachwork. Ryland had had the foresight to bring along a map of the Highlands, which Langham spread out on his lap.

The twilight soon deepened into darkness and the Ford's headlights cut two brilliant cones through the driving rain.

They came to a crossroads and Ryland braked. He peered through the windscreen, the wipers merely smearing the rain back and forth so that visibility was minimal.

'Can't make out a signpost, Don.'

Langham thumbed on the overhead light and peered at the map in the dim glow. He traced the road they had come along from Inverness, and, when his finger arrived at a likely looking crossroads, said, 'I think we're here. Take a left and continue for about twenty miles, then we'll come to the town of Glenross. We need to take a right there and head north-west. The castle's about four miles from Glenross.'

Ryland had conveniently marked the position of the castle with a big biro'd X beside a body of water shaped like a dolphin.

Ryland lit up a Woodbine and stuck it in the corner of his mouth; Langham followed his example, stuffed his pipe with Navy Cut and applied a match, sucking until the tobacco caught.

Ryland gunned the engine and turned left down a narrow lane.

Soon they were tooling at thirty miles an hour between forests of fir, the trees blurring by on either side. Their headlights were assisted by the illumination of a full moon which cut a phosphorescent halo through the clouds.

'Reminds me of the old days, Don,' Ryland commented at one point.

'The old days?'

'Madagascar,' the detective said.

Langham peered out at the pelting downpour, and then at Ryland. 'In what way, Ralph, does this remind you of that sultry tropical island?'

Ryland laughed. 'Not the island, but you and me, out on patrol, heading into potential danger.'

'Well, I hope it's not danger we're heading towards,' Langham said. 'What I want from this weekend is to find that the major is entirely mistaken in his fears; that the food is good, the whisky excellent and the castle warm and hospitable.'

Ryland grunted. 'I reckon we might get the last three.'

'We'll see. I'm looking forward to meeting the guests. I've never encountered Hungarian royalty before.'

'That's why I wanted you along, Don. Didn't fancy hobnobbing with stuck-up foreign royals, or retired professors, for that matter.'

Langham glanced at his friend. 'You'll be fine,

22

Ralph. These people are no better than you – they just think they are, that's all.'

'That's a great help. Meself, I'd rather socialize with me mates down the local.'

Langham smiled around the stem of his pipe and admitted to himself that, on that score, he agreed with the detective.

'Anyway,' Ryland went on, 'you'll be pleased to know that I've brought me service revolver along, just in case.'

Langham smiled. 'That's reassuring.'

Thirty minutes later they came to Glenross – and tore through it almost before Langham had registered the arrival of the small, dark houses on either side of the road. He made out the blue light of a police station and a decrepit-looking hotel. Ryland slowed down, searching for a right turning. Langham wondered if all the signposts in the vicinity, removed for reasons of security during the war, were still gathering dust in some corporation warehouse.

He turned on the overhead light and consulted the map. 'The turning should be just past the town.'

'This must be it,' Ryland said, slowing to a crawl and taking the turn.

'And now it's straight on – with a number of twists and turns along the way – until we come to the loch.' He consulted his watch. 'It's just after five. We should arrive in time for dinner.'

'Hallelujah,' Ryland said. 'I could eat a whole stag.'

'Wouldn't be surprised if venison's on the menu

at some point. Hello,' Langham exclaimed. 'Who the blazes can this be?'

Picked out in the glare of the headlights, like an actor on a stage, a tall figure stepped into the middle of the lane and signalled dramatically, as if attempting to halt a train. Ryland swore under his breath and braked, and as the car rolled to a halt Langham had a better view of the man. He wore a long cape, an improbable fedora and affected a cane. With the moonlight at his shoulder and his cane raised, he struck Langham as a very Chestertonian figure.

Langham wound down his window, admitting an icy blast of wind and a scattershot of hail. The man lowered his head from a considerable height and peered into the car.

'Would I be presumptuous in assuming you gentlemen might be travelling as far as Loch Corraig Castle?'

Ryland gestured to the back seat with his thumb. 'Hop in!'

The rear door opened and the man squeezed himself into the confined space; as well as being tall, he was bulky and carried an overstuffed valise. 'I'm in your debt, gentlemen. I didn't expect to meet another soul out in this foul weather.'

Ryland squinted over his shoulder. 'What? You mean you'd've walked it all the way to the castle?' He started the car and they set off along the lane.

'I've done it before, though admittedly in more clement weather,' the man replied. He was, Langham saw now, younger than he'd first

24

assumed – perhaps thirty, with a long, aquiline face and a Byronic mane of jet-black hair. He clutched his cane in both hands as he leaned forward between the front seats, and Langham noted that it was no ordinary staff but an expensive-looking silver-knobbed Malacca.

Langham squirmed around to offer his hand. 'Donald Langham,' he said, 'and my chauffeur is Ralph Ryland.'

'Hey, less of the chauffeur, Capt'n,' Ryland quipped. He then asked their passenger, 'But how come you're out 'ere in the middle of bleedin' nowhere?'

'I caught the sleeper from London yesterday. To cut a long story short, I kicked my heels in Inverness this morning until I picked up a lift as far as Glenross. I'm Gabriel, by the way – Gabriel Gordon.'

'You're not the major's son, by any chance?' Langham vaguely recalled the major mentioning a fifteen-year-old son while in India.

'Indeed, I have that misfortune,' Gabriel said. 'How do you know the old man?'

Ryland had lit up another Woodbine. The cigarette dangled on his lower lip as he said, bridling somewhat at the young man's disrespectful tone, 'We had the honour of serving under your father in the last war.'

'The honour, you say? Well, I've never met any of his war chums. Be interesting to hear your stories around the fire with a whisky apiece, hm? But what brings you to the castle at this godawful time of year?'

Ryland hesitated and Langham filled the breech.

25

'Just a visit for old times' sake. We both had a little time off work and thought we'd pay a call on our commanding officer.'

Gabriel hung his handsome head between the seats and regarded the pair. 'And what jobs might those be, if you don't mind my asking?'

Langham told Gabriel that he was a freelance writer.

'A hack?' the young man asked in lofty tones. 'Or do you aspire higher?'

Langham smiled. 'I write thrillers, and I like to think I do so to the best of my ability.'

'And you?' Gabriel asked, fixing Ryland with eyes as dark as Indian ink.

The detective had a ready reply. 'I travel in Hoovers.'

'A door-to-door salesman, hm?' His disdainful tone might well have been translated as, *Well, someone has to do it.*

Langham glanced at the young man. 'And you? What do you do?'

Gabriel raised his head. 'I am a *poet*,' he said. It was almost a declamation.

Langham thought that he certainly looked, with his languid hauteur, like an aspiring poetaster imitating Lord Byron. 'And have you had anything published?' He'd met many a would-be versifier whose heartfelt quatrains had seen print only in their imaginations.

'A couple of dozen pieces in various literary magazines,' Gabriel said, 'and my first volume is out next spring from the small but select firm of Harris and Thomson.'

Langham had never heard of them – no doubt

26

some fly-by-night printers who turned a profit by persuading thwarted poets to subsidise the publication of their own works.

The Ford puttered through the driving rain. With the addition of a third body to the car's cramped confines – and a large, perspiring body at that – the temperature had risen and was almost tolerable.

Langham asked, 'What brings you to the castle? I take it you live in London?'

'Muswell Hill,' said the young man. 'I'm part of a commune of a dozen like-minded artists and poets.' He cleared his throat. 'And to answer your question, I look in on my father from time to time. Not that I care to remain for long.'

Ryland sucked on the tab end of his Woodbine and glanced at the poet. 'You don't like the place?'

'I don't mind the castle, and to a certain extent I admire what my father has done with it – resurrecting it from the moribund state to which history had consigned it. Let me say that I admire the idea, the *ideal*, of the castle. But, gentlemen, I *deplore* the use to which the old man has put it.'

'The use?' Ryland asked, nonplussed.

'I mean, a hotel, for heaven's sake? Is there anything more *infra dig* than an ancient establishment catering to the ignorance of common tourists?'

'Oh, I dunno. I quite like the idea of a beer and whisky chaser in front of a roaring log fire while a Highland wind whistles around the eaves.' And to show that he knew what he was doing, Ryland gave Langham a wink.

'So is this your first visit to the castle this year?' Langham asked.

'As a matter of fact, I was up here a month ago.'

'For long?'

'Just three days. I found the company hardly conducive to a longer stay.'

'Oh, in what way?' Ryland asked.

'Don't get me started!'

'Go on, what was wrong with 'em?' Ryland prompted, glancing at Langham. 'I'm curious, seeing as how some of 'em might still be hanging around. I heard there was some Hungarian queen or something?'

'Hungarian queen?' Gabriel spluttered. 'She's no more a member of the Hungarian royalty than you or I, but she likes to think she is. You'll find her something of a remote and icy woman.'

'How long has she been in Britain?' Langham asked.

'That I don't know, but she's been staying at the castle on and off for two or three years. I think she's taken a shine to my father.'

'And the major?' Langham asked. 'Does he reciprocate her feelings?'

Gabriel snorted. 'I rather think the old man's past all that.'

'I take it that you and your father don't get on,' Ryland said.

'We're not close. Chalk and cheese. The man doesn't have a sensitive bone in his body. Doesn't appreciate . . .' Whatever Gabriel was about to say, he stopped himself from saying it rather abruptly.

28

'Yes?' Langham prompted.

'He doesn't appreciate the finer things in life, like art, literature, poetry.'

Nor his own son's attempts at the latter, Langham thought; hence Gabriel's resentment, perhaps.

Langham asked, 'And isn't there some professor staying at the castle, conducting psychic research? Have you met him?'

'Met him? I've been bored to death by Professor Hardwick on more than one occasion. He's made it his life's work to track down some spook or other said to haunt the pile. Practically taken up residence at the castle. He's an old friend of my father's. Apparently they went to the same school, way back before the First World War.'

'They're on friendly terms?' Langham asked.

He felt Gabriel's eyes bore into him. 'What an odd question—'

Ryland was quick with, 'Don's like that. Comes of being a scribbler, see? Interested in how people get on. Isn't that right, Don?'

'Relationships fascinate me. But I apologise if you thought—'

'No, that's perfectly all right, Langham.' Gabriel was silent for a second or two, then said, 'Are they on friendly terms? I always thought they were, but then I overheard my father and Professor Hardwick arguing.'

'About the professor's work?' Ryland asked.

'I didn't hear enough to make out what the fuss was all about,' Gabriel said. 'But my father was furious, stormed out of the room and nearly skittled me in the process.'

29

'As for the professor's work,' Langham said, 'what do you make of it?'

'If you want my candid opinion, the man's utterly bonkers and his research an exercise in futility. He's one of these boffins who thinks he can detect occult goings on with all manner of up-to-the-minute scientific devices. The castle's festooned with 'em, as you'll see. Come to think of it,' he mused, 'I wonder if *that* was what the brouhaha was all about that time? Was my father concerned about guests coming a cropper on all the wires and machinery around the place?' He leaned forward suddenly. 'I say, slow down or you'll miss the sharp right turn when the firs end in about a hundred yards. It's deceptive.'

Ryland slowed, turned the corner and urged the ageing Ford up the incline. The rain had abated and the clouds cleared; the full moon illuminated the surrounding moorland in a brilliant silver light.

'And when we get to the top of the hill,' Gabriel instructed, 'stop a second and admire the view. The castle's about a mile away, and with the moon reflecting on the loch the panorama should be exquisite.'

They gained the summit and Ryland braked as instructed.

Langham whistled. 'My word, you're right. Beautiful.'

'Like something from a film,' Ryland added.

Loch Corraig was a crescent of silver embedded in the inky hills, and on the southern shore rose the stark outline of the castle. It had been a four-sided edifice at one point, with round towers at each corner and high battlements between. The centuries had eroded the northern and western walls and two of the towers; all that remained now were the two towers on the eastern side and the high, crenellated wall between them, as well as a length of the southern wall ending in ruins, so that the whole resembled a back-to-front letter L. The scene presented such a picture of serenity that Langham found it hard to believe that the castle harboured a man in fear of his life.

Ryland released the brake and the Ford coasted down the hillside towards the loch.

Gabriel said, 'The only other guest present when I was last there was an unpleasant cove called Vermeulen. The man's uncultured and thunderingly dull, as you'll find out.'

Langham couldn't help himself. 'So he doesn't read poetry?' But Gabriel, if he was aware of the barb, didn't bite.

'The man's an engineer. Need I say more? In my opinion he's a scheming opportunist out to bleed my father dry.'

'In what way?' Ryland said.

'That way,' Gabriel said, leaning forward and pointing through the windscreen. They were travelling along the bank of the loch, the castle a shadowy bulk in the distance. Beside the castle, extending into the silvered waters of the loch, Langham made out a low timber platform.

'Ah,' he said, 'the pontoon. But what's it for?'

Gabriel laughed but without humour. 'It's my father's greatest folly,' he said. 'But I'll let the old man tell you about it himself, which no doubt he'll be delighted to do. And here we are, turn right under the gatehouse arch and park before the tower.'

Ryland steered into the grounds and braked the Ford between an old Bentley and a Morris Oxford. As soon as the car stopped, Gabriel opened the back door and climbed out. 'Right, this is where I make myself scarce. I don't want the old man to know I'm here yet, so mum's the word, OK?'

'But why—?' Langham began.

'Let's just say that I need to see someone before I let the old man know I'm here.' And with a cryptic wink Gabriel disappeared into the darkness.

Ryland and Langham exchanged a glance, climbed from the car and unloaded their travelling bags. They crossed to an oak door the size of an upended dining table; it creaked open before they could yank on the bell pull. Silhouetted in the lighted doorway stood a portly little man in plus-fours, with a full set of pork chop sideburns, a vast moustache and a head as bald as a bollard.

Langham resisted the urge to drop his bag and salute the major.

'Langham! Splendid! Ryland said you were coming along – capital. Ryland, m'boy! Wonderful to see you both. Now come inside and warm yourselves. How about a whisky before dinner?'

They shook hands and Ryland was unable to stop himself from essaying a quick salute.

'I wonder if I might make a quick phone call, sir?' Langham asked.

''Course y'can. And less of the "sir". You'll find phones in your rooms. I'll take you up.' Major Gordon's expression became suddenly serious. 'And then I'll tell you what's been going on up here,' he said, and led the way into the castle.

Four

Maria's meeting with Travers went well, all things considered. He was an editor of the old school, pinstripes and bowler hat, whose idea of how to do business harked back to before the war. His word was his bond and he frowned upon contracts as if such legal niceties cast aspersions upon his integrity. He looked upon literary agents as a form of parasite, and the thought of an author being represented by a woman – and a young slip of a thing at that – went against everything that was right and proper, or so Maria had heard from a third party.

For her part, she knew from experience that the way to handle such old fossils was to employ a subtle combination of flattery and feminine charm. To this end she praised recent additions to Gollancz's fiction list, even though she didn't represent these authors, and did not demur when he insisted that he foot the bill for lunch.

When it came down to business, she was forceful in her representation of her author, whose previous novel had done well for Gollancz.

She let it be known that Secker and Warburg had expressed interest in his next book, and that, for Travers to secure the author's continued loyalty, a two-book deal with an increased advance might be prudent. The editor hemmed and hawed over his pudding, but by the time he'd downed his second brandy Maria had talked him into believing that it was he who had won the day and secured a deal that would keep the up-and-coming scribe with the venerable firm of Gollancz.

All in all, she thought as she shook the old man by the hand and took her leave, an excellent lunchtime's work. She would phone her author later and break the good news, then chase up the editor for the contract later in the week. Charles would be delighted; the author was one of Charles's prodigies. 'A veritable banker, my dear girl, whose books combine literary merit with mass appeal; ergo, happiness all round!'

In the taxi on the way to Oxford Street, she considered Charles and his imminent release. She and Donald had visited him at Wormwood Scrubs every week, bringing him up to speed with business at the agency and all the gossip of his social circle; he had lost a little weight, deplored the standard of cuisine on offer at the Scrubs and let slip that he had made a 'special friend' – but would say no more. 'He's due for release a little after my own liberation, and I will present him to the world then and only then.'

On Tuesday morning she would meet Donald off the train at King's Cross at seven thirty, then drive across London and collect Charles from Wormwood Scrubs. In the evening she would cook a meal at her apartment, and at some point insist that Charles take the week off work. He would protest on that score, but she would stand firm; he deserved a little time to rest and ease himself back into the good life before he returned to the cut and thrust of the literary battlefield.

She returned home to her Kensington apartment via Harrods, where she bought Charles an expensive box of Belgian chocolates and a silver tiepin, depicting a cherub, to add to his growing collection. She was making herself a cup of tea when the telephone bell shrilled.

A broad Scottish voice said, 'Teddy Troon here, calling from the Trossachs.'

'Donald, you big buffoon. Did anyone tell you that your Scottish accent is abominable?'

'And did anyone tell you that your French accent melts a man's heart?'

She sank into the sofa, hugging the phone. 'It's lovely to hear your voice again, darling. How was the journey?'

'Long and a tad cold – or rather the last leg was. I think Ralph hired the slowest, coldest car in Scotland. Anyway, we arrived safe and sound and we're just about to have a whisky with the major before dinner. I must say, it's rather an impressive pile he's got here.'

'I'm missing you already, Donald.'

'Me too. I wish you were here.'

Maria told him all about lunch with the publishing fossil, the deal she'd secured and the presents she'd bought for Charles.

'He'll love those,' he said. 'What are you doing this evening?'

'I think I'll make myself cheese on toast and a big mug of tea. Oh, I have the third draft of a novel by a certain Donald Langham to go through with a red pen.'

She could almost see him wince. 'Well, don't be too severe, my darling.'

She laughed. 'I promise I'll just prune where absolutely necessary.'

The chatted for another minute, then Donald said, 'Hey-ho. I'd better dash – the major is waiting.'

'Take care, darling. I love you.'

'Love you, too. And I'll see you on Tuesday morning.'

No sooner had she replaced the receiver and was basking in the bittersweet emotion of her love being stoked by the fact of Donald's absence, than the phone rang again.

'Maria, my dear! I hope I do not call at an inconvenient time?'

'Why, Dame Amelia, how lovely to hear from you. No, not at all.'

'I am in town! Business brought me up, and I had cocktails with Reginald at three, but he's been called away to some ghastly literary dinner this evening. I was wondering . . . I know it's short notice, my dear, but would you and your young man care to dine at my hotel this evening?'

'My young, man, Amelia, is about to dine five hundred miles away in the Scottish Highlands. But I'd love to come.'

'The Highlands? My word, what on *earth* is he doing up there?'

'I'll tell you this evening, Amelia. What time should I arrive?'

'What say about seven? We can have a little drink in the bar and then dine. They do a very passable Dover sole and their cellar is better than average. I shall look forward to your company.'

Dame Amelia Hampstead came up to London once a month and always stayed at an exclusive little hotel in Highgate. As well as Amelia being a bestselling crime writer, the star of the Elder and Dupré Literary Agency, Maria considered her a great friend and, if the truth be told, something of a mother substitute. She had the piercing diction and the imperious manner of a Kensington dowager from before the Great War, but a refreshingly forthright manner which combined modesty and a loathing of all pretension.

Maria took a taxi to Highgate and arrived at the Marquis Hotel a little after seven.

'My darling!' Dame Amelia called out, rising from her table. 'But you look absolutely divine!'

Maria removed her hat and arranged the shoulder strap of her scarlet A-line dress. 'Givenchy. Donald bought it for me when we had a weekend in Paris in August.'

'It shows your figure off to perfection. Oh, if only I were forty years younger! I think of the abominations we young gals were forced into and I shudder! But here I am, and I haven't even asked what you would care to drink!'

They settled down with their drinks – a G&T

37

for Maria, sweet sherry and seltzer for Amelia – and the dowager said, 'Now, before I forget – I am so excited about the wedding. When is the happy day?'

'Sometime in late May, but we've yet to finalize the exact date. It should be either the second to last or the last Saturday in the month.'

'I shall put both in my diary, Maria. There is nothing like a wedding to invigorate an ageing heart!'

Maria laughed. 'I would have thought yours needed no invigorating, Amelia. How is Reginald, by the way?'

Amelia had stunned her friends earlier that year by announcing her 'friendship' – she was being coy – with an editor at Collins, Reginald Harrop. Widowed in the last month of 1917, Amelia had remained single until the late thirties when she had fallen madly in love with and married an RAF officer, only for tragedy to befall her a second time when, in 1942, her husband was killed in action in Africa. She had rallied with characteristic fortitude, but vowed never to marry again.

There was a sweepstake amongst her close friends as to when wedding bells would transform that vow into so much hot air.

'Reginald is perfection rolled up in the form of a slightly chubby, impeccably dressed, beautifully mannered bachelor who treats me like a princess!' Amelia laughed with deprecation. 'I really am too lucky for words.'

'In my opinion, Amelia, it's Reginald who's the lucky one.'

38

'Tut tut! Look at me! On the wrong side of sixty – and my face! Is it any wonder, girl, that *foundation* cream is so called? Without it my visage would crumble! But finish your drink and let's dine.'

They moved through to the restaurant where Dame Amelia's valet was on hand with her Belgian Schipperke named Poirot; he carried it to the dowager's table – the management had granted Dame Amelia special dispensation and allowed the dog dining rights – and placed the ball of fur on a chair beside Amelia, where it sat with impeccable manners upon its own silk cushion.

'Now,' Amelia said as they dispensed with starters and ordered poached Dover sole and winter greens, 'what is all this about your young man leaving you all alone and haring off up to the Highlands? Shooting, I take it?'

'I hope not,' Maria said. 'No, he's gone with a detective friend of his – you've met him, Ralph Ryland.'

Dame Amelia fed Poirot a morsel of fish. 'I recall. That ferrety-looking little cockney. But, if memory serves, he did the job.'

'He's one of the best, according to Donald.'

'He's not on a case, is he?' Dame Amelia asked with foreboding.

Maria winced. 'I think perhaps he is,' she said, and told the dowager all about the major and the threats upon his life.

'My word, it sounds like something from one of my own capers! I'll have to grill Donald when he gets back.'

'I'm sure he'll be delighted to regale you with all the details.'

'It has the hallmarks of a first-rate tale, my girl! A Scottish castle, much skulduggery – and the weather! Mark my word, the snow will fall with a vengeance and they'll be cut off from civilization – and then, and *only* then, will the murderer strike!'

'Don't! You're making me shiver . . .'

Dame Amelia smiled reassuringly. 'But the good thing about Donald's being all the way up there, my girl, and your being down here in the Smoke is that you won't be drawn into assisting him on *this* case, mark my word!'

'I should certainly hope not,' Maria said, and took a gulp of Chardonnay.

Five

Langham sank into the wing-backed armchair as if it were a chintz quagmire. Across from him Ryland did the same, falling into his chair's embrace with a surprised exclamation, his feet barely touching the Persian rug. A log fire roared in a vast hearth, above which a stag's head gazed down imperiously.

Major Gordon poured three generous measures of whisky. 'Single malt, from the local distillery. One of the finest. See what y'think.'

Langham took a sip and the liquid slipped down his throat like honey. 'I say, this is excellent, Major.'

40

'Just what I needed after a bitter cold journey,' Ryland said.

The major stood before the fire, roasting his tweed-clad buttocks, and gestured around the room. 'This is where I've been holing meself up for the past week. Tactical vantage point, y'see? High ground. Only one staircase winding up the tower so only one damned entrance, to which I have the key.'

The library was a big oak-beamed room at the very top of the castle's northern tower; in daylight it would command an impressive view of the loch and surrounding moorland.

'I call it the library,' the major went on, 'but it's really pretty limited. Me collection on India, a few tomes on hunting and shooting and a travel section. Keeps me amused on cold nights, though.'

Major Gordon was that peculiar specimen of Scottish aristocracy – a Scot born and bred who sounded more English than any blue-blooded Englishman. Langham suspected that a public school education had knocked the edges from any Scottish accent he might once have possessed.

The old man was chewing his moustache. 'You never appreciate it when you're tootling along in neutral, minding your own damn business, and then something crops up to shatter your complacency.' He gazed into his Scotch, took a sip and went on, 'I mean, there I was, the hotel side of things picking up, thank you very much, and the project progressing apace.'

Langham interrupted. 'The project?'

'I'll get to it, Captain,' the major grunted,

forgetting that he was no longer in the officers' mess. 'I had no complaints. My aim when I bought this pile was to get it up and running. It was a complete ruin when I shelled out on it back in 'forty-seven. But little by little I've brought it back to the land of the living. I don't charge an arm and a leg and the food's second to none. Word got around and the bookings increased. And if that wasn't all tickety-boo, to put the icing on the cake I heard about the plane.'

Langham glanced at Ryland. 'The plane?'

'Earlier this year I had a letter from an engineer based in London. Apparently he'd holidayed in the area and heard a few local tales – about a plane coming down in the loch near the castle in early 'forty-five. He asked if he could come up and do some exploratory diving, and I must admit I got rather interested in the whole thing. To cut a long story short, this summer he travelled up with his team, made a dive or two and after a bit of poking around came up trumps. There was a plane on the loch bottom – a German Dornier, don't y'know – sitting there relatively undamaged. The engineer suggested how he might go about raising the bird, and I set them on.'

'Which is where the pontoon comes in,' Ryland said.

'Precisely. They built the structure over the wreck and did a lot more diving. The good news was that the plane was intact so they could lift it in one piece. The bad news was that, just as we were about to start the haul a few weeks ago, things turned stormy. So it's all on hold now until the weather clears up.'

He eyed Langham and Ryland. 'It's me project, boys. I'm interested in seeing the plane up, and maybe even restored, but it goes beyond that. I'm fascinated by what the plane might have been *doing* here. A Dornier was a light bomber, not a heavy duty long-range monster like the Luftwaffe's Junkers. And it was flying alone. There were no raids at the time – this was February 'forty-five. So, I ask meself, what was this lone plane doing flying over the Highlands towards the end of the war?'

'Have the divers been able to enter the plane to see what, or who, it might have been carrying?' Langham asked.

The major shook his head. 'Like a pea-souper down there. Visibility a matter of inches. There must be bodies *in situ* – well, skeletons by now – but the divers couldn't get into the cockpit.'

Ryland shook his head. 'Fascinating.'

The major laughed. 'As you might imagine, I was like a boy in a sweetshop. I lived and breathed the project. Fair champing at the bit to get the kite up.' He fell silent. 'And then this . . .'

He swigged off his whisky and suggested a refill. Langham drained his glass and accepted a second.

The major went on, 'The dashed thing is you expect it in wartime, y'see. The enemy are out to get you, and vice versa, and it's no hard feelings. The honour of war and "may the best man win" kind of thing. Remember the assault on Diego-Suarez? Bullets raining down like hail and we didn't bat a bally eyelid. All part of the show. But this . . . this is different, gentlemen.

43

Somebody's out for blood. They're playing dirty and I don't like it one little bit.'

Langham shook his head. 'On the phone to Ralph you weren't too sure about exactly *whose* blood?'

'That's the ruddy thing, young Langham. I don't think I've an enemy in the world. A few old coves in the regiments I didn't see eye to eye with and the odd paper-pusher on the Inverness council who opposed me rebuilding this place.' He paused. 'But, y'see, I might not have been the intended target. The hell of it is not knowing.'

'I think it might help,' Ryland said, 'if you told us exactly what happened.'

The major nodded and limped across to the window. 'Come over here and take a gander.'

Langham lodged his glass on a side table and joined the major before the high leaded window. The loch was an expanse of beaten silver, scaled in the moonlight, and from this elevation they had a bird's-eye view of the pontoon. Langham thought that the best way to describe it would be like a picture frame – a timber deck, perhaps forty yards square, surrounding the area of loch where the plane was submerged. A long, railed gangway connected the pontoon to the castle's jetty directly beneath the window.

The major pointed to a great machine comprising booms and cogged wheels sitting on the near deck of the pontoon. 'See that ugly-looking apparatus on the platform? That's the crane that'll do the job of lifting the Dornier. Anyway, I was on the pontoon last Wednesday

44

afternoon, discussing a minor repair to the crane with me chief engineer, Hans Vermeulen, when I heard a couple of shots – one after the other. One whistled right between us – a matter of inches from me head. It ricocheted off the frame of the crane, and the second shot went right through the timber of the deck a yard or two before us. There was no doubt that we were the intended targets – either me or Hans, or both of us. Bally lucky we were, too. We dived for cover behind the crane and I tried to see where the shots had come from.'

'Were you able to . . .?' Langham began.

The major shook his head. 'The inhabited east wall of the castle overlooks the pontoon,' he said. 'Someone could have taken a potshot from any of the upper windows – or then again the gunman could've been concealed on the hillside across the road from the castle. Impossible to tell.'

They returned to the fireside and the major eased himself on to a settee.

'Did you manage to get back to the castle without being shot at again?' Ryland asked.

'This was late on – three thirty. So we waited till dusk then hot-footed it back inside. I went straight to the gunroom and checked me rifles. But the room was locked and, as far as I could tell, none of the rifles'd been used.'

'Does anyone have access to the keys to the gunroom, other than yourself?' Langham asked.

'No, and I keep them in a locked box in the hall. The keys to that are on me person all the time.'

Langham looked across at Ryland and said,

'We'll take a look at the pontoon in the morning, Ralph, not that it'll tell us much. You called the police in, I take it?'

'That's right. PC Ross came and took a poke around. He said he'd make a report and send it to Inverness.'

'Who was resident at the castle when the incident occurred?'

'Just friends, Renata Káldor and Professor Hardwick. And Elspeth, of course.'

'Elspeth?' Ryland asked.

'Elspeth Stuart, slip of a thing I took in a few years ago when her mother and father died. She works as a housemaid, though these days I consider her part of the family.'

'What about other staff?'

'Mr and Mrs Fergusson live in and do all the cooking and cleaning – they run the hotel side of things, if truth be told.'

Langham took a mouthful of Scotch and contemplated the fire.

'What we've got to work out,' Ryland said, 'is a motive. Why might someone want you or Vermeulen out of the way?'

'And that, gentlemen, is what's concentrating me thoughts. Fair sets me skin crawling, I must admit.'

A tap sounded at the door; it opened a fraction and a fair, thin-faced girl peered round and smiled. 'Major, dinner is almost ready.'

'Capital, Elspeth. If you'd care to sound the gong and serve drinks in the Stewart room . . .'

The major turned to his guests. 'And now, gentlemen, I suspect you might be a tad peckish?'

46

'And curious to meet the other diners,' Langham said. 'I take it they'll be joining us tonight?'

'We should have a full table, Langham. This way.'

Langham and Ryland followed Major Gordon from the library and down the twisting stone staircase.

Six

Eight suits of armour stood sentry around the grey walls of the Stewart room like so many medieval mannequins. Raised on timber plinths, they loomed over the major and his guests as they made small talk with glasses of dry sherry in hand.

Langham noted a tall, elegant woman in a stylish green two-piece dress suit; her auburn hair was coiled on one side of her head, emphasizing her high cheekbones and long face. She had the most amazing light green eyes, which raked the room with an expression of disdain, and she smoked a cigarette in an exaggeratedly long holder. This, he told himself, must be Renata Káldor, the Hungarian aristocrat.

She was engaged in languid conversation with a stocky man with a porcine face who Langham took to be the Dutch engineer, Hans Vermeulen. The Hungarian looked as if she had never been so bored in her life. The elfin Elspeth stood beside the pair, a glass of sherry clutched to her flat chest.

There was no sign as yet of Gabriel Gordon, and Langham wondered whom he'd been so eager to meet before he announced his presence to his father. The major's old retainers, Mr and Mrs Fergusson, moved around the room ensuring that the guests were supplied with sherry.

'Dates from thirteen forty-five,' the major was telling Langham and Ryland. 'Which makes the pile a tad over six hundred years old. But let me introduce you to someone who knows even more about the castle than I do.'

Langham noticed a tall, stick-thin gentleman slip into the room. He stooped diffidently like an elderly stork, and his snow-white hair, as upright as whipped cream, was retreating up the pink slope of his forehead.

'Hardwick, may I introduce Donald Langham and Ralph Ryland, colleagues of mine in the last war, don't y'know. Gentlemen, my esteemed friend, Professor Hardwick.'

They shook hands and Hardwick said, 'Emeritus, these days. Long gone are the days at the lectern. How delightful to make your acquaintance.' He had a gentle smile and a benign manner which bordered on the seraphic; Langham took an immediate liking to the man.

'Langham and Ryland were under me in Madagascar and India,' the major said. 'And one wouldn't wish to serve with finer fellows. Langham here was mentioned in despatches.'

'Saved me life in Diego-Suarez,' Ryland chipped in.

Langham winced; he disliked talking about the

incident, still less reliving the assault on the Vichy French machine-gun emplacement.

'While I was lying there,' Ryland went on, 'pinned down by machine-gun fire, Don stormed the enemy position, did for a geezer with a grenade and dragged me back to our lines.'

'My word, how absolutely astounding. Such bravery. We really do owe our freedom to the likes of you sterling fellows.' The professor sighed. 'I, for my part, served the entirety of the war behind a desk in Intelligence.'

Langham changed the subject. 'Major Gordon mentioned that you're here to conduct psychic research in the castle?'

'I lectured in psychology at St Andrews,' Hardwick said. 'But after my retirement my interests turned to the paranormal – and the human apprehension of such phenomena termed paranormal and supernatural. I see you're a non-believer,' he went on, surprising Langham who thought he'd kept his sceptical expression well concealed. 'But let me tell you that there are things out there which we, and our sciences, are only just beginning to understand.'

Langham raised his glass. 'I like to think that science is beginning to explain phenomena we ascribed, in days of superstition, to the occult.'

'I'm in the sceptic's camp,' the major opined. 'Been living in this pile for five years and I've yet to come across the faintest whiff of a ghost.'

Ryland asked, 'You really can detect spooks and such with scientific apparatus, Professor?'

Hardwick smiled. 'What we can do at the

49

moment is set up experiments which monitor the environment where occult phenomena might manifest. We're in the early days of such experimentation at present. My work here consists of temperature and sound readings. Alas, my funds are not sufficient to rig up a comprehensive coverage of cameras.'

'But you do have some cameras set up?' Ryland asked.

'One or two in what I call prime positions, though ideally I would like more.'

'And,' Langham ventured, 'have your experiments come up with anything conclusive?'

'I have various items of data which prove, on close examination, to be very interesting indeed. Perhaps at some point I might have the pleasure of showing you gentlemen around the castle and explaining my research further?'

Langham nodded. 'I'll look forward to that.'

The vast door at the far end of the room swung open and Gabriel Gordon, looking even taller and more Byronic in the glare of the chandelier, made his entrance.

'Why,' the major exclaimed, 'the prodigal son returns. But I thought you were in London, Gabriel?'

The poet snatched a glass of sherry from the tray proffered by Mrs Fergusson, quaffed it in one and took a second. He joined Langham's group, nodded to the professor and said to his father, 'Just got in. Managed to hitch a lift from Inverness.'

The major made the introductions. 'Langham and Ryland, meet my son and heir – my only son and heir. Gabriel reckons himself a poet. Can't do with the stuff, meself.'

'The old man's literary education started and finished with Kipling,' Gabriel said, 'who was very good as far as he went.'

Gabriel and the major stood side by side, and a greater physical mismatch Langham had never seen: the poet stood head and shoulders over his diminutive father.

'But Gabriel,' Professor Hardwick enquired, 'what brings you back to the castle from the gay metropolis of London?'

Major Gordon chuntered something to himself, which Langham didn't catch.

'A period of recuperation, Professor. For the past month I've been overseeing the design and production of my first volume of poetry, to be published next year. An artist friend of mine is illustrating the cover. We've been going over a few last-minute emendations.'

Hans Vermeulen joined the group; clutching his empty sherry glass, he stared at the poet and said, 'That must have been very taxing, Gabriel. No wonder you need to recuperate. Is a friend also *printing* the pamphlet?'

Not to be fazed, Gabriel stared down at the engineer and replied, 'It's coming out from a respectable company – who, moreover, pay.'

The professor said charmingly, 'And I for one shall look forward to purchasing a copy, Gabriel. When did you say it was out?'

While the poet and the professor chatted of matters literary, the major drew Langham and Ryland across to where Renata Káldor stood in

51

conversation with Elspeth Stuart. 'Renata, Elspeth, may I have the pleasure of introducing my friends?'

They shook hands, Elspeth smiling shyly at the men. A second later she excused herself and said she must go and help Mrs F in the kitchen.

The Hungarian gave the impression of staring down from a great height, even though only her stiletto heels elevated her above Langham's five feet eleven.

'Welcome to the Highlands, gentlemen,' she said in a rich contralto with a slight Hungarian accent. 'Have you come for the shooting? I, myself, shoot – I was taught the art of gunmanship when I was just five years old. Every winter as a girl my father took me to Lake Balaton and we shot wild duck. My father was a great man, the son of a prince. Sadly he lost everything when the communists under Béla Kun briefly seized power in 1919.' She applied the cigarette holder to her cranberry lips, sipped and exhaled an elegant plume of smoke. Langham took in her pearls, the gold rings on her fingers and her film-star poise.

Ryland, Langham noted, was watching her like a mesmerized stoat. 'You live in London?' the detective asked.

'I have a little place in Belgravia, but I prefer to winter in the Bahamas with old family friends.'

Langham asked, 'But you would rather spend this particular winter in the Highlands?'

Renata's lips compressed themselves into a thin, steely line as she regarded Langham. 'I have a fondness for the major,' she said, 'and I find the solitude conducive to peace of mind.'

The door opened and Mrs Fergusson announced that dinner was about to be served. The party trooped from the Stewart room, along a short corridor to a timber-panelled room dominated by a beamed ceiling and a long oak table set before a blazing fire. Stern portraits of clan leaders, all kilted and posing amidst rocky terrain, gazed down from the walls.

'The great dining hall,' the major explained. 'Much as it was back in the days of yore.'

The meal was every bit as good as Langham had hoped, with cock-a-leekie soup followed by haggis, potatoes and mashed turnips. Ryland tucked in like a starving man, and across the table Gabriel Gordon ate with speed and gusto.

A small voice with a fetching Scottish lilt sounded beside Langham. 'The major tells me that you write thrillers, Mr Langham. I very much like a good mystery.'

Elspeth smiled up at him and then looked away, and Langham gave his full attention to the girl. She was pretty in a fey, waif-like way, though seated so close to Renata she was somewhat eclipsed by the Hungarian's confident poise and hauteur.

He told her about his books, describing a few action sequences, and she hung on his every word.

'When I'm next in Inverness, Mr Langham, I shall order a couple of your books from MacGilvie's.'

'That's most kind of you. I hope you'll enjoy them.'

From across the table, Gabriel said, 'You'll read Langham's thrillers but not my verse?'

Langham glanced at Elspeth, expecting her to blaze with embarrassment, but to his surprise she gazed defiantly across the table and, with an insouciance that made him wonder, stuck out her tongue at the poet. Gabriel dabbed his lips with a napkin, hiding his smile.

Vermeulen was answering a question from Ryland in his rather monotone Dutch accent. 'I was only twelve when the war broke out, Mr Ryland. But when I was sixteen I joined the Dutch resistance. I saw my father badly beaten by an SS officer in the street, and a week later my older brother died fighting with the British in Africa. To join the resistance was the least I could do.'

'Dashed brave, I say,' the major put in.

Vermeulen shrugged modestly. 'I really did very little. I helped to print and distribute a few leaflets, and once I helped to move an injured British pilot from one hiding place to another. It was really nothing, but I thought at the time that I was doing my bit to oppose the Nazi occupation.'

'And so you were,' Professor Hardwick murmured from the other end of the table. 'So you were.'

'It was a terrible time in Holland,' the engineer went on. 'People were starving while the Nazi pigs were eating like kings and killing our people for the most minor infringements.'

The major said, 'And they would have put you up against a wall and shot you had they known of your work with the resistance.'

'Come on,' Gabriel said, turning and staring at the Dutchman. 'You were a teenager and loving it. I bet you didn't even think of the danger. Resistance was instinctive. You can't claim to be a hero.'

Vermeulen, to his credit, smiled and said equably, 'But my dear Gabriel, I have never claimed anything of the sort. As I said, I really did very little.' He chewed a mouthful of haggis ruminatively, then asked, 'But what did you do in the war?'

'I was fifteen when it finished, Vermeulen. A little too young to enlist.'

'But had you been old enough,' Elspeth said with uncharacteristic bravado, 'you would have written first-rate verse in honour of our nation, wouldn't you?'

A mixed expression crossed the poet's long face, a half-amused twist of the lips and a sharp look in the eye that flashed a telegraphic message across the table to Elspeth. *Whose side are you on?*

Renata, at the head of the table, set down her glass and regarded the assembled diners, 'All this talk of Nazis. They are dead now and no threat. They cannot rise from the grave and cause mayhem yet again.'

Vermeulen turned to her and smiled. 'What are you trying to say, Renata?'

'I am saying, why all this preoccupation with the past, with Nazi atrocities, when a real danger threatens Europe and the freedom of all democratic countries?'

The professor smiled beatifically. 'The danger, Miss Káldor?'

'I speak of the communists, yes, the Soviets who as we debate the past are now, at this very minute, committing atrocities across the nations of Europe every bit as barbaric as the Nazis. If you could hear the stories from Poland and East Germany, and from my own country, then you would not be sitting here so complacently and talking about one's bravery against a defeated foe.'

Langham spoke up. 'I think we know, and acknowledge – at least most of us do – the depravities carried out under communism's name by Stalin during his rule. But there's little we can do now, politically or militarily, to counter what the Soviets are imposing on the countries you mentioned.'

'I think Renata,' Vermeulen said, 'would like to fund her own little army to oppose the Russians, wouldn't you?'

Professor Hardwick spoke up. Raising his glass to the firelight, he said, 'I must say, Gordon, old man, you do keep a wonderful cellar. This Burgundy is the most magnificent I've tasted in many a year. Don't you think so, ladies and gentlemen?'

A chorus of approbation and general appreciation of the wine passed around the table, and the moment of conflict was defused.

At one point the major cleared his throat and announced, 'We shall have an extra guest at breakfast, ladies and gentlemen. My good friend Ulrich Meyer is returning for a few days. Unfortunately he won't be in until midnight, but Mr Fergusson is staying up to greet him.'

'And how long will our German friend be staying with us?' Gabriel asked pointedly.

'Ulrich will be my guest for an indefinite period,' the major said. 'Needless to say,' he went on, looking around the table, 'I would appreciate it if you refrained from bringing into the conversation any mention of the last war, and specifically the Nazis. Ulrich is a good man, and sensitive to the imputation that, merely due to his nationality, he was in any way implicated with an ideology he regards as abhorrent.'

'We shall treat him with the respect he deserves, father,' Gabriel said.

'It will be pleasant to catch up with Herr Meyer and hear about his travels,' Professor Hardwick said.

'Ulrich stayed for a day or two last week,' the major explained to Langham, 'before taking off again on a tour of the Highlands. He is an expert on Second World War aircraft, and plans to write a short treatise on the salvaging of the Dornier.'

The meal ended an hour later without further caustic dialogue from any quarter, and the guests finished off with brandy and coffee.

A little later Langham drained his glass and, claiming tiredness after a long day's travel, thanked the major for the splendid meal and excused himself. This began the exodus, and Vermeulen, Elspeth, Ryland and Gabriel made their exits.

As they moved along the corridor, Langham heard Vermeulen murmur to Gabriel, with an affected off-handedness, 'And by the way, I was passing through Inverness last week and, do you know something, I could have sworn I saw you leaving the Three Thistles. But I must have been mistaken, yes, as you say you were in London? Goodnight, Gabriel,' he said, and disappeared up a narrow staircase.

Gabriel hunched his ox-like shoulders and hurried on without a word.

Langham glanced at Ryland beside him. 'Odd,' he commented.

'No love lost between those two, Don,' Ryland said as they continued to their rooms.

'I wonder if it's over Elspeth?'

'What?' Ryland sounded surprised.

'I might be wrong, but at dinner I rather received the impression that there was something going on between Gabriel and Elspeth.'

'You mean . . .?'

Langham shrugged. 'As I said, I might be wrong. But it's worth keeping in mind.'

Ryland nodded. 'A very interesting mob, I thought.'

'Yes, very interesting,' Langham agreed.

He said goodnight and took himself off to bed.

Seven

The following morning, at breakfast, he made the acquaintance of Ulrich Meyer.

Langham came down early and breakfasted alone, served kippers and scrambled eggs by Mrs

Fergusson. He found, despite the heavy meal the previous evening, that his appetite was undiminished and the kippers were excellent.

He was finishing off with a second cup of Earl Grey when the door opened and a tall, stiffly upright man limped into the room, leaning all his weight on a walking stick. He wore grey slacks and a white polo-neck sweater, and his silver hair was cropped close to his skull. The most striking thing about Meyer, however, was the fact that he wore a tooled-leather patch over his right eye.

Langham rose as the man approached the table. They shook hands, Meyer with a stiff formality entirely in keeping with his demeanour, and introduced themselves.

'Ah, Herr Langham,' Meyer said as he lowered himself, grimacing with pain, on to a chair. 'The major mentioned when I spoke to him on the phone yesterday that you were arriving. You served with the major in India, I believe, and now write thrillers?'

'That's right. And I hear that you write books yourself.'

Meyer waved that away. 'Three or four monographs on various aspects of German aviation, that is all. Of specialist interest only, unlike your novels.'

'Looking at my sales figures,' Langham said self-deprecatingly, 'I sometimes wonder.'

Meyer asked Mrs Fergusson for toast and black coffee.

'The major said you were arriving late last night,' Langham said. 'How was the journey?'

'It was after midnight when I did eventually get here,' Meyer said. 'The ice on the road was treacherous and I underestimated the time it would take for me to drive from Fort William.'

'Are you staying for long?'

Meyer smiled. He had a long, grey, rather severe face on which the smile sat uneasily. 'That all depends on how long it takes Herr Vermeulen to raise the aeroplane. I was here initially last month, when the signs were that it might be brought to the surface within weeks. That was not to be, though Herr Vermeulen is confident that he can complete the operation before Christmas.'

'And you plan to write about the plane itself, or the operation?'

Meyer sipped his coffee before replying. He moved with a kind of wincing circumspection, as if fearful of causing himself more pain than was absolutely necessary. 'I hope to combine both, Herr Langham. You see, I am intrigued by both the plane itself – or rather what it was doing here, back in 'forty-five – and the nature of the salvage operation. I have never witnessed such an attempt before, and from an engineering point of view I find it fascinating. And of course the question of the plane, and its mission, only adds to my interest.'

'What do you think it *was* doing here?'

Meyer took a precise bite of toast – buttered, but without jam or marmalade – chewed for a time and then replied, 'That is a mystery, and it might remain so. You see, bombing raids on Britain had ceased well before 'forty-five, so it

60

cannot be that the plane was separated from its formation, veered off course and crashed into the loch. I venture to say that it must have come over alone on a specific mission.'

'The plane is a Dornier, I understand?'

Meyer inclined his head. 'Though what specification of Dornier we have yet to ascertain. The pictures obtained so far are not clear – it could either be a Dornier Do 17, or a Dornier Do 217. They were both bombers, though the 217 was a later, larger and improved model.'

Langham sipped his tea and ventured, 'Were you a pilot yourself, Herr Meyer?'

Meyer smiled frostily. 'Sadly, no. During my boyhood I dreamed of qualifying as a pilot. Indeed, it was all I thought about. However, fate decreed another destiny. I was injured in an automobile accident in my hometown of Leipzig in 1930, when I was just sixteen. I broke both my legs, my pelvis and my back. The surgeons said that it was a miracle I survived, never mind learned to walk again. Of course, that put an end to my dream of flying.'

'I'm sorry.'

'I could tolerate the physical pain, Herr Langham – one learns to live with pain; it becomes the norm – but it is more difficult to live with the mental pain of thwarted dreams. I live with pain that tortures me still daily . . . To this day I find it impossible to accept the fact that I will never fly.'

Langham nodded. 'I can appreciate that.'

'So during the war, while many of my friends went off and joined the Luftwaffe, I remained on

61

the ground. As the next best thing to being a pilot, I managed to get a job as a clerk on an airfield near Hamburg. At least then I could be close to that which I loved.'

He dabbed his lips with his napkin. 'But all that is in the past, my friend. I am still fascinated by all aspects of aviation and I have made it my hobby – as well as my vocation.'

'What is your occupation, if you don't mind my asking?'

'Not at all. I'm the director of an aeronautical museum in Frankfurt.' He sipped his tea, then went on: 'The major wrote to me earlier this year when the Dornier was located. I was lucky enough to make his acquaintance in nineteen fifty at a meeting of the British–German Friendly Society in Edinburgh. We "hit it off", as you say, immediately.'

The door opened and Gabriel Gordon, looking tired and hungover, nodded to Langham and Meyer and moved through to the kitchen.

Meyer rose, bowed stiffly from the waist – Langham almost expected him to click his heels – and excused himself. 'I will now lie down and rest before I write a little before lunch.'

He bowed again and departed. Langham finished his tea and was about to return to his room when the door leading to the kitchen swung open and Gabriel sauntered through with a plate of toast. He paused at the table and poured himself a coffee.

'Did you have to sit through a catalogue of Herr Meyer's misfortunes, Langham? He bores everyone with his sob story. I'm sorry if I sound intolerant, but it's enough with one literal-minded engineer around the place in Vermeulen without having to suffer Meyer as well.'

Langham murmured something non-committal and managed to steer the conversation around to London and Muswell Hill, and for the next five minutes, before the poet excused himself and took his breakfast to his bedroom, he told Langham about his life in the artists' commune.

Immediately after breakfast Langham returned to his room, dialled the operator and got through to Maria.

He lay on his bed, twirling the braided telephone flex around his forefinger as he listened to the dialling tone. He smiled as Maria picked up the receiver and said, ''Ello,' in that typically French fashion.

'Maria, it's wonderful to hear your voice. The line's so clear you could be in the next room.'

'Oh, I wish I were, Donald,' she said wistfully. 'But tell me, what is happening in the Highlands? What is the castle like?'

'The castle's ancient and imposing.' He looked at the window recess. 'The walls are about five feet thick and the stonework pitted and grey.'

'But is it cold and draughty?' She *brrr*'d her lips. 'I imagine you're freezing up there!'

He laughed. 'On the contrary, the place is warm and palatial. The major has done a fine job of restoration.'

'Ah, the major . . . Do you think that someone is out to kill him?'

'Well, it pretty much looks that way – him, or his chief engineer.'

He told Maria all about the German plane, the major's salvage project and the shooting incident. He described the guests, the dinner last night and the various animosities that had come to light during the meal.

'Do you think that it is one of the guests who might be responsible, Donald?'

'Well, there's the rub. It might very well be. That's where I need your help.'

'My help?' She sounded surprised.

'There are a few of the guests I'd like you to check up on, if that's at all possible. They all have connections to London and I'd like to ensure that they're bona fide.'

'I'll do what I can. One second while I fetch a pen.' He imagined her striding across the Axminster, fetching a pen from her bureau and returning. 'There. Now go ahead, Donald.'

'The first is Gabriel Gordon, the major's son. He claims he was in London from around a month ago until yesterday, but I have reason to believe he's being economical with the truth. He lives in some kind of artists' commune in Muswell Hill.'

'I wonder if it's the one at Carmody House? If not, then they're sure to know of any other communes in the area. I'll make up some story and check up on him.'

'Wonderful. Now the other chappie is a Dutch engineer called Hans Vermeulen.' He spelled out the surname. If the gunman's intended target had been Vermeulen and not the major, then Langham wanted to know as much about the engineer as possible. 'He has a company

64

registered in London and he worked for the Dutch resistance during the war. I wonder if you could call a friend of mine, Lew Cramers? Lew was in the resistance, you see. Pretty high up, by all accounts. I'd like to know if he's heard of Vermeulen.'

'Right. Do you have Cramer's number?'

'That's the thing,' he said. 'I'd contact him myself but I left my address book back at the flat. You'll find it in the top drawer of my desk.'

'I'll pop over and get it,' she promised.

'Attagirl.'

'Anyone else?'

'Didn't you once mention that you had a Hungarian émigré friend?'

'That's right – Marguerite Selasny.'

'And you're still in contact with her?'

'I saw her perhaps a year ago. But why are you asking?'

He described Renata Káldor and her claims to Hungarian royalty. 'I was just wondering if your friend might know anything about her. I suspect that the Hungarian émigré community in London can't be that extensive.'

'I will contact her and ask if she has heard of this Renata Káldor.'

'I'm sorry to make you work like this, but I really think it might help with the investigation.'

'I don't mind in the least, Donald. Is there anyone else?'

He thought about it. 'An old retired professor who's into spooks, but he seems tame enough to me and he hails from St Andrews, so I suspect there's not much to be learned about him at your end. And a certain Ulrich Meyer, a German. But he's based in Frankfurt.'

'So what are you doing now? Have you had breakfast? Porridge?'

'I have, and porridge was on the menu but I plumped for kippers and scrambled eggs, which were excellent. Washed down with Earl Grey, of course.'

She sighed. 'Well, think of me, Donald, with my soft-boiled egg and soldiers.'

He laughed at her playfully glum tone. 'I promise to bring you some kippers back with me.'

She laughed. 'You can keep your kippers! How you English assault your palates with such things at breakfast!'

A tap sounded at Langham's door. 'Ah, that must be Ralph. We're just about to have a look-see at the pontoon.'

'I'll ring you back when I find out anything about these people – but I need the castle's number, Donald.'

He recited the number and rang off.

He pulled on his overcoat, scarf, gloves and hat, and set off with Ryland through the castle.

'I had an interesting natter with the prof at breakfast, Don.'

'What did he have to say?'

'He's a decent old cove, isn't he? I'm not usually comfortable with academic types but the prof doesn't put on any airs. He was telling me about the ghosts that haunt this pile. Apparently there was a murder committed in the cellar a couple of hundred years ago. The laird got a maid in the family way then had her strangled when she tried to kick up a fuss. According to Hardwick, her spirit still haunts the cellar where the murder took place.'

'Well, let's hope it's another two hundred years before the next murder at the castle.'

'The other ghost is that of an infant who died of cholera – it's said to haunt our landing, Don. Fair gives me the shivers, it does.'

Langham grunted. 'You shouldn't believe such rubbish.'

'I don't, but I do like a good ghost story, and the prof tells them well.'

They came to the door, stepped out into an icy but dry gale and took an uneven footpath around the walls of the castle.

The loch presented a glorious spectacle. A brilliant winter sun sparkled on the wind-ruffled waters and the hills rose green on either side. A railed gangway extended for twenty feet to the pontoon in the shadow of the castle's northern tower.

A small figure stood at the far end of the gangway. Vermeulen waved when he saw them and called out, 'Just push the gate open and jump the gap.'

Langham did as instructed, the loose boards of the gangway rattling underfoot.

Vermeulen was dressed in a camel-coloured canvas coat which came down to his ankles, and a curious flat cap. He saw Langham's gaze and explained, 'A bargeman's cap, Mr Langham. My father was captain on a timber ferry and this belonged to him.'

He led them across the deck to the crane and patted its red-painted cab. He launched into a spiel about the specifications of the rig, its tonnage and lifting capacity.

The engineer said that this was the first time he'd been involved in any kind of salvage operation and he was proceeding with extreme caution. 'We've attached buoys to the wreck of the plane, which we will inflate when the time comes, in order to ease the lifting operation.'

Langham's attention wandered and he noticed a long scar on the superstructure of the crane.

He touched the flaking paintwork and looked at the engineer. 'I take it that this is where one of the shots . . .?'

Vermeulen nodded. He pointed to the deck a few feet away. 'And that was where the second bullet struck.'

'And where exactly were you and the major standing?'

The engineer took up a position three yards from the crane. 'Here, facing away from the castle.'

Langham looked back at the rearing grey edifice. 'So, as the major said, the shots might have come from either the castle itself or from the hillside over the road.'

'It was hard to say. And at the time we were more concerned about getting out of the line of fire, yes? We took cover behind the crane.'

'Pretty lucky it was there,' Ryland said.

Vermeulen looked from Langham to Ryland.

'The major said that you wanted to examine the pontoon, gentlemen, which I considered a little odd – until something occurred to me. I wonder if I might ask a question?'

Langham glanced at Ryland. 'Go on.'

'You are police, no?'

Ryland said, 'Not police. I'm a private investigator and an old colleague of the major. He called us in when this happened, but I'd appreciate it if you kept that under your hat for the time being.'

Vermeulen nodded. 'Of course.'

Langham said, 'I wonder if you have any thoughts about what happened last Wednesday, Mr Vermeulen?'

The Dutchman frowned. 'I have been wondering two things, gentlemen. One is why, if the major was the target of the shooting, would anyone wish him dead? I concluded that the gunman might have wished to halt the salvage operation. You see, with the major out of the way, the project would grind to a halt.'

Langham shook his head. 'But who might gain from not having the wreck recovered?'

'That's what I've been asking myself for the past few days,' Vermeulen said. 'And I cannot begin to guess who it might be.'

Langham looked at the engineer. 'Of course, it might have been you who was the intended victim. Have you any idea why you might have been targeted?'

The Dutchman shook his head and his porcine jowls – mottled in the freezing wind – juddered. 'That's what I've been trying to work out. But no, I have no idea at all.' He shrugged. 'If I were no longer around then my deputy would take over the project, so if I were the intended target then the motive cannot be to halt the project.'

'And to the best of your knowledge you have no enemies, no one who might gain from your . . . removal?'

'No one that I can think of, Mr Langham.'

Ryland looked along the shore of the loch, his eyes screwed up against the wind. 'Have you noticed any strangers in the area? Any cars not belonging to guests or locals?'

'No one at all, no.'

Langham heard footsteps on the gangway. 'Hello, here's the major.'

The portly figure of the old soldier, buttoned up in a tweed overcoat and sporting a deerstalker, hailed them from the gangway, slipped through the gate and joined them.

'My word, but it's dashed freezing.' The major indicated the sky, louring indigo in the east, and went on, 'Snow on the way, according to the BBC, and scads of it. Place'll be under a couple of feet by nightfall.'

'Hope we don't get snowed in,' Ryland said.

'Hans was just telling us about the shooting.' Langham indicated the gunshot marks on the crane and in the deck. 'I'd like to talk to the police about this.' He turned to Ryland. 'You up to driving over to Inverness this afternoon?'

The major interrupted: 'You don't have to do that.' He pointed along the near shore of the loch, indicating a small croft on the hillside. 'PC Ross

70

lives there. He's the fellow who came and poked around the other day.'

'We might just wander up there this afternoon and have a natter, if he's at home.'

'I can tell you're not a country boy, Langham,' the major said. 'See the chimney? Old Ross is too much of a skinflint to be burning peat when he's not at home.'

Langham looked up and made out a faint skein of smoke rising from the croft's tiny chimney.

He turned and regarded the major and Vermeulen. 'No doubt it'll be redundant of me to suggest that you both should take extreme care. Are you armed?'

The major pulled a revolver from his waistband. 'Not that this'd stop anyone if they were really determined to do me in,' he said.

Vermeulen said, 'For that reason, Mr Langham, I do not carry a weapon.'

The major rubbed his hands against the cold and changed the subject. 'I came out to see if you gentlemen would care for tea and crumpets?' he said. 'Mrs Fergusson's just cooked a fresh batch.'

'That sounds splendid,' Langham said. 'It'll set us up for the hike to the croft.'

'And a hike it is, my boys. It's deceptive. The croft looks close but the lane winds like an angry snake before it gets to the place. C'mon! Let's get inside.'

They made their way from the platform, Vermeulen and Ryland going on ahead. Langham accommodated himself to the major's limp and assisted the old man from the gangway and on

71

to the jetty. In the shadow of the castle, out of the wintry sun, the temperature dropped appreciably. Langham hunched in his overcoat.

'I was chatting to Gabriel over breakfast,' he said. 'He was telling me about the commune at Muswell Hill.'

'Terrible, filthy place. Full of bohemians who think they're artists. Want my opinion – half of these so-called artists are no more than professional shirkers.'

'Including Gabriel?' Langham asked playfully.

The major grunted. 'The boy has his attributes, I'm sure. One or two people I've asked think his verse not at all bad.'

'He has been published, Major. That's no small achievement.'

'But, dammit, the fellow lacks backbone. If only he'd been old enough to see a bit of active service during the war. That's what he needed. A good dose of discipline and combat – a crack at the Bosch! Done him the world of good.'

'If,' Langham said in an undertone, 'he'd survived.'

The major went on, oblivious, 'And some of the women he consorts with down there . . . He brought one floozy to the castle a couple of years ago. My God!'

'I noticed Elspeth at dinner last night. I think she's smitten.'

The major spluttered. 'I forbade it, Langham! They had a fling earlier this year which I got wind of and put me foot down. I was adamant. Read Elspeth the riot act. She's a sweet child who's led a sheltered life. Gabriel's a rogue, and

72

I don't mind saying that of me own flesh and blood. He treats women shockingly and I wasn't going to let Elspeth get hurt.'

Smiling to himself, Langham opened the door and followed the major into the warmth of the castle.

Eight

Maria phoned Marguerite Selasny at ten o'clock on Sunday morning, only to be informed by the maid that she was away for the day; she left a message, requesting that Marguerite call her back.

She had spent most of the morning reading Donald's latest manuscript to make up for not doing so the previous night when she'd dined with Dame Amelia and returned home well after eleven. The novel was another thriller in his Sam Brooke series, which sold steadily and was proving popular with lending libraries up and down the country. In this instalment, Brooke had fallen in love – an unusual development for the usually lonely private eye – and was attempting to thwart a jewel heist while dealing with affairs of the heart.

Maria smiled as she read of Brooke's feelings for the novelist Celia Turner. 'She brought light to his life where before he had dwelled only in darkness,' and, 'For so long he had lived without the hope of love that his feelings for the tall, beautiful, intelligent Celia swelled within him like a brimming glass of wine.' She scored a red line through 'beautiful', and wrote in the margin: 'I suggest a better simile than the rather clichéd "a brimming glass of wine".'

At noon she set aside the manuscript and gazed through the window.

Snow was falling steadily over Kensington. There was no wind and the snowflakes floated down vertically, almost hesitantly, as if reluctant to inflict on the citizens of London any further winter mayhem. Already a dozen trains out of King's Cross and Euston had been cancelled due to excess snowfall, and according to the radio news the bus timetable was in chaos. *The Sunday Times* forecast continuing bad weather and warned Londoners to brace themselves for some of the lowest temperatures since the infamously severe winter of 'forty-eight.

She decided to make her way to Muswell Hill before the snowfall became any heavier and pulled on her gabardine, belted it at the waist and adjusted her scarlet beret at an angle. She hurried down into the street and slipped in behind the wheel of her Sunbeam saloon.

The car started at the second time of asking and she pulled out into the preternaturally quiet street; not only was it Sunday, but motorists were reluctant to venture forth thanks to the incessant snow. She encountered only a dozen other vehicles on the road between Kensington and Muswell Hill, and two of them were exhaust-belching omnibuses finding the slush-covered inclines too much of a battle.

Maria was aware of one artists' commune in

the area, a dilapidated mansion overlooking the serried rooftops of the staunchly middle-class suburb. It seemed an odd place for a group of radical artists to set up a communal studio, but one of their number, an unsuccessful sculptor, had been left the mansion by his millionaire father. In a fit of egalitarian magnanimity that had appalled the rest of the family, he had thrown its twenty-five rooms open rent-free to his indigent creative friends.

This was where Maria suspected the poet Gabriel Gordon made his London base.

The Sunbeam laboured up the steep, seemingly never-ending hill, its tyres slipping in the slush. At one point Maria feared she might slide all the way back down to the bottom, but she managed to arrest the Sunbeam's slithering retreat and make it up to the crest of the hill without mishap.

The mansion was a dark, snow-encrusted hulk against a sky like curdled milk. The stonework and mouldings were chipped and neglected and the windows – those not boarded up – were cracked and lacking curtains. She pulled up to the kerb directly before the commune and wondered what kind of person would willingly make this their home – then smiled to herself as she realized that she was sounding like her father. The type of person willing to live in such a commune would be young, idealistic and more than eager to put up with physical hardship in the furtherance of their art. And good for them, she thought as she left the car and hurried through the snow towards the broken front gate.

75

She found that the bell pull was in a similar state to the rest of the house – in a word, defunct – and resorted to knocking on the scabrous paint-work with her gloved knuckles.

She reasoned that in a house of over twenty occupied rooms there must be at least one person at home. But as a minute elapsed, and then two, without anyone answering, she began to give up hope. She rapped again, then, bent to the letter box, pushed it open and called through, 'Hello; is anyone there?'

Almost instantly the door was pulled open, leaving her bent double and feeling a little silly as she straightened to see a chubby young man in clay-encrusted corduroy trousers and a ripped shirt staring at her with ill-concealed animosity.

'Not another one?' he said.

She blinked. 'I beg your pardon?'

'You're after Gordon, right?'

'But how did you know?'

He turned his back on her and walked away, grunting, 'It's not difficult.'

She stepped inside and closed the door behind her.

The young man gestured to the heavens with a palette knife. 'Second floor. The room at the back of the house with the green door. But mind the stairs to the second – they're treacherous.'

The mansion had obviously been palatial once, but the neglect that came from multiple inhabit-ants, none of whom took responsibility for its upkeep, had resulted in period features like oak panelling and plaster cornices falling into disre-pair. Attempts had been made to paint the walls,

76

but the overall effect was a patchwork hotchpotch of close but not matching shades.

Maria climbed a wide, carpetless staircase and came to a corridor of bare floorboards. In the distance she made out another, narrower flight of stairs – the treacherous flight the sculptor had warned her about. She made her way along the corridor and passed several rooms whose doors were open to reveal young men and women either working at their art – painting or sketching at easels – or engaged in earnest discussion. Their talk ceased and they stared at her in silence as she passed along the corridor.

She came to the staircase and saw that the tread of the second stair was missing. She stepped over the gaping hole and climbed gingerly, testing every step as she went.

She made it to the top without injury and found herself standing before a railed mezzanine over-looking the floor below. On the far side of the mezzanine, at the back of the house, was a door daubed a sickly shade of bright green.

She made her way to the green door and knocked.

There was no reply, but a neighbouring door opened and a waif of a girl looked out. She wore at least three jumpers of various colours and hugged herself against the freezing temperature. Maria could not help but notice that her legs were bare.

She leaned against the woodwork and looked Maria up and down. 'Classy,' she said.

Maria found herself begging an artist's pardon for the second time that day.

'He must be reverting to type,' the girl went on.

'I must say, I have no idea what you're talking about.'

'And foreign, too. Spanish?'

'French.'

'Sorry, it's the dark complexion. Gabriel prefers blondes, usually. And working-class girls. But as I said, he must be reverting to type, him being an aristocrat.' The girl leaned forward and whispered, 'But I wouldn't knock too hard or you'll wake Sophie, and she'll kill you.'

Maria stopped herself just as she was about to blurt, 'I beg your pardon?' for the third time. 'I take it that Sophie is a friend of Mr Gordon, no?'

'A "friend" is one way of putting it,' the girl said.

'Then I need to speak to her.'

'You sure? I mean, she'll take a knife to you as soon as say hello. Jealous as a cat, Sophie.'

'I assure you that she has no reason to be jealous.'

The girl laughed. 'It's your funeral,' she said, pushing past Maria and turning the handle of the green door. She pushed it open and called out, 'Sophie! A visitor.'

She turned to Maria and said, 'Go on in, but be careful. And don't say I didn't warn you.'

Eyeing the girl, Maria warily stepped into the room and closed the door behind her.

The first thing that struck her about the room was that, in contrast to the rest of the house, it was warm – a fire blazed in a hearth to her right.

78

The second thing that caught her attention was the abundance of canvases – virgin white, half-finished or completed – that hung on the walls or were stacked against them. The paintings were figurative, great daubs of colour depicting, for the most part, naked men and women.

Last of all, she became aware of a mattress positioned on the bare floorboards before the fire and a figure stirring beneath a mound of blankets.

A small, drowsy face peered out, for all the world like a timid animal surveying the lie of the land after a long spell of hibernation. 'Gabriel . . .? Is that you? Gabriel?' She blinked and saw Maria, then sat up and pulled the covers around her nakedness. 'What do you want?'

'I am enquiring after Gabriel Gordon.'

The girl stared at her with puffy red eyes. '*Enquiring?* Why don't you go to hell!'

'Please, I think you're mistaken.'

'He's sent you to do his dirty work! That's just like Gabriel. Tell the bastard to come and tell me himself, or isn't he man enough!'

'Please, Sophie, you don't understand.'

Maria looked around, found a rickety fan-backed chair and repositioned it before the mattress. She sat down. 'I know what you think, but I have nothing to do with Gabriel in that sense.'

Sophie backhanded her nose. 'I don't believe you.' She glanced at the fire, saw that the flames were dying down then reached under the blankets for something.

Maria watched as Sophie pulled out a cylinder.

Scowling with the effort, she bent it in half and fed it into the fire.

The roll was a canvas and, coated in primer and flammable paint, it ignited with a roar. A pulse of heat surged from the hearth.

Maria leaned forward, concerned. 'What are you doing?'

'Oh, I have plenty under here. Dozens. Enough to keep me warm all day and night. They burn beautifully, don't you think?'

'Sophie . . .'

'Look,' the girl said, pulling another rolled canvas from beneath the mound of sheets. She unrolled the painting like a scroll and held it down for Maria's inspection.

The painting depicted a tall, well-built man, naked and sprawling on a mattress – perhaps the very mattress on which Sophie sat now. The man was handsome, with a strong jaw and black flowing hair.

'Who is it?' Maria asked, though she suspected the subject was Gordon himself.

Sophie sneered. 'As if you don't know, you bitch!' She released the canvas and it clenched itself back into a loose cylinder. Sophie bent it in half with a grunt and fed it to the flames.

'And here's another one,' the girl said, unrolling yet another painting of Gordon for Maria's inspection.

'It's very good.' She peered at the bottom of the canvas and read the signature: 'Sophie Miller'.

Sophie made to consign the painting to the fire, but Maria reached out and pulled it from her grip. She cast the canvas to one side and said, 'You have talent, Sophie. You should never destroy works of art. One day you'll regret it.'

'I'll regret nothing! You'd destroy them if . . . if you . . .' She shook her head. 'Just you wait. You'll see. You'll know what it feels like when he's used you and leaves you to rot!'

'Sophie, please . . . You're mistaken about Gabriel and me.' She reached into her purse and produced a business card. 'Here,' she said, proffering it to the girl.

Hesitantly, Sophie took the card.

'Maria Dupré,' she read. 'Literary agent, Elder and Dupré.'

She looked up, shaking her head. 'This doesn't prove anything. Or rather it does. He's tired of slumming it with the likes of me.'

As she stared at the girl, naked under the sheets and suffering, Maria felt an immense pity. 'Sophie . . . Please believe me. I've never met Gabriel Gordon in my life.' She considered her next words and thought the lie justified. 'I'm here in my capacity as a literary agent. I've heard about his poetry. Someone recommended it. I can't locate anything he's done, but I'd like to read some of it and . . .' She shrugged and smiled at the girl.

Sophie sat up straight, letting the sheets fall from her body. She was as slim as a child, with small breasts and quite beautiful in an etiolated, elfin way. 'You're not . . . you're not just another of Gabriel's women?'

'Sophie, I've never met Gabriel in my life.'

'I don't believe you!'

Maria sighed. 'Look.' From an inside pocket

of her coat she took a small brown envelope, hesitated and then opened it. She had shown no one the contents of the envelope until now.

She passed Sophie a small photograph. 'My fiancé, Donald Langham.'

Suspiciously, Sophie took the picture, stared at it and smiled. 'He's very handsome.'

The picture was from the agency files, showing Donald at his typewriter, pipe clenched between his teeth.

'And this . . .' she said, passing the girl a small, square card with a heart on the front.

Sophie opened it and read the inscription, '"To Maria, with all my love, Donald."'

She returned the card and the photograph and pointed to a nearby chair. 'Could you pass me . . .?'

Maria handed the girl a paint-covered man's shirt, which she slipped over her head. Three sizes too big for the girl, it had the effect of making her appear even younger.

'Now how about passing me the rest of those canvases,' Maria suggested, 'and I'll put them safely out of harm's way, no?'

The girl smiled timidly and nodded. Maria took the rolls and stacked them on the floorboards away from Sophie's reach.

'I'd offer you tea,' she said, shrugging, 'but I'm out of everything at the moment.'

'I know it's hard,' Maria said, 'but you really shouldn't neglect yourself.' She thought back more than a year to when a young man – ironically enough an artist himself – had proved himself unworthy of her . . . not that she had

82

looked at it in quite that way at the time. She had suffered for a while and neglected herself. She knew what Sophie was going through.

In a small voice, the girl said, 'I know I shouldn't have become involved with Gabriel. I knew it was a mistake. Tania, the girl next door . . . she told me I was a fool.' She shrugged. 'But I couldn't help myself. He . . . he's like an animal, Maria, and he came after me. Do you know something: a part of me hates myself for giving in to him, while another part wanted nothing more than to submit. I am stupid, aren't I?'

Maria shook her head. 'No, of course you're not.' Not stupid at all, she thought; just young and vulnerable and unfortunate in falling victim to someone as unscrupulous as Gabriel Gordon.

'I knew his reputation, knew he couldn't keep his hands off . . .' She smiled up at Maria. 'But I thought that with me it might be different. I thought that maybe I could . . . I know it sounds pathetic but I thought I could tame him, if only I showed him love.'

'I'm sorry.'

'But then I heard he was chasing after a woman in Hampstead – a married woman. He said it was a lie and claimed he only loved me. And a month ago he disappeared up to Scotland. His father lives there, you see.'

'And he hasn't been back since?'

Sophie shook her head. 'That was the last I heard from him. Oh, he said he'd be back, but he was lying. I suspect he has someone up there.'

Maria leaned forward. 'And what makes you think that? I'm sure there's an obvious explanation for why he hasn't returned. I mean, look at the weather – and it must be even worse in the Highlands.'

Sophie shook her head. 'But then why hasn't he rung? He should at least have rung, shouldn't he?'

'Perhaps he hasn't had the time,' she said lamely. 'And he is in an out-of-the-way location. The phone connection can't be that reliable.'

Sophie stared into the flames and murmured, 'Yes, that's possible, isn't it?'

'Of course it is. I wouldn't fret, if I were you.'

Sophie went on with an optimism that Maria found pitiable, 'He's a wonderful man, Maria, for all his . . . for all his faults. He's sensitive and talented and . . .' She regarded the flames. 'He can't help what he is, you know? I mean, we're all products of our upbringing, aren't we?'

Guardedly, Maria agreed.

'And Gabriel . . . Well, his mother died when he was a child and his father was something of a martinet. A soldier. They never saw eye to eye about *anything*. His father never understood his poetry. During the war his father was somewhere in the Far East and Gabriel was packed off to boarding school. You see, Gabriel was never *loved*.'

And poor Sophie had assumed, mistakenly, that that was all the spoilt young man would need.

The girl stood up suddenly and darted across the room. She found a sheaf of foolscap and hurried back to the mattress. 'Here. I think they're terribly good.'

84

Maria took the sheets and smoothed them out on her lap. She read a verse or two and smiled at Sophie.

'What do you think?'

How could she tell the girl that the poems were mediocre? 'There's certainly something there,' she said, placing the poems on the floor beside the mattress.

She looked around the room at the stacked canvases. 'Are you managing to sell much of your work, Sophie?'

The girl pulled a sour face. 'I flog one once in a blue moon for half a crown,' she said. 'You see, I'm self-taught. I never went to art school or college, and the art world is so full of snobs.'

'You're very talented. I hope you realize that? Keep working and don't be downhearted by rejection. I know it's easy for me to say that, but please persevere. The only way you'll fail, with a talent like yours, is if you stop painting. So don't stop. Carry on.'

Sophie smiled. 'I will do. Thank you.'

Maria looked around at the paintings again and thought how nice it would be to help the girl. Perhaps she could commission Sophie to do a portrait of Donald – fully clothed, of course.

She reached out and took Sophie's hand. 'I must dash before the snow gets any worse. It's been nice talking to you.'

'Thank you,' Sophie said, with pathetic gratitude.

'And don't burn any more canvases, OK?'

Maria made her way from the room and back down the dilapidated staircase. She left the house, hunched against the wind and the snow. Perhaps in reaction to Sophie's pitiable love for the poet, she thought of Donald, and then recalled something that a novelist had once said to her: 'Having a novel on the go is like having a boiler burning in the basement – it's a constant source of warmth.'

As she started the Sunbeam and eased it out into the grey, slush-covered street, she thought that her love for Donald Langham was very much like the novelist's boiler: it warmed her.

She considered driving over to Notting Hill and looking for his address book, but she wanted nothing more than to return to her apartment and make herself a cup of tea. She would pop round to the flat first thing in the morning.

In the meantime, she would ring Donald later today and give him the news that Gabriel Gordon had lied to him and had been in the Highlands all along.

Nine

'Do you mind,' Ryland panted, 'if we take a breather? I'm fagged.'

'Damned good idea. There's a rock over there.'

They crossed to a large boulder at the side of the track and sat down. Ryland lit up a Woodbine, cupping the match in both hands against the wind. Langham stuffed his pipe and soon had it going. He looked down at his brogues. 'Wish I'd thought to bring my boots but I didn't think we'd be doing much hiking.'

Ryland lifted his right shoe. Like the rest of him, his foot was long and thin, more like a flipper. He stuck a finger into a hole in the sole. 'Look at that! Me sock's sopping!'

The tarmac'd lane had petered out a mile back, turning into a rutted cart track. Langham peered up the hillside; PC Ross's tiny croft was still a mile and a half away.

Ryland puffed on his cigarette. He was garbed in a wholly unsuitable raincoat and a flat cap, and looked for all the world like a disreputable, down-at-heel greyhound trainer. He shook his head. 'I spend too long behind the desk. Don't do enough footwork.'

'I'm the same. And I've put on a few pounds since meeting Maria.' He patted his stomach. 'We dine out far more often than I used to. And I'm partial to sticky desserts.'

'What you need,' Ryland said, 'is to join the agency. Then you can do all the footwork and the pounds'll fall off you.'

Langham smiled. 'And deprive you of exercise?'

He gazed down the hillside at the loch. It was a couple of miles long and, from this elevation, more than ever resembled a leaping dolphin. The castle rose, bleak and severe, against the silver water.

He gazed around at the stark terrain; the land rolled away to the east, hillside after hillside gaining elevation until, on the horizon, the distant line of the Cairngorms showed hazily purple.

Above all this, a vast bruise-blue sky confirmed the BBC's forecast of snow to come.

Ryland shivered. 'My God, I find all this depressing.'

Langham looked at his friend. 'But you deal with evil-doing every day.'

Ryland laughed. 'Not the attempted murder business, you duffer! This' – he indicated the landscape –'gives me the jitters. Give me Clapham Common any day.'

Langham smiled. 'It's because we're not accustomed to its grandeur, Ralph. We feel reduced by the dimensions. There's nothing like gargantuan geography to make one feel insignificant.'

Ryland peered at him. 'That sounds like it's come straight out of one of your books.'

'It hasn't,' Langham said, 'but it might.'

The wind intensified, stinging his cheeks with its sub-zero chill. He lowered his hat and looked up the hillside. 'Should we push on?'

Ryland ground out his tab end with his leaking shoe and they continued up the cart track.

'How should we play this, Don?'

Langham considered. 'Show Ross your PI accreditation and explain the situation. We're more likely to gain his cooperation that way.'

Thirty minutes later they approached the tiny white-washed croft. Along with the rich aroma of burning peat they were greeted by the gamey scent of cooking meat.

Langham was about to pound on the weathered timber door, but their approach had obviously been noted. The door opened and a huge man, surely too vast to inhabit such a tiny house with any degree of comfort, loomed on the threshold.

'Ah, and you'll be the detectives up from London, no doubt? Come in.'

The door opened to reveal a kitchen-cum-living room. A huge leaded range occupied one wall, steaming with pots. On a big oak table in the middle of the room lay the empurpled remains of a skinned rabbit, and next to it a lethal-looking carving knife embedded in a chopping block.

'Excuse the carnage, gentlemen. I prepare a broth on Sundays to last me the week.'

Langham made the introductions. Ryland attempted to show Ross his PI card but the constable waved this aside. He was a broad, raw-boned giant with a thatch of ginger hair, a jaw like an anvil and smiling blue eyes. Langham put him in his early thirties. 'Tea? I've no milk, but plenty of sugar. Take a seat.'

'That'll do me,' Ryland said. 'Three sugars.'

Langham sat down at the table. 'But how did you know . . .?'

Ross interrupted, his great back to them as he prepared three mugs of tea. 'I was speaking to the major the other day. He said he'd be calling someone in from London.'

He lodged the mugs on the table and took a seat himself.

'Nasty business,' Ryland said, slurping his brew. 'What did you make of it?'

'It was as it appeared. Someone had taken potshots at the major and the Dutch fellow. Pity we couldn't locate the bullets – that would have helped. Anyway, I took a statement from them

89

and forwarded everything to Carter in Inverness. I reckon he'll be along tomorrow . . .' He glanced through the tiny window, '. . . weather willing.'

'How's the major regarded in the area?' Langham asked.

'Everyone's known him for years. He's been around here since he was knee high. He's well liked.'

'So you can't think of anyone with a grudge against him?'

Ross shook his head. 'As I say, he's well liked.'

'And the engineer, Vermeulen? Do you know anything about him?'

'I've met him once or twice but I can't say I know him. Nor do I know much about him, either. Isn't it more likely that the gunman was after him, rather than the major?'

'We're keeping our options open at the moment,' Langham said.

'We did wonder,' Ryland said, 'if you'd noticed any strangers in the area over the past week or so? Any vehicles not belonging to locals?'

'Interesting you should mention that,' Ross said. 'I did see a vehicle the other day – last Tuesday. An old Morris Commercial van backed into the woods on the shore of the loch.'

'Did you see who was driving it?' Langham asked.

Ross shook his head. 'I went to have a look but there was no one about. It was locked up and all I saw in the cab was a couple of old news-papers. It was gone the following morning.'

'You didn't happen to take its registration number?'

Ross smiled. 'I did, out of habit. After the shooting incident on Wednesday, I rang the registration number through to Inverness, to be on the safe side. Just a jiffy while I get my notebook.'

He ducked into the adjoining room. Langham said, 'What do you make of that? The van was around just before the shooting.'

'Worth looking into,' Ryland said.

Ross returned with a tiny black notebook and read out the Commercial's number. Langham copied it into his own notebook and thanked the constable. 'We'll probably wander down and take a look-see when we leave here. Where did you say you saw the van?'

Ross pointed through the window. 'Directly below the croft – the only woodland on the shore. You can't miss it, and there's a path through the bracken from here that joins the road. It'll only take you ten minutes to reach the woods.'

Ross cupped his mug in both hands and looked from Ryland to Langham. 'We don't get much crime in these parts, gentlemen, and the bit of trouble there is . . . well, it's soon cleared up. I don't see my job as an investigator as such but more of a peacekeeper, helping sort out disputes and disagreements. When something like this happens it brings back bad memories.'

Langham had been studying the stretched, purple meat of the rabbit's carcass on the table, but he looked up at Ross now. 'Memories?'

'Do you know how many murders there have been in these parts since seventeen hundred?'

'I heard about the servant girl being strangled

91

a couple of hundred years ago,' Ryland said. 'The story is her ghost still haunts the castle.'

Langham smiled; he rather thought that Ross's 'bad memories' were not occasioned by this particular homicide. 'Has there been a more recent murder?'

'Aye, there has. Ten years ago. I'd just taken up the beat, fresh from training, and it was my first ever crime. I don't mind admitting that it shook me up.'

'What happened?' Ryland asked.

'February 'forty-five. Over yonder.' He pointed through the window. 'See that tiny croft on the far shore?'

Langham peered and made out a small, square outline of tumbled stone against the heather. 'It looks more like a ruin.'

'Aye, well, it is now. But back then it was the home of Fergus Bruce. He owned a smallholding, a few sheep and some chickens. A bachelor. Peaceable man, he was. Wouldn't harm a fly. I'd known Fergus all my life.'

He fell silent, staring into his mug. 'I found the body. I was in the habit of calling on Fergus every few days for eggs. His birds produced the finest eggs this side of Glenross. The door was open . . . which was unusual seeing as it was winter, and raining hard . . . so I went inside and found Fergus. He was on the floor.'

'It must have been a hell of a shock,' Ryland said quietly.

'I couldn't believe what I was seeing, Mr Ryland. Fergus had been bludgeoned around the head. And I don't mean hit just once or twice.

He'd been beaten again and again with something blunt and heavy. Turned out to be the starter handle of Fergus's own car. His skull was battered to pieces. There was nothing left of . . .'

He fell silent again, reliving the scene.

'I was twenty-two, gentlemen, and I'd never even seen so much as a bloody nose. Never even seen a fistfight in all my years. And then that happened . . . After the shock, all I felt was anger. Who could have done such a thing to old Fergus? He didn't deserve that end.'

'Who was responsible?' Langham asked.

Ross looked up, his expression bleak. 'That's the thing, gentlemen. I felt rage then and a sense of frustration now. Because, you see, they never did find his killer.'

'It must have been someone local, surely?' Ryland said.

'That was the frightening thought – that we had a killer on our doorstep. The big guns arrived from Aberdeen and investigated but they came up with nothing. Not even a motive. There was nothing stolen from the croft – not that there was much to steal, mind. But the little money in the place was still there, untouched, on the dresser. There was no reason why anyone should have killed old Fergus like that, no reason at all.'

'When in February did it happen?' Langham asked.

'Late on.'

'Do you know the exact date?'

Ross shook his head. 'You'd think something like that would imprint itself on the memory,

93

wouldn't you? But all I recall is that it was late in the month.'

'I'm sorry we've stirred such unpleasant memories.'

Ross smiled. 'Don't be. They're always there, not far from the surface, every time I look across the water. It's the not knowing that rankles, gentlemen. The fact that we just don't know who did it and that they're still out there, unpunished.'

'You never know,' Ryland said. 'One day . . .'

Langham finished his tea and said, 'You've been very generous with your time, Constable. We'll go take a look at the woods.'

'I'd hurry if I were you. The snow's starting and it looks set in.'

Langham peered out as he donned his hat and wound his scarf around his neck. Snowflakes as large as feathers drifted past the window.

Ross showed them to the door. 'Call again if you need anything else,' he said. Langham thanked him again and led the way from the croft and across the track.

He indicated a worn dirt path that led steeply through the gorse and bracken. The loch was a cold grey expanse far below, with the woodland a dark smudge on its near shore.

'What did you make of that?' Langham called out above the wind as they tramped down the hillside.

'Didn't learn much more than we knew already.'

'And what about the murder of Fergus Bruce?'

'February, 'forty-five,' Ryland said. 'The German plane . . .' He was silent for a time as they hurried along. 'Too much of a coincidence *not* to be connected, Don?'

'You're right. Two events like that . . . a gruesome murder and the crash-landing of a Nazi plane, taking place just days apart.'

'I can't help wondering, Don, if this plane might be at the bottom of the whole damned business.'

Langham pulled his scarf up around his mouth and nose, leaving only his eyes free, and leaned into the wind. Already the snow was an inch deep, and more than once he almost lost his footing on the slippery ground.

'Not far to go now,' Ryland said, pointing ahead.

They were halfway down the hillside; the woods were a forlorn tangle of leafless sycamore and elder backed by the pewter waters of the loch.

Five minutes later they crossed the road and paused on the margin of the woodland. It covered a narrow strip perhaps a mile long, still and silent in the falling snow.

'Here!' Ryland called out, indicating the ground under the cover of the trees. Langham joined him and stared down at a pair of tyre tracks imprinted in the mud and leaf mulch. They followed the tracks through the woods, where the wind lessened and the tangle of foliage overhead kept out much of the falling snow, and came to the loch.

Langham stood on the bank, hands in pockets, and stared across the water at the castle, its lights shining invitingly. From this angle, the ruins of the northern and western battlements, and the abbreviated southern wall, could not be seen; the two remaining towers stood tall and imposing, with the crenellated battlements in between.

'Stop your sightseeing, Don, and look at this.'

Ryland was kneeling beside the water and peering down at something. 'See . . .?'

The detective pointed to a mess of mud and pebbles lapped by the cold loch water. 'What do you make of that?'

'I don't see . . .' Langham began – and then made out what Ryland's eagle eyes had spotted. A deep rut cut through the mud. He turned, following its trajectory up the bank.

'My word, it ends directly between the tyre's tracks.'

'You know what it is, Don?' Ryland said, and went on before Langham could reply. 'It's the mark made by the keel of a boat – a rowing boat in this case – when it's dragged ashore.'

'So whoever owned the van used a boat on the loch last Tuesday or Wednesday.' He stared at the detective. 'Surely it's no coincidence that that was when the shooting took place?'

'I'll get on the phone to London when we get back, Don, and get a contact to check on that registration number.' He blew into his bare hands and rubbed them together. 'Come on, we've seen enough here. I could murder a cuppa.'

They left the woods and walked along the road, bending into the headwind.

The snowfall was relentless. Langham hunched his shoulders and stared down at his feet; he could just about make out the surface of the road

96

as he trudged along, but the rest of the landscape was lost in the blizzard.

He had never been more grateful, thirty minutes later, to behold civilization in the form of electric lighting behind the windows of the castle a hundred yards ahead.

They gained the refuge of the castle with gasps and curses, and only when he was shrugging off his overcoat in the warmth of the hallway did Langham realize how cold he was. He stamped his feet and rubbed his hands, attempting to restore sensation to his frozen extremities.

Mrs Fergusson appeared at the end of the corridor and hurried towards them, maternal concern on her features. 'You look like refugees from an Arctic expedition, gentlemen! How about a nice pot of tea with a wee dash of brandy?'

'That sounds like the best idea I've heard all day,' Langham said.

'Then hurry along to the Stewart room and I'll serve it there. There's a fire burning and do draw up a couple of chairs.'

'Give me the Commercial's number, Don, and I'll phone my contact in Bethnal Green.'

Langham handed over the note then made his way to the Stewart room. He pulled up a couple of armchairs and settled himself before the roaring fire. Vitality returned slowly, and it dawned on him that the crumpets he'd had at eleven were but a distant memory; he was famished.

Ryland entered a couple of minutes later. 'All done. My contact'll get back to me pronto if he comes up with anything.'

Mrs Fergusson bustled in bearing a tray; Langham espied a plate of buttered scones and a pot of marmalade, and could have kissed the woman in gratitude.

'Now help yourself and ring the bell if you require anything further, gentlemen.'

Langham thanked her and sat back in the armchair with his tea and a scone, wondering if this was the closest – excepting his time with Maria, of course – he had ever come to heaven.

'Wait till I ring Annie and tell her about this,' Ryland said. 'Tea and scones in a Highland castle, and me supposed to be working!'

'After battling through that blizzard, I don't feel the slightest bit guilty.'

They ate in silence and Langham closed his eyes and stretched his feet towards the fire.

His reverie – he was considering his return to London and holding Maria in his arms – was interrupted a few minutes later. He sensed a presence beside him and heard a genteel cough.

He opened his eyes and struggled upright.

Renata Káldor towered over him, stunning in a navy blue pinstriped skirt and blazer.

'I wonder if I might talk for a minute with you and your friend, Mr Langham?'

'By all means. Pull up a pew.'

She found a high-backed chair and set it between the two armchairs. 'Mr Ryland seems dead to the world,' she observed.

Langham stretched out a leg and kicked the sleeping Ryland's foot. 'Ralph, on your toes. We have company.'

Ryland came awake instantly and shot up like a startled jack-in-the-box. 'What? Oh, sorry. Taking forty winks.'

Renata tugged on the bell pull and when Mrs Fergusson arrived she requested a pot of Darjeeling.

On closer inspection, Langham thought, the Hungarian possessed a rather severe glamour. With her high, Slavic cheekbones and those peculiarly light green eyes, her thin face was striking rather than conventionally beautiful. Her dominant expression was disdain, though whether this was a true indication of her prevailing mood or merely an impression given by her habit of tilting her head back when regarding anyone, Langham was unable to decide.

She produced a gold case and offered a cigarette to Langham, who declined, and then to Ryland, who accepted and tapped the cigarette on the back of his hand before lighting up. He inhaled, pulled a face and peered at the smoking cylinder with suspicion.

'Helmar. They are Turkish,' Renata explained, fitting a cigarette into a long holder.

Mrs Fergusson returned with a tray of tea and Renata poured herself a cup.

She took a sip, then replaced the cup precisely on the saucer before saying, 'Am I correct in the assumption that you are private detectives, gentlemen?'

Ryland glanced across at Langham. 'Word certainly gets around.'

'Brought in by the major?' she asked, drawing on her cigarette.

Langham said, 'How did you come by this information?'

Renata regarded the men through narrowed eyes and blew out a nonchalant stream of smoke. 'It was something I overheard, a snatch of conversation between the major and Vermeulen a day or two ago.'

Langham knew she was lying. Vermeulen had been unaware of the major's idea to invite them up here until Langham had told him on the pontoon that morning.

Ryland said bluntly, 'We're here to find out who might want the major, or Hans Vermeulen, dead.'

Langham watched her reaction. She took a quick breath and stared from Ryland to Langham as if in disbelief. 'But who might want such a thing? The major is such a harmless soul, and Hans . . .'

'But you must have known about the incident on the pontoon,' Langham said, 'if you overheard the major speaking with Vermeulen?'

'I heard only the briefest snatch of conversation, about bringing in a detective. But what incident?' she asked.

He briefly recounted the shooting and Renata shook her head. 'I cannot begin to imagine who might do such a terrible thing,' she murmured. 'You are doing all within your means to ensure their safety and get to the bottom of this matter?'

'We have things in hand,' Langham assured her.

'That is reassuring,' she said, smiling from Langham to Ryland.

Langham changed the subject, 'How did you meet the major?'

'Quite by chance, as it happens. I wanted to take a holiday, a break in Scotland, where I had never been before. This was three years ago, and I saw an advertisement for the Loch Corraig Castle Hotel in *Tatler*. I booked for two days, came and fell in love with the place, then stayed for a further week. I have returned often since then.'

He glanced at her as he refilled his tea cup. 'If you don't mind my asking, what do you find to do here, other than relax?'

'I usually come in summer, and I enjoy walking and taking a boat out on the loch. When I was a young girl we had a family boat and a lake of our own.' Her eyes became distant as she regarded her lost past. 'I also go out with the major and shoot.' She laughed, and it was the first time Langham had seen amusement animate her usually severe features. 'Are you surprised, Langham, that a lady should shoot?'

He glanced at Ryland, who raised an eyebrow. 'Not at all,' Langham said. 'You mentioned it at dinner last night. You said that your father taught you as a child.'

Her expression misted over and became almost melancholic. 'Did I also say that the communists killed my father?'

He regarded her as she stared into the flames. 'No,' he murmured. 'No, you didn't.'

'Oh, it was described as an accident at the time. He was out hunting, and "someone" – who, it was never found out – shot him in the back. By that time we were already outcasts in our own land, our estate taken from us. We rented a small apartment in Budapest and my father worked as a private tutor to a German family, but he was writing articles for a nationalist pamphlet and the communists wanted him out of the way. It was an ignominious end to a proud life, Mr Langham. A year after my father's murder, my mother fell ill and died. This was in nineteen twenty; I was just seven.'

'I'm sorry,' Langham murmured.

'I do hate to recall those times, gentlemen. They are filled with sadness, with no hope at all. Sadness and grief and despair. I had a distant relative in Munich whom I called an aunt, though really she was nothing of the kind. She took me in and I lived with her family for many years. She was married to a German industrialist, a gross man whom I despised, and they had two girls a little older than myself, whom I hated also. They treated me abominably, the entire family.'

She fell silent, gazing at the smoke coiling up from her cigarette. She looked from Langham to Ryland. 'When I was eighteen I met and married a friend of my "step-uncle". He too was a businessman, and much older than me. It was not a love match but, on my part, an escape. He was a good man, in his own way, and he loved me, or said he did, though I found it hard to reciprocate those sentiments. He died five years later and I inherited his considerable wealth.' She smiled bitterly. 'But if you think for a minute, Mr Langham, that this new-found prosperity in any way made up for my lost life, the life that the communists had destroyed – my lost happiness – then you are sadly mistaken. Those without money often assume that all their troubles, all their woes, would magically vanish if only they had money. But that is not so. While money might buy you a certain freedom, it does nothing to liberate you from the horrors of the past that haunt you. Nor can money buy one health . . .' She waved. 'But all that is in the past,' she said, 'and the future is uncertain.'

Langham stared at the woman and knew that appearances – in this case of a beautiful, wealthy, sophisticated socialite – were deceptive.

Ryland finished his tea. 'When did you leave Germany?' he asked.

She drew on her cigarette, regarding him. 'I came to England in 'thirty-six. I knew a few people in London. As the years passed I watched the rise of communism in Russia and its satellites, and the thankfully abortive attempts of the republicans in Spain . . . and before and during the war I ran anti-communist fundraising events. I met many prominent people and tried to make them see the evil of the Soviet regime, but they were stupid and ignorant and blind.' She twisted her face into an ugly sneer. 'I was proven correct, Mr Langham, with events in Eastern Europe after the war, wouldn't you say? The repression in Poland and East Germany . . .'

'Though I'm of the Left,' Langham said diplomatically, 'I have no love for the Soviets.'

'Their evil is all the worse for their assumption of moral superiority,' she said, 'and their

103

egalitarian ideals. I despise their dictum that the end justifies the means.'

Langham finished his tea and replaced the cup and saucer on the tray. 'I take it you've never been back to Hungary?'

'That would be impossible. The memories . . .'

'And do you mind if I ask if you ever remarried?'

'I do not mind, and I never remarried. I could never bring myself to trust anyone with my liberty.'

What a strange way of expressing it, he thought. And what an oddly complex woman – a little like the Turkish cigarettes she affected to smoke, he fancied: an elegant exterior disguising a smouldering, toxic interior.

Mrs Fergusson appeared in the doorway and called out, 'Mr Langham, you have a phone call.'

Ryland stretched, yawned and said, 'I think I'll go for a little kip before dinner. I'm bushed.'

Langham climbed to his feet as the detective left the room. 'Excuse me,' he said to the Hungarian, and crossed to where Mrs F was waiting

'A Maria Dupré, calling from London,' she said. 'Would you care to take it in the morning room, or in your own room?'

'Ah . . .' His own room was a fair hike along the corridor and up a flight of stairs, whereas the morning room was situated in the tower beside the castle's entrance.

Mrs Fergusson went on, 'The phone in the morning room is a direct line out, you see. But the ones in the bedrooms are party lines.'

104

He stared at her. 'Party lines? You mean . . .?'

'Aye, other guests might accidentally overhear your conversation, sir.'

'In that case I'll take the call in the morning room,' he said, and followed Mrs Fergusson along the corridor towards the southern tower.

He picked up the phone and flung himself into a chintz-covered armchair. 'Maria!'

'Donald, I'm missing you! Do you know, this is the first time we've been parted since you proposed to me.'

'My word!'

'Yes, we've seen each other every day.'

'Well, that must account for my melancholy: withdrawal symptoms.'

'Melancholy? You're joking, Donald!'

'Only a little. But I'm missing you like crazy. I was thinking that when I get back I'll take you to a slap-up meal in the West End.'

'That sounds wonderful. And you *will* be back on Tuesday morning? I mean, the investigation . . .?'

'Is getting nowhere fast, to be honest. But come tomorrow afternoon, if we're still at an impasse, then Ralph can stay up here and I'll take the sleeper back to London. Weather permitting, of course.' He peered through the tiny window at the driving snow. 'It started snowing just after breakfast and it's six inches deep already.'

'You must come back, even if you have to walk to Inverness!'

He laughed. 'I'll do that, my darling.'

'Anyway, I have been doing what you asked me, Donald. I went to Muswell Hill this morning and found the commune.'

'Jolly good. And?'

'What a strange place! Gabriel Gordon must be an exceedingly odd young man if he lives there.'

'Well, he certainly is on the decadent side.'

'I mean, it was filthy for one thing, falling to pieces and daubed with mismatched paint. And the people . . .'

'Go on.'

'I met a young girl who is in love with Gabriel Gordon. She was in a terrible state. She thought me one of Gordon's lovers, until I showed her my agency card and said I wanted to see Gordon about his poetry.'

'And? What did she say? Did you find out if he's been back to London?'

'The poor girl said he'd gone off to stay with his father in Scotland over a month ago and hadn't been back since.'

'That's very interesting. Great work, Maria. Oh, did you get the girl's name, by any chance? I might drop it into the conversation when I confront him.'

'She was called Sophie Miller. She looked as if she had been lying naked on a filthy mattress for a week and she was burning paintings of Gabriel Gordon one by one – until I stopped her.'

'Now I wonder why he lied about being here all the while?' Langham mused. 'I did half suspect he hadn't been back to London.' He told her about Vermeulen having thought he'd seen the poet in Inverness last week. 'I'll put it to him and see what he says.'

'Be careful, Donald. I don't want—'

He interrupted. 'He's a poet, Maria, not a pugilist.'

'Still, be careful.'

'I promise. I'll take Ralph with me, OK?'

She laughed. 'He's hardly my idea of a body-guard,' she said. Then: 'Oh, I rang my friend Marguerite, the Hungarian.'

'Any luck?'

'Her maid told me that she was away for the day, so I left a message asking her to call me back. I did mean to pop over to your flat, Donald, and find your address book so I could ring your Dutch friend, but when I left Muswell Hill the snow was falling again. I'll go over in the morning, I promise.'

'That's fine. Take your time.'

'What are the other guests like?' she asked. 'Any beautiful women you've taken a fancy to?'

'Not many . . .' He laughed. 'The Hungarian, Káldor, is a strange fish – remote and as cool as you like. Then there's a girl the major took in – adopted, really – called Elspeth, as timid as a church mouse. And Mrs Fergusson, who runs the place with her husband, is sixty and tweedy in sensible shoes.'

Maria sighed. 'I love listening to your voice, Donald.'

He laughed. 'Oh, I forgot to tell you: the propo-sition from Ralph. He wants me to join him at the agency on a part-time basis.'

'He does?' She sounded surprised. 'And will you?'

'I think I'll seriously consider it. I get on well with Ralph, and the extra spondoolicks will come in handy, especially as I refuse to have your father continuing to pay for the apartment.'

'We'll talk about it when you get back, Donald. And on Tuesday morning we'll meet Charles from gaol.'

'I can't wait to see the old boy,' Langham said, and the thought of Maria, Charles and London made him homesick.

They chatted for a further five minutes, then Langham rang off and sat staring through the leaded window at the snowfall.

Finally he moved himself to leave the morning room; he'd find Ryland and tell him about Gabriel's deception.

On his way up the stairs to the bedrooms, he bumped into Mrs Fergusson – almost literally – as she rounded a corner bearing a pile of bedlinen. He danced around her, then asked, 'I don't suppose you might know where I'd find Gabriel? Is he in his room, by any chance?'

'Young Mr Gordon is reading in the Macgregor room, sir. Go back to the morning room and take the corridor along the southern wing. Ground floor, the third door on the left. Young Mr Gordon likes to hide himself away there and bury his nose in a book.'

He thanked her and continued up the stairs.

He knocked on Ryland's door, heard the detective's cockney voice call out: 'Who is it?' and opened the door. Ryland was lying on the bed, hands clasped behind his head.

Langham leaned against the door frame. 'Just been on the blower to Maria. Interesting developments on the Gabriel front.'

108

Ryland sat up. 'Go on.'

'Turns out he never went back to London,' Langham said, and recounted his conversation with Maria.

'Wonder why he lied?'

'That's what I hope to find out. But I was wondering how we should go about asking him. He doesn't know the real reason why we're here, after all.'

Ryland chewed his straggling ginger moustache. 'I think we should come clean. Tell him about the shooting and see how he reacts. Then we hit him with the fact that we know he's been up here for the past month and watch him squirm.'

Langham nodded. 'That sounds sensible.'

'If he gets bolshy,' Ryland said, 'I'll come down on him like a ton of bricks. You play the good cop.'

Langham smiled. 'That'll suit me.' He pushed himself from the wall and led the way through the castle to the Macgregor room.

'Come,' Gabriel Gordon called.

Langham opened the door and entered, followed by Ryland. The room was smaller than the Stewart room – not as ceremonial – with no sentinel suits of armour, tapestries or old oil paintings. It struck Langham as more like the lounge of a traditional hotel.

Gabriel sprawled in a small Queen Anne chair before an open fire, his bulk at odds with the delicacy of the chair, especially as he had his left leg slung over one of its arms. His languorous posture seemed an abuse of an object so elegant.

109

'Gentlemen, to what do I owe the honour? I would have had a decanter on hand had I known you were joining me.'

He set aside a slim volume of poetry – Ezra Pound, Langham noted – on a small table and pushed himself further upright, but still affected to slouch.

Ryland positioned himself with his back to the fire, his hands clasped behind him. Langham sat in an armchair across the hearth from the poet.

'We've just come for a little chat,' he said.

'I suspect you have no idea why your father called us here?' Ryland said.

Gabriel swept a big hand through his dark locks and smiled a little unsurely. 'I thought you said you were old friends? Said you were taking a break. What's all this about him calling you up here?'

'You have no idea at all of the . . . prevailing situation?' Langham asked.

'Gentlemen,' Gabriel's expression was a mixture of bemusement and frustration, 'I have no idea what you're talking about. What "prevailing situation"?'

Langham glanced at Ryland, who nodded. Langham said, 'We have reason to believe that someone wants your father, or Hans Vermeulen, dead.'

That had the effect of galvanising the poet from his lassitude. He sat up, staring at Langham. 'What? Someone wants . . .? What the hell's going on here? What do you mean?'

Ryland said, 'Don's put it in a nutshell,' and

proceeded to tell the poet about the shooting incident.

Gabriel heard him out, staring into the flames of the fire, his long, handsome face a mask of concentration. He looked up when Ryland came to an end. 'But who could do such a thing? And why?' He stopped and stared at Langham. 'Is it an outsider or a resident in the castle?'

Langham looked up at Ryland, who said, 'We don't know that at the moment. It could be either.' He removed a card from his jacket pocket and passed it to the poet, who gave it a cursory glance and handed it back.

'Your father called us up to look into the situation,' Ryland said, 'which is what we're doing. We're investigating the movements of *everyone* in the castle.'

Gabriel looked surprised. 'Everyone? Why, you can't be saying that you suspect that I would do something like . . .?'

'We're saying nothing of the kind, at the moment,' Langham said. 'But we must be thorough in our investigations. What we need is for everyone to be open with us when asked about their movements over the past . . . the past month, say?'

'In order to rule out certain individuals from suspicion,' Ryland said, smiling, 'we require the *truth*.'

Gabriel sat back in the chair, his legs outstretched. 'Of course. I fully understand.'

'So,' Langham said, smiling with reassurance, 'where were you over that period?'

'As I told you yesterday when you gave me a

111

lift,' Gabriel said, 'for the past few weeks I've been in London.'

'At Muswell Hill?'

'That's right.'

'And you're quite sure about that?'

The poet's eyes flashed. 'Of course I'm sure. Do you doubt my word?'

Before Langham could reply, Ryland said, 'Of course we doubt your word, Gordon. Look, there are two ways of doing this. You can tell us the truth, plain and simple, right now – or we get the police in to give you a grilling.'

Gabriel looked across at Langham, who turned a hand in an eminently peaceable gesture. 'If I were you, Gabriel, I'd save myself a lot of time and trouble and tell us what you've been doing up here for the past month. You see, I, for one, seriously doubt that you'd harm a hair on your father's head. And to be honest I can't see you wanting Vermeulen dead, either—'

'But *I* wouldn't be so sure,' Ryland snarled. 'You stand to gain quite a packet when the old man shuffles off. This castle must be worth a fortune. And you've said yourself that you dislike the engineer.'

'If you think for a minute I'd—'

'And it must be galling,' Ryland went on, 'to watch your father fritter away all those hundreds, or even thousands, on a project you yourself have called a folly. The sooner he's out of the way the sooner you can wind up the salvage operation and get your paws on all that cash in the bank.'

Gabriel looked horrified. 'I don't know what you're talking about,' he said.

Ryland smiled. 'Is your old man a bit tight with the old cash? Is he reluctant to subsidise your indulgent lifestyle? It must be so frustrating to see all those thousands tied up in this old pile and not be able to get your hands on them.'

Gabriel stared at Ryland, defiant. 'I didn't do anything.'

Langham leaned forward and tapped the poet on the knee conspiratorially. 'Do yourself a favour, Gabriel, and tell us what you were doing in Inverness.'

Gabriel closed his eyes and murmured, 'I didn't take a potshot at my father or Vermeulen, so I don't see that what I was doing in Inverness has any relevance.'

'That's for us to decide,' Langham said. 'What were you doing there?'

Gabriel sighed. 'If you must know, I was seeing someone.'

Ryland grinned, enjoying himself. '"Someone"? Someone as in a business partner, perhaps? A publisher? Or could it have been a butcher, a baker or a candlestick maker?'

'For Christ's sake!' the poet exploded. 'I was seeing a woman.'

Ryland smiled at the disclosure. 'There, you see – that wasn't so painful, was it?' he said in a mock-soothing tone. 'There was no reason to keep it from us, was there?'

Langham asked, 'Who was the woman?'

Gabriel avoided his gaze. 'If you don't mind, I'd rather keep that to myself.'

'But we *do* mind,' Ryland snapped. 'We need

to know in order to verify your story. Otherwise,' he went on, 'how the hell do we know you weren't sneaking around the castle, taking a pop at your father and Vermeulen?'

'Who was she?' Langham asked gently. 'You have my word that it'll go no farther than the two of us.'

Gabriel leaned forward and hung his head in his hands, silent.

At last he looked up and said, 'I'm sorry, I can't tell you. You can suspect me if you like, but I can't tell you who I was seeing.'

Langham leaned back in his chair and said, 'Is that because you wish to protect this person? Because you fear your father's anger if it ever got out?'

Gabriel ran a hand through his dishevelled hair and stared at Langham.

'You have my word,' Langham said, 'that I'll tell no one, least of all your father, who you were seeing.' He paused, then said, 'It was Elspeth, wasn't it?'

Gabriel's eyes widened. 'How the hell . . .?' he began.

Langham smiled. 'It doesn't take a degree in psychology to see that the girl is head-over-heels in love with you. And at dinner last night, the way you two interacted . . . Well, it was pretty obvious that something was going on.'

Gabriel sighed. 'We've been seeing each other for the past year, when I can make it up here and she can escape down to London. But London wasn't ideal – the old man doesn't like her going away even for short breaks. And when I was up here . . . Well, what with the Fergussons on my father's side, it was awkward.'

'So you decided to hole up in Inverness,' Ryland said, 'and have Elspeth come over for a bit of slap and tickle when she could make it?'

Gabriel looked up at the detective. 'You are a rather crude and despicable little man, aren't you?'

Ryland grinned. 'At least I'm honest, guv,' he said, emphasizing his cockney drawl. He smiled across at Langham. 'What was the name of his squeeze in Muswell Hill? Sophie, wasn't it?'

Langham leaned back in his chair, watching Gabriel closely.

Anger blazed in the poet's eyes. 'That's been over for ages! And it was never even that serious anyway.'

'And Elspeth is?' Langham asked. 'Or is she just another fling? Which is why your father was so concerned and so determined to keep you apart? Your reputation in that department precedes you, Gabriel.'

'I like Elspeth very much,' Gabriel said. 'My father's proscription on our relationship was intolerable—'

'But entirely understandable, given your track record.'

'What does my father know about these things?'

Langham stared at the young man. 'He was – is – acting in what he sees as Elspeth's best interests, surely you can see that? Or do you merely see it as vindictive curtailment of your pleasure?'

'Sometimes,' Gabriel said, trembling, 'I find

115

myself hating my father with a passion, hating his conservatism, his bigoted, reactionary view of the world.'

'Hating your father,' Ryland said, 'enough to want him dead?'

The poet stared down at his hands. 'Of course not,' he muttered.

Langham looked at Ryland and made a silent gesture towards the door.

'Thanks for your time,' Ryland said. 'We'll see you at dinner, no doubt.'

Gabriel looked up, something pleading in his eyes as he stared at Langham. 'And you'll keep your promise? Not a word about this to my father?'

Langham nodded. 'Not a word,' he said.

They left the Macgregor room and strolled down the corridor. 'There's something about the man,' Ryland admitted, 'that puts my back up.'

'It was pretty obvious, Ralph. You gave him a hard time.'

'Well, I did say I'd play the bad cop, didn't I?'

'And you played it to perfection. So . . . what do you think?'

'About whether he wants his old man out of the way?' Ryland made a facial expression Langham had seen before when the detective was weighing up the options: he inflated one cheek and then the other in quick succession, as if shuttling a marble back and forth in his mouth. 'Much as I don't like the man, I doubt he was behind the shooting.'

'For what it's worth, I agree,' Langham said.

'Though of course he might have been going after Vermeulen for reasons we haven't yet fathomed.' He looked at his watch. 'An hour and a half before dinner. I think I'll go to my room and catch a bit of shut eye.'

'You do that,' Ryland said. 'I'll try and scrounge another cuppa from Mrs Fergusson.'

Langham retired to his room, lay down and went over what Gabriel Gordon had told them. He thought of Sophie in Muswell Hill, then considered Elspeth Stuart, and couldn't help feeling sorry for the orphan.

Ten

Langham was awoken by a light tapping at his door.

'Mr Langham,' Elspeth said, 'dinner will be served shortly if you'd care to come down.'

'I'm on my way,' he called.

He washed, changed then hurried down to join the diners; they were filing from the Stewart room by the time he arrived. 'There you are, Langham,' the major said. 'For a minute I thought we had another absentee.'

'Another?' he asked.

'Renata's ill. She hasn't mentioned . . .?'

'"Mentioned"?' Langham prompted.

'Her condition? Obviously not. I'll tell you another time, Langham. Now's neither the time nor place.' He changed the subject. 'Hey-ho!

Suckling pig! You recall those boars we roasted in Kashmir? Those were the days.'

Langham followed the major into the dining hall, wondering about Renata Káldor's 'condition'.

The seating arrangements were the same as the night before: Langham sat between Ryland and Elspeth, while across from him were ranged Vermeulen, Gabriel and Professor Hardwick. Ulrich Meyer occupied Renata's place at the opposite end of the table from the major.

'Renata not joining us this evening?' Vermeulen asked as he spooned his French onion soup.

'As I was telling Langham,' the major said, 'she's not feeling quite the ticket.'

Gabriel knocked back a glass of red wine in one go, reached for the bottle and refilled his glass. It was not, Langham judged, his first; the poet's face was flushed and his hand trembled as he poured the wine. He wondered if his inebriation was a result of their interview that afternoon.

'It is unfortunate that Mrs Káldor is indisposed,' Meyer said between spoonfuls of soup. 'I have yet to speak to her since my arrival. I recall we had some stimulating conversations during my last visit.'

'About the bad old days in Germany?' Gabriel asked.

'About the evils of communism, as a matter of fact,' Meyer said.

Vermeulen rolled his eyes. 'I might have guessed.'

'I hope Mrs Káldor recovers soon,' Meyer said, 'so that we can continue our discussion.'

The major said, 'Renata likes to present a stiff upper lip to the world, but between you, me and the gatepost it's all show. She's as fragile as they come.' He shook his head sadly. 'Not surprising, really, considering what she's been through.'

'And that is?' Professor Hardwick asked with his trademark benign smile.

'Hounded out of her homeland by the communists,' the major said, 'then persecuted by the Nazis.'

Langham looked up. Káldor had said nothing about that when they'd spoken earlier. 'Persecuted? On what grounds?'

'Something to do with her then husband, apparently,' the major said.

'Was he Jewish?' Ryland asked.

'No, but he opposed the Nazi regime. He died in the mid-thirties, and according to Renata the Nazis had her name in their little black book and made her life uncomfortable. So when she could, she took the opportunity and skedaddled to Blighty.'

'With her inheritance comfortably stashed away,' Gabriel muttered drunkenly.

To Langham's right, Elspeth jerked as she landed a warning punt on Gabriel's shin. The poet looked up suddenly and scowled at her. She bent innocently to her soup.

'What was that, my boy?' the major asked.

'Nothing,' Gabriel muttered, staring down at his plate.

'Your trouble, young man,' the major said, pointing at his son with a thick forefinger, 'is a distinct lack of respect.'

119

Gabriel took another draft of wine. 'I apologise – wine speaking and all that . . .'

The tension was diffused when Mrs Fergusson flung open the doors and pushed in a serving trolley, upon which sat an enormous silver salver. She pushed the trolley to the table and lifted the lid of the salver to reveal a whole suckling pig.

'Please allow me to assist you,' Meyer said, rising stiffly. Together they lifted the salver on to the table.

'My word,' the major declared, 'you've done us proud, Mrs F.'

Beaming her satisfaction, she bustled from the room.

'I'll do the honours, if you don't mind,' said the major, brandishing a carving knife.

The diners tucked into the pork, accompanied by roast potatoes and steamed vegetables. Langham sipped his wine; he would have preferred beer – red wine was Maria's favoured tipple – but he had to admit that the Burgundy slipped down a treat. Beside him, Ryland was on his second glass.

A little later, Vermeulen asked of Gabriel, 'And what are you working on at the moment, if I might ask?'

'A poem,' Gabriel answered shortly. 'A long poem.'

'About?'

Gabriel sighed and said, 'Are you really interested, Vermeulen?'

'Of course.' The Dutchman's eyes twinkled. 'That is why I asked.'

'Very well, I'm working on an epic poem in the manner of Eliot, about post-war austerity in Britain and how it relates to the cultural desert in which we find ourselves . . .'

'How fascinating,' Vermeulen interrupted dismissively and turned to address Herr Meyer.

Conversation fragmented; Vermeulen, Meyer and the major spoke of matters concerning the project. Langham divided his attention between Ryland – comparing tonight's feast with the last time they had dined together, at a policemen's charity event in Southwark last year – and Elspeth, who asked him where he got his ideas for his novels.

Gabriel moodily tucked into his meal, polishing off half a bottle of wine and opening another. Professor Hardwick, away in a world of his own, ate slowly and from time to time beamed dreamily around the table like a cleric with a predilection for laudanum.

At one point, during a lull in the conversation, the major said, 'I was speaking to Fergusson before dinner. He came down to tell me he'd had a call from Fraser, a landowner up the valley. Apparently the road's cut off at the pass.'

Ryland looked up. 'Don't tell me we're stranded here? Not that I'm complaining – there are worse places to be stranded.'

'I do hope,' said the professor from the far end of the table, 'that we're well stocked with provisions?'

'Don't worry y'self on that score,' the major reassured him. 'The Fergussons keep a well-stocked larder. And even if the worst came to the

121

worst and the electricity went down, we have our own generator. We'd be able to see the winter out!'

'I wasn't thinking of remaining here that long,' Langham laughed.

Elspeth asked, 'When were you thinking of returning to London, Mr Langham?'

'We're booked on the London sleeper from Inverness tomorrow evening.'

'No chance,' Gabriel belched. He turned to Vermeulen and said, 'Well, this scuppers your plans, eh?'

'And what do you mean by that?'

'What did you say yesterday? That you hoped to raise the plane before Christmas? Are you still as optimistic now?'

'The long-range forecast from the BBC indicated that the snow will pass within a week,' the Dutchman replied, 'and a period of clear weather will follow. I plan to reconvene my team from Edinburgh and go ahead with the salvage. I see no reason why we cannot have the plane out of the loch by Christmas, as originally planned.'

'In your dreams, more like,' Gabriel slurred.

'And even if we are delayed until the New Year,' the engineer went on, 'we shall successfully accomplish the salvage sooner rather than later.'

'I raise my glass to that happy day!' Meyer said.

'And all the while,' Gabriel said, 'my father's paying through the nose for your services.'

'I'll have you know,' said Vermeulen, 'that I

122

am not charging the major for my services during this period of inactivity.'

'I should jolly well hope not,' Gabriel rejoined.

The major leaned forward, across Vermeulen, and tapped his son's hirsute wrist. 'And whatever the financial arrangements of the project might be, my boy, it is a matter between Hans and myself. Restrict yourself to your blessed verse and leave the engineering to the men, hm?'

Gabriel glared at his father and was gathering himself to launch some barbed reply; to forestall him, Langham said to Professor Hardwick, 'You mentioned showing us around the castle at some point, Professor.'

Hardwick beamed. 'Perhaps after breakfast tomorrow, if you are free? Yes, a guided tour – why not? You can listen to my tapes and I'll tell you all about the place.'

'Splendid,' Langham said, despite his scepticism.

Gabriel drained yet another glass of wine. 'Chasing spooks'll make a change from all the snooping around you've been doing recently, eh, Langham?'

Langham held the poet's gaze and said, '"Snooping around"? Whatever do you mean by that?'

'C'mon! Tell everyone why you're really here, man!'

'Gabriel,' the major warned, 'that's quite enough.'

Gabriel wiped his lips and flung down his napkin as if issuing a challenge. 'No, it's not. It's not enough by a long chalk.' He pointed across the table at Langham and Ryland and said, 'This pair, Ryham and Langland . . . whatever they call themselves . . . burst in on me this afternoon and . . .' He paused and smiled. 'Well, why don't you tell everyone what's going on here?'

Langham sighed. 'Everyone? I think only Professor Hardwick, Herr Meyer and Elspeth don't know what is "going on", as you say.'

Gabriel leaned forward. 'Well, why don't you tell *them* what's happening?'

'Happening?' the professor blinked.

Meyer blotted his lips with a napkin. 'What is happening, precisely?'

Beside Langham, Elspeth was agitated. 'I don't understand – what is all this about?'

'Go on,' Gabriel laughed, 'tell them. Tell them you burst in this afternoon and accused me of trying to kill my own father.'

Ryland said, 'We said nothing of the kind. We merely asked you for an explanation of your whereabouts over the past few weeks.'

Langham glanced at Elspeth. She sat stiffly, staring at Gabriel as if frozen.

'We were endeavouring,' Langham said, more in explanation to the major who was looking non-plussed, 'to account for everyone's movements and whereabouts while all this has been going on. Gabriel, for personal reasons we need not reveal here . . .' and he stared across the table at the poet, '. . . took exception to our investigations.'

Elspeth screwed up her napkin, her face drawn. 'But what is happening, Mr Langham? What "investigations"?'

'Elspeth,' the major said, 'listen to me, please. I wasn't going to say anything about this, until this drunken young fool' – he glared across the table at his son – 'started shooting his mouth off.'

Hardwick asked blandly, 'Is something not quite right, Major?'

The old man sighed. 'Everything is under control, let me assure you. Langham and Ryland are on hand, and I have every confidence in their ability.'

'But Major, please . . .?' Elspeth pleaded.

Meyer said, 'I think an explanation might be in order.'

The major regarded the girl. 'Elspeth, I'll be blunt. There was an incident the other day on the pontoon . . .'

'Go on,' Gabriel said. 'Go on, say it! Very well, I will. Someone is out to kill my father, or Vermeulen – there seems to be some confusion on the matter. Someone took a potshot at 'em and Langham and Ryland think it's one of us.'

'We said nothing of the sort, Gabriel,' Langham said. 'At the moment,' he said, looking around the table at the diners, 'we're trying to eliminate individuals from suspicion.'

Elspeth gasped, her face as white as her napkin.

'And as y'can see, girl,' the major said, 'I'm as hale and hearty as I've ever been, and Hans is still in the land of the living.'

Professor Hardwick was all aflutter. 'But I say, this is quite extraordinary.'

'If there is anything at all I might do to assist you in this matter . . .' Meyer said.

'I appreciate that,' Langham said. 'But—'

With a cry, Elspeth rose to her feet and rushed from the room. The major stared at his son. 'And look what you've done! If I were you I'd go and ensure she's . . .' He stopped himself. 'On second thoughts, you've caused enough harm this evening. I'll go and have a word with the gal.'

He flung his napkin to the table, glared at Gabriel, then excused himself and limped from the room.

Without a word, Gabriel drained the remains of his wine, surged to his feet – skittling his chair in the process – and staggered from the table.

Silence descended as he left the room.

'Well, well,' Professor Hardwick said. 'On that rather tempestuous note, I shall take my leave, though I doubt whether I shall sleep very well tonight. Goodnight, gentlemen.'

'I, too, shall retire,' Meyer said. He rose from the table, bowed formally to those who remained and made his way slowly from the room.

Vermeulen looked across the table to Langham and Ryland. 'I don't know about you, but I could do with a stiff whisky.'

They repaired to the Stewart room and had Mrs Fergusson fetch the decanter.

'I sometimes wonder about Gabriel,' Vermeulen said when they were ensconced in armchairs before the fire. 'I don't know why the major tolerates his presence here.'

'Flesh and blood,' Langham said. 'You accept behaviour you wouldn't put up with from a stranger. Gabriel must have his good points.'

Ryland grunted. 'He keeps them well buried.' He wielded the poker and stirred the fire to greater vigour, then sat back with his whisky.

The Dutchman smiled. 'Perhaps the major's partly to blame for indulging him. If he were my son I'd cut him off without a penny and then see how he fared. The old man can't afford to keep on funding his indulgent lifestyle.'

Langham peered at the engineer. 'I was under the impression that the major was pretty well off.'

Vermeulen pursed his lips, eyeing the glass which he balanced on his slightly protuberant stomach. 'Between you and me, he's on his "uppers", as you say. The restoration of this place cost him a fortune, and its running and upkeep has almost bankrupted him. He puts up a good show, but that's what it is – a show to disguise the fact that he's almost broke.'

'But surely . . . the guests? It can't be cheap, staying here, and he told me the other day that he was fully booked for much of the year.'

'What he recoups in revenue from running the castle as a hotel is hardly a drop in the ocean compared to what he owes his creditors.'

Ryland pointed a nicotine-stained finger at the Dutchman. 'Hold on a sec, correct me if I'm barking up the wrong tree. What about the project – the salvage operation? If he's so broke how come he's paying you hundreds, at least, to raise the plane?'

'That's just it, Ryland. He isn't. What I said over dinner, about not charging the major while I'm technically redundant, was said in order to

127

placate Gabriel. The fact is I'm not charging the old man anything at all, full stop.'

Langham jerked his head back, staring at the engineer. 'What?'

Ryland said, 'You mean to say, the pontoon, all that equipment, raising the wreck? You're doing it all for free?'

'Major Gordon paid me a fee for some initial survey work and for the first day or so of diving to establish the precise location of the plane. But all the rest I agreed to do for free.'

'Might I ask why?' Langham said.

Vermeulen smiled. 'Either I'm a fool or I am an inspired businessman. I will let you decide.' He refilled his glass, asked the others if they wished for more – Langham covered his glass with a hand while Ryland held his out for a top up – then sat back and went on, 'I gave the major a quote for the preliminary work and told him that the overall cost would be determined by what I found down there. Well, I did the easy work. I found the plane – in one piece, thankfully – and then worked out the salvage fee and presented the quote to the old man. It was obvious that the sum was beyond his means. He didn't beat about the bush, but came straight out and told me so. Well, by this time I was fired up about the idea of salvaging the plane. My company was doing quite well, and I decided to offer to do the work for free.'

'That was incredibly generous of you, I must say,' Langham said.

The Dutchman shrugged. 'Oh, I would not say that. I was satisfying my own professional and personal interest in raising the plane – and it would be very good publicity for my company, no? I could absorb the loss across my various business interests and the major would get his wreck up and restored. Everyone would be a winner.'

Langham nodded, staring into the amber depths of his Scotch. He said at last, 'As we asked ourselves this morning, if someone wants the major dead so as to stymie the salvaging of the plane – why? Why might anyone want it to remain down there?'

Ryland glanced at him. 'You sound as if you have a theory, Don?'

Langham shrugged. 'It's just occurred to me: perhaps the plane was carrying something important and someone doesn't want the fact to come to light?'

Vermeulen looked dubious. 'That sounds a little far-fetched, I think.'

'It's just a notion,' Langham said.

'OK, but what can that *something* be?' Ryland said. 'I don't get it. What can be so important to someone that they want it to stay at the bottom of the loch?'

'All I can think of . . .' Langham began. 'How about this – aboard the plane were papers, documents, incriminating someone high up in the British establishment—'

'But incriminating them in what?' Ryland frowned.

'Collusion,' Langham said. 'And if the facts came to light they'd implicate someone who was working with or for the Nazis . . .?' He fell silent;

even to himself it sounded more than a little unlikely.

'And papers and documents,' Ryland pointed out, 'wouldn't last that long under thirty feet of water, surely?'

'Or perhaps,' Vermeulen said, 'someone is out for the major's blood for another reason? Or perhaps *I* was the intended victim of the shooting?'

The fire crackled and a log crumbled and slipped, sending up a flurry of sparks. Beyond the leaded windows the snow continued to fall.

They chatted for a while about other matters. The engineer asked where in London Langham lived, and when he said Notting Hill, Vermeulen laughed. 'What a small world! I too lived in Notting Hill after the war. Where exactly, may I ask?'

Langham told him just off Portland Road, around the corner from a wireless repair shop. 'I have a small flat on Kenley Street but I'll be upping sticks and moving to Kensington when I'm married.'

'You lucky man. The marriage, I mean, though I envy you living in Kensington, too.'

Ryland said, 'I take it you're not married yourself?'

Vermeulen laughed and shook his head. 'Too busy working,' he said.

A little later he glanced at his watch, drained his glass and said that he must be turning in.

Ryland stirred himself. 'Midnight. I'm bushed, Don. I think I'll toddle off.'

Langham finished the last drop of his whisky. 'Ghost hunting in the morning, Ralph.'

130

'It'll make a change from hunting criminals. Nighty-night.'

Alone, Langham moved to the window and stared out. Through the falling snow, he made out the hillside they had climbed that afternoon. Under the silver light of an almost full moon, the land was upholstered in a thick mantle of snow.

He made his way to his room, undressed and was asleep as soon as his head hit the pillow. He had a succession of vivid dreams – a German plane racing through the night, the spectral image of a woman in a cellar . . . and then the same woman, screaming.

He came awake suddenly and lay very still, listening. The scream came again, but not in his dreams this time. It was the exclamation of a woman experiencing pleasure, not pain.

The sound of her cries came from the adjacent room – the one occupied by Renata Káldor – and as he lay and listened to the animal sounds of a couple making love, her cries rose in pitch and then abruptly ceased.

He stared into the darkness, aware of his pulse, and listened for movement. He heard hushed voices, then the sound of a door creaking open.

He climbed from the bed and crossed the room. With infinite care he opened the door a fraction and peered out. He made out a tall figure pacing along the corridor away from the Hungarian's room.

In the moonlight slanting through a small window at the end of the corridor, Langham recognized Gabriel Gordon.

He returned to bed, cursing the poet, and slept fitfully until the winter sun rose on a landscape rendered motionless beneath its silent burden of snow.

Eleven

Langham rose early, drew himself a bath and soaked awhile, then went down to breakfast.

He was the first person at the table, and Mrs Fergusson met him with a cheery, 'It's a raw one, Mr Langham, so it is. And what will you be having?'

'Just toast for me this morning, Mrs F. Bit of a thick head. And a pot of Earl Grey would be wonderful.'

He slathered marmalade on the toast when it came and ate it leaning against the deep window embrasure, staring out at the transformed landscape. The land rose steeply on the far side of the loch, a brilliant white fleece climbing to a pewter sky. It was so cold out there that the margin of the loch, extending for about five feet from the shore, had frozen over. The wind stirred the waters, fracturing the extremities of the ice which floated like panes of shattered glass.

He replayed the image of Gabriel Gordon leaving Káldor's room last night; the poet had been bare-footed and bare-chested, padding away like an untamed animal after a successful feast.

'It's started snowing again, Mr Langham,' said a voice behind him.

He turned, smiled at Elspeth Stuart then peered through the window. 'Well, so it has. I hadn't noticed. I was miles away.'

'Plotting your next novel?'

'Something like that.' He considered Elspeth and an image rose unbidden in his mind's eye: Gabriel Gordon reclining on the Queen Anne chair yesterday, his lumberjack's frame abusing its fragility.

'I'm glad I bumped into you,' the girl said. 'Look what I've found.'

She was clutching two hardback books to her light blue cashmere cardigan, and presented them for Langham's attention.

'My word. Two of my early ones.'

'I found them amongst my father's collection. When he died and the major took me in, I had all my father's books brought over here. My father loved crime novels. He had thousands of them.' She held up *Murder at the Museum*. 'I found this an hour ago, and I must say I can't put it down.'

'That's what I like to hear, a satisfied customer.'

Elspeth buttered a slice of toast, spread it with marmalade and poured herself a cup of tea. She moved to the window and stood beside him, nibbling her toast.

'Beastly day, Mr Langham. Did you know the telephone lines are down? Mrs F told me earlier.'

'And I presume the road's still impassable?'

She nodded. 'Mr F trekked up to see Mr Fraser

133

at first light to see if he could help clear the snow, but even Mr Fraser's plough couldn't make an impression. It looks as if we're stranded.'

So much for the idea of taking the train back to London later that day, Langham thought.

Elspeth looked at him, her expression hesitant. The idea of her in Gabriel's bear-like embrace was at once incongruous and unsettling.

'About last night,' she murmured.

'I'm sorry that I couldn't disclose the true reason for our presence here,' Langham said. 'I hope you understand?'

'Oh, that. Yes, of course. But I meant Gabriel's outburst. He'd drunk too much and he gets . . . argumentative when he's had too much wine. Gabriel is misunderstood, Mr Langham. He's a good man, really.'

'I'm sure he is,' Langham said soothingly. 'We all say things we regret when under the influence.'

He glanced at the carriage clock on the mantelshelf. It was almost nine; the others would be down for breakfast soon and he wanted to continue his conversation with Elspeth without interruption.

He pointed to the books on the table. 'Did you say you found those amongst your father's collection? I'd love to cast an eye over it.'

She smiled, delighted. 'The books are in the south wing, where I have my apartment. Would you care to have a look?'

'I would,' he said, placing his cup on the table.

She led the way from the dining hall along the corridor to the southern tower, where they turned right along the truncated wing, the shorter length of the reversed 'L'.

She pressed the books to her chest like a schoolgirl and chattered away. 'The major was ever so kind to take me in. I did wonder what might happen to me. I lived with mummy and daddy at the lodge a few miles beyond Glenross, and I'd been tutored privately and hadn't travelled much. I think daddy wanted to marry me off to some rich laird. But then he drowned in a boating accident off Colonsay and a month or so later my mother had a stroke. At least I was with her when she collapsed. But to lose my parents like that so quickly . . . It makes you think, doesn't it?'

Langham smiled sympathetically, but was unable to find even a halfway adequate response.

The odd thing was that the girl recounted the tragic events without an ounce of self-pity or bitterness, and he detected a kind of stoic fortitude in her manner; she was much stronger than her slight appearance might suggest.

They came to the end of the corridor and climbed a spiral staircase, the wedge-shaped steps so worn over the years that they resembled butcher's chopping blocks.

'The major and my father were great friends. When the major's wife died back in the thirties, the major was in a bit of a state and could hardly look after himself, never mind Gabriel. So my parents took the major and Gabriel in and they lodged with us for almost a year. Then the war came along and the major volunteered his services as he'd served in the Great War. My father often said it was the major's salvation, finding himself of use again.'

They came to the head of the staircase and turned along a corridor hung with tapestries and oil paintings depicting hunting scenes.

'So you spent a year of your youth with Gabriel?'

'Well, I was only very young. Five, I think. Gabriel was a little older – seven or eight. We became fast friends, thrown into each other's company like that. We'd set off and explore the burns and forests and be away all day. We'd have fabulous adventures. It was like something from a children's book.'

'What happened to Gabriel when the war came?'

'Oh, he was packed off to some ghastly boarding school in England. I was devastated, of course. Here we are.'

She opened a door and he stepped into a room that was more Langham's idea of a library than the major's so-called library in the northern tower. One wall was given over to Elspeth's father's crime collection, while other bookshelves dotted around the room were stocked with encyclopaedias and children's books. A fire burned in the grate and an old sofa was pulled up close to the hearth.

'I call this my lounge,' Elspeth said. 'My bedroom is next door. I even have a small kitchen for when I want to prepare my own meals. But I mainly dine with the major and whoever might be staying here.'

Langham crossed to the crime novels and

whistled. 'Impressive. Your father was quite a connoisseur.'

Elspeth smiled. 'He forever had his nose in a detective story.'

He noted a pristine collection of R. Austin Freeman first editions and a comprehensive run of green-jacketed Penguin crime novels, as well as the complete works of Conan Doyle, Christie and Sayers.

'This certainly brings back memories,' he said, then explained. 'During the war I served in India. The major was my commanding officer. I was in Field Security and at one point I had to hobnob with a maharajah at his palace.'

'How romantic!'

'It was pretty amazing. The maharajah was an anglophile and collected crime novels. He was very proud of his haul.' He smiled in recollection. 'We spent many a happy hour chatting about whodunits. He would have been in his element here.'

'I'm so grateful to the major for allowing me to bring all my things and my parents' possessions with me. He's been like a father to me.'

'You're obviously close to him.'

'Well, as close as I can be. I mean, he's a little distant, wrapped up in his own obsessions. But then he is old, in his mid-seventies now, and he never had a daughter. I sometimes think he no longer knows quite how to relate to women.' She stopped suddenly and looked at Langham. 'What you said last night, about someone wanting . . .'

'I'm sorry that Gabriel felt the need to blurt it out as he did.'

'That was the wine talking, and I suspect his concern for his father.'

'Even so . . .' he began, then stopped himself.

Elspeth said in a small voice, 'But why would anyone want to harm the major?'

'Well, to be honest we don't know that the major was the intended target. It might have been Vermeulen. That's what we're trying to find out. I'm as concerned as you are, Elspeth.'

'Surely you don't think it was one of the guests, do you? It's got to be some madman.' She gestured vaguely to encompass the world beyond the castle walls.

'I honestly don't know. But we're doing all we can to find out.'

He moved across to the fire and stood before it, looking back at the tiny girl diminished before the façade of books. 'I hope you don't mind if I ask you a question or two?'

She shook her head. 'Of course not.' She moved to a high stool situated before the window and hitched herself on to it.

'I know that Gabriel and the major don't see eye to eye on a great range of things, but how would you describe their relationship in general?'

She swept a tress of blonde hair from her high forehead, frowning. 'That's a difficult question, Mr Langham. There is a lot of animosity between them, the result of neither being able to understand the views of the other. That's a generational thing – I sometimes find myself exasperated by the major's entrenched views – but their temperaments are entirely opposite, too.

The major is pragmatic and literal-minded; Gabriel's a romantic day-dreamer.'

'And never the twain shall meet?'

'Exactly.' She smiled. 'But, that said, they have an obvious if grudging affection for each other.'

Langham considered his next question. 'I hope you don't mind my asking how Gabriel reacted when the major forbade him from seeing you?'

Elspeth coloured quickly and stared through the window at the driving snow. 'So you know . . .?' she said, twisting her fingers in her lap.

'I'm sorry,' he said. 'I hope you don't think I'm prying. But it is important.'

'No. I understand.' She hesitated. 'Gabriel was enraged. We . . .' She stared down at her fingers and murmured, 'We were close when we were younger, Mr Langham, and then when I came here and Gabriel came up to stay for a month earlier this year . . . Well, it was as if we were young again. We explored, spent a lot of time in each other's company, so I suppose it was natural that . . .' She trailed off, staring through the window.

Langham said, 'Gabriel was angry that the major forbade him to see you, so when he came up a little over a month ago he arranged to stay at a hotel in Inverness and have you visit him?'

Blood flared in her hitherto pale face.

'I'm sorry. All these personal questions might seem out of order, but I assure you that they're necessary, and I promise I'll say nothing about any of this to the major. But I must ask you in order to corroborate Gabriel's story, you see?'

139

She nodded. 'Of course I understand. It's just a little upsetting that someone should know all about . . .' She gathered herself. 'But yes, Gabriel booked a room and, usually every other day, I drove over to Inverness for the afternoon on the pretext of going into the town on errands.' She smiled at him with spirit. 'I'd phone through to Gabriel in the morning with a list of things I needed and he'd go out and buy them for me to take back later that day.'

He smiled. 'Ingenious.'

'Oh, I didn't like deceiving the major like that, especially after he'd been so good to me, but there was no other way I might contrive to see Gabriel. We were driven to deception, Mr Langham, and I do love him so much.'

Langham looked away, seeing again the poet creeping away from Renata Káldor's room in the early hours.

'We hope,' she said from her high stool, smiling across at him with an ecstatic expression, 'to get married next year.'

'Gabriel promised this?'

'Not in so many words, but he's told me again and again that he wants us to be together. Are you married, Mr Langham?'

An aching well opened in his chest as he considered his happiness with Maria and the heartbreak lying in wait for Elspeth.

'As matter of fact I plan to get married next May. Bit late in the day, I know, with me in my forties – but better late than never, as they say.'

He sensed that Elspeth wanted to quiz him

about his bride-to-be and his forthcoming nuptials, but the thought of Gabriel's deception made him ill at ease.

'Gabriel doesn't much care for Hans Vermeulen, does he?' he said.

'They have their differences, Mr Langham. Hans is forever goading Gabriel about his poetry and the fact that he doesn't work – or doesn't do anything that he, Hans, would call a proper job. And Gabriel for his part is like a small boy taking the bait.'

'But you don't think that Gabriel would do anything to harm Hans?'

Elspeth looked shocked. 'Oh, I'm sure he wouldn't. Gabriel wouldn't harm anyone!'

He changed the subject and they chatted for another five minutes before he glanced at his watch and made an excuse. 'I hope you don't mind my shooting off, Elspeth, but Professor Hardwick promised Ralph and me a spot of ghost hunting.'

'Not at all,' she said. 'I hope you see something.' She pointed to his novel, which she had placed on the sofa. 'I think I'll snuggle up before the fire and finish your book. I have an hour before I help Mrs F with the housework.'

He moved to the door. 'I appreciate your answering my rather intrusive questions,' he said. 'And thank you for showing me the collection.'

He slipped from the room, made his way back through the castle and found Ryland breakfasting alone when he entered the dining hall.

'Meyer and Professor Hardwick have been and gone,' Ryland said. 'According to Mrs F, the major is breakfasting alone in the tower. The prof said he'll see us in half an hour in the armoury.'

'The armoury? If we can find it.'

'I know. They should have given us a map of the place when we arrived. But don't worry, Mrs F told me how to get there. It's in the cellar, next to the dungeons.'

Langham sat down and helped himself to coffee.

'Oh,' Ryland said around a mouthful of scrambled egg. 'Nearly forgot. I had a call from my contact in Bethnal Green first thing, about that Morris Commercial.'

'That's odd. Elspeth told me the lines were down.'

'Bert rang at the crack of dawn. Ten minutes later I tried to ring Annie but couldn't get through.'

'What did he have to say?'

'The van was stolen from outside a fruit and veg place in Glasgow eight days ago and found by the rozzers near Edinburgh a few days later.'

'So whoever stole the van didn't want to be traced, which rather casts suspicion on their presence here. But what might they have been doing? Why would they have taken the boat out on to the loch? The shooting was from the other direction entirely . . .'

He stared through the window. 'By the way, the road's still blocked. Looks like we're stranded here for the duration.'

He sipped his coffee and thought about Maria snug in her apartment and Charles's release from Wormwood Scrubs tomorrow morning. He'd really wanted to greet his agent and celebrate his new-found freedom.

'You look all in,' Ryland observed. 'Too much booze last night?'

Langham smiled. 'A tot over the limit – and it didn't help that I was awoken in the early hours. You'll never guess.'

'Go on.'

'Gabriel, paying our Hungarian aristocrat a nocturnal visit.'

Ryland's mouth hung open. 'You mean . . .?'

'I was awoken around three and treated to the full soundtrack. When I heard the door, I looked out and saw our Gabriel sneaking off in the moonlight.'

'Well, blow me down. Poor Elspeth.'

'That was my first thought. Or second, after calling Gabriel all the names under the sun.'

'So he's stringing Elspeth along, having a bit on the side with the Hungarian. And then there's that bit in Muswell Hill.'

'And that's just the three we know of . . . . The thing is Elspeth's smitten. I was talking to her just now. She's got it into her head that he wants to marry her.'

'He needs taking down a peg or two.'

The door opened at the far end of the room and Renata Káldor strode in, paused to take in the scene then selected a chair at the far end of the table. 'Good morning, gentlemen.'

'Renata,' Langham said. 'I'm pleased to see that you're feeling better.'

'Must have had a good night's sleep,' Ryland muttered under his breath.

143

Renata helped herself to coffee. 'A migraine. I'm feeling much better now, thank you.'

Mrs Fergusson entered, took the Hungarian's order of poached eggs on toast and departed.

'I understand I missed quite a fracas at dinner last night,' Renata observed.

'How come you heard about that then?' Ryland asked.

'Word gets around,' she replied.

'Gabriel excelled himself,' Langham said, sipping his coffee, 'even outdoing his usual display of bad manners.'

The woman's lips quirked as she tried not to smile. *Boys will be boys*, her expression said. 'Gabriel is prone to speak the truth as he sees it. There is nothing wrong with that. Though, I have noticed, you English with your impeccable manners and delicate reserve often find the truth unpalatable and prefer to take cover behind a screen of banalities.'

She sipped her coffee and smiled across the table at them.

'You might be right,' he said, and realized that he was taking cover behind a banality.

'He was as drunk as a skunk,' Ryland said, 'and announced what Don and I were doing here.'

'But I assumed everyone knew that?' Renata said loftily.

'Certainly not Hardwick, Meyer and Elspeth,' Langham said. 'He frightened the girl with the news that the major's life had been threatened.'

Renata snorted ever so genteelly. 'Elspeth? Well, she'll soon get over the fright. She's no

144

more than a child. I don't know what Gabriel
. . .' She stopped herself.

'Yes?' Langham prompted.

'It's nothing.' Her poached eggs on toast arrived
and she busied herself with cutting them up.

Langham waited until Mrs F had departed, then
said, 'You were about to say that you don't know
what Gabriel sees in the girl, am I right?'

He wondered if he detected a blush beneath
the woman's artfully applied make-up.

Ryland elbowed Langham and said, 'Gabriel
sees only one thing in a woman, Don – what he
can get.'

'My friend puts it crudely but pithily,' Langham
said to the Hungarian.

Renata laid down her knife and fork and stared
across the table at Langham. 'Have you bothered
to read any of Gabriel's poetry, Mr Langham?'

'The experience has eluded me,' he admitted.

'Because if you were to do so, you might
discover another side to the man's nature. Gabriel
is not only very talented, gentlemen, but sensitive
and—'

Ryland clutched his chest. 'Me heart bleeds.'

'In that case it's a great pity,' Langham said,
'that this sensitivity isn't on display when it
comes to his dealings with other people.' He
looked at his watch and, before the woman had
time to reply, said, 'Isn't it time we were meeting
the professor, Ralph?'

He nodded to Renata as he left the table and
followed Ryland from the room.

'Now if only I can remember Mrs F's directions
to the armoury . . .' the detective said.

Twelve

At nine thirty on Monday morning Maria phoned Molly and told her that she would not be in until after lunch. Mondays were always quiet at the agency and Molly, an efficient Oxford graduate, was more than capable of holding the fort alone.

She was about to leave for Donald's flat to collect his address book when the phone bell rang.

'Hello?' she said, hoping that it was Donald.

A deep-throated woman's voice called out, 'Maria, my sweet. It has been too long! What, a year? I have been remiss. Do you forgive me?'

Whenever Maria heard Marguerite Selasny's rich, mid-European accent she was always reminded of molasses. Marguerite was a well-heeled Hungarian émigré who had fled her homeland when the Nazis invaded and now wrote popular books on European history.

'Forgive *you*?' Maria laughed. 'But *I* haven't been in touch for ages. We'll have to meet for lunch soon.'

'That would be wonderful,' Marguerite said. 'You have *so* much to tell me, after all. I have heard the news on the grapevine. Now tell me all about him. One of your authors, so I hear?'

Maria told Marguerite about Donald, said that she was so happy she felt as if she were walking on air, and that they were to be married in May.

146

'So not content with taking your agency cut,' Marguerite said, 'you want this author's body and soul!'

'Whatever it takes to keep a popular author on our books,' she laughed.

She went on to say that she hoped Marguerite might be able to help her. 'I was wondering if you know a fellow Hungarian émigré who lives in London, a Renata Káldor?'

'Renata?' Marguerite said. 'Do I know her? As well as anyone can know the woman. But why do you ask?'

'Someone I know has recently made her acquaintance and wanted to know a little more about her.'

'Wouldn't we all!' Marguerite laughed, and Maria thought of molasses bubbling in a pan. 'Renata Káldor is an odd character. I don't take to her, myself. But she has her admirers.'

'In what way is she odd?'

'She is aloof and distant and gives away very little about her past. All I know for certain is that she comes from an aristocratic family and that her father fell on hard times in the twenties. Apparently Renata fled to Germany and married young, and here the stories diverge.'

'They do?'

'There are some people I know who say she came to London before the war after the death of her German husband, fleeing the Nazis.'

'And others say?'

'That she remained in Germany, had a liaison with a Gestapo officer and only fled to Britain after the war. But as I said, Renata says absolutely nothing of her past in Germany, though she will reminisce about her childhood in Hungary.'

'That's intriguing,' Maria said. 'What does she do now?'

'Do? She does nothing. She is independently wealthy – her German husband was a rich industrialist, the story goes, who left her a fortune. She lives in Belgravia, holds soirées and salons and likes to think herself an intellectual. She reads Sartre,' Marguerite sniffed, 'and patronizes the occasional young poet.'

'That's very interesting, Marguerite. Thank you. I'll pass that on to my friend.'

'I am happy to be of service, and remember, we must meet up for lunch.'

They chatted about various mutual friends for a while before Maria promised that she would be in touch soon, thanked the Hungarian again and rang off.

She wondered whether to ring Donald now with what she had discovered about Káldor, but decided to do so after she had found his address book and contacted his Dutch friend about the engineer, Vermeulen.

She pulled on her hat and coat and left the apartment, her breath taken by the cold. Snow had fallen throughout the night – though it had stopped now – and the city was oddly still and almost silent under a six-inch coating. One of her neighbours, a man in his eighties, was scattering ashes across the pavement.

The road was treacherous and Maria steered her Sunbeam with care across London towards Notting Hill.

148

She reminded herself that later this afternoon, when she had rung Donald's Dutch contact and then spoken to Donald himself, she must do a little shopping to restock Charles's larder for his return home. He had a little flat above the agency and resided there during the week; Maria had the key and would buy a nice bunch of flowers and a bottle of Chardonnay. She would also purchase a few luxuries to which Charles occasionally treated himself – and which would have been in short supply in the Scrubs – such as a jar of caviar, liver pâté and a cob of crusty bread.

The street outside Donald's flat was full of parked cars, so she turned the corner and found a place in front of Barton and Bone's wireless repair shop, then picked her way along the pavement.

Donald's second-floor flat comprised a small living room, a tiny kitchen, an even smaller bathroom, a bedroom and a room he used as his study. It was poky, badly furnished and bore all the hallmarks of being the transient domicile of a bachelor whose aesthetic sensibility was matched only by his apathy regarding matters of decoration and furnishings. The sofa, armchair, standard lamp and rugs in the sitting room were all second-hand, and the flowered wallpaper was a throwback to the early thirties.

She moved into his study, where books lined every wall and his desk and chair were the only furnishings. She stood in the doorway and smiled at how neat and tidy everything was in here, in contrast to the rest of the flat. Donald prided himself on the fact that his book collection was

149

ordered not only alphabetically but chronologically.

She looked to her right, frowning. A pile of manuscripts – Donald's fiction output of the last two years – was stacked in folders on the floor, or rather should have been. The stack was toppled, a manila avalanche that spread across the floor before the window. She was sure that the last time she had been here . . .

Then she saw toecaps protruding from the hem of the full-length curtains, and her stomach turned.

Someone was hiding behind the curtains in the bay window recess.

Heart thumping, Maria backed silently from the study, turned and crept towards the hall. As she did so, she caught a glimpse of movement from the corner of her eye.

She jumped, gasping with shock, as someone slipped out of the bathroom and made for the door. The intruder saw her and turned, pulling a knife from his pocket. 'Move. In there. Now!'

The man was small, thick-set and wore a donkey jacket. From the little that he'd said, Maria thought his accent was German. His face was heavy, lantern-jawed and darkened by a five o'clock shadow.

He gestured with the knife. 'I said move!'

She nodded, trying to swallow, and backed into the study.

'Sit down!'

She moved to Donald's writing chair and slumped into it, her legs weak.

The second burglar – for surely she had

150

interrupted thieves at work in the empty flat –
moved from behind the curtains and muttered
something to his companion, his words too indis-
tinct for her to catch.

The second man was a little taller than the first
and wore a dirty raincoat and a trilby, but his
distinguishing feature was a jagged scar that ran
the length of his left cheek.

'What do you want?' she said, trying to keep
the tremor from her voice. 'There is money on
the mantelshelf in the living room, through there.
A few pounds. Please take it and go. There is
nothing else of value here.'

Please, she thought, just take the money and
go.

Scarface leaned against the bookshelf, pushing
back a section of L to M crime hardbacks. She
found herself thinking that Donald would be most
displeased.

The thug with the knife leaned against the door
frame, the knife held loosely in his right hand.

They adopted the pose of people who were in
no hurry to go anywhere. She wondered, incon-
sequentially, how they had entered the flat, as
neither the lock on the communal door on to
the street nor the lock to the flat had been
damaged.

'We're not interested in money,' Scarface said.

Maria nodded, attempting to maintain a poise
she did not feel. If they did not want money,
then . . .

The thug with the knife said, 'Who are you?'

She shook her head, wondering why it mattered
to them who she was.

Scarface said, 'You know Donald Langham, yes?'

She stared him in the eye, trying not to show her fear. 'Why do you want to know?'

'Just answer the question!' the knifeman said. 'I am not afraid to use this, do you understand?' And he jerked the knife towards her. The blade reflected the winter sunlight pouring in through the window.

She said, 'Yes, I know Donald Langham. Why do you want to know?'

She reassured herself that Donald could not be in immediate danger as he was hundreds of miles away.

The thugs exchanged a glance and Scarface said, 'What is he?'

The question wrong-footed her. She shook her head. 'What is he? I don't understand.'

'A private detective, yes?' Scarface asked.

The other thug said, 'Or a policeman?'

'A policeman?' Maria's initial urge was to laugh. 'What is all this about? Of course he isn't a policeman!'

'A private detective, yes?'

'No. No, of course not.' She gestured around the room at all the books, then indicated the Remington on the desk at her elbow. 'Donald is a writer. A novelist.'

The thugs looked at each other as if they had never heard of the term.

'You're lying,' Scarface said.

She turned and picked up something from the desk – the Blunt Instrument award for the best thriller of 1950.

152

The man with the knife stepped forward, his blade outstretched, then stopped when he realized that Maria had no intention of attacking him. She held out the award. 'Read that.'

Cautiously, Scarface stepped forward and peered at the inscription on the base of the trophy: *Awarded to Donald Langham for his novel* A Dark Sunset.

'He's a writer,' Maria repeated.

The knifeman said, 'His friend, Ryland – Ralph Ryland?'

Her stomach turned. She knew, then, that their presence here had something to do with what was happening in the Highlands.

'What about him?'

'What does he do? He is an investigator, no? A private investigator?'

She looked the knifeman in the eye and said, 'I don't know him. I've never heard of . . . whatever his name was?'

'You're lying. He is a friend of Langham!'

'I don't know all of Donald's friends.'

'You're lying!'

'How did you get in here?' she asked. 'How did you know where Donald lived?'

The knifeman resumed his casually menacing stance against the doorframe. 'We are asking the questions.'

He looked across at his friend, who murmured something in their own language.

Maria wondered if she could take up the blunt instrument, launch it at the knifeman and dart through the doorway, into the hall and down the stairs before they recovered and gave chase.

The knifeman said, 'So Donald is a writer, yes. But Ryland? Tell me.'

She shook her head. 'I told you. I don't know. I've never heard of . . .'

The knifeman took a single quick step forward and lashed out at her. A stunning blow impacted the side of her head. She gasped, shocked as much by the unexpected assault as by the pain. At first she thought he'd struck her with the knife, then realized that he'd used his left hand.

'Next time, I will cut your pretty little face.'

Scarface reached up and, with blunt fingers, traced the ragged line that bisected his cheek. The gesture revolted Maria with its sensuousness.

'How would you like to have a scar like this? No? But I think it would suit you. It would contrast with your beauty, yes?'

'So . . . Ralph Ryland?' the knifeman said.

'I . . .'

'Tell me!'

She nodded, swallowed and said, 'He's a private detective.'

The knifeman lowered his weapon.

Scarface laughed. 'Excellent.'

'His address?' the knifeman asked. 'He has an office, yes?'

'I . . . I don't know—'

The knife came up again.

Maria said, 'Wandsworth. The High Street. Above a fish-and-chip shop. I don't know the number.'

Another guttural exchange in a foreign language that Maria did not think, now, was German. She dared not look up. She stared at the rug, noticing how threadbare it was. When Donald moved in to her apartment she would buy a new rug for his study.

Scarface moved to the door. The knifeman said, 'Stay there and don't move.'

He grabbed the telephone cord, looped it and sliced the flex with his blade.

He hurried to the door, paused to look back at her and repeated, 'Stay there!'

He slipped through the door and disappeared. Maria was suddenly aware of her thumping heart. She sat, paralysed and gripped by the fear that they might return.

She listened for the sound of the front door closing but heard nothing. Bracing herself, she crossed to the window and peered out. The men were on the pavement below, hurrying away; as she watched, they turned the corner.

Crying out with relief, she stared at the severed cord of the phone on the desk and almost wept, 'You fools!'

She moved into the sitting room, lunged for the telephone beside the sofa and dialled 999. 'Hello! I want to report . . . I've been—'

The telephonist told her to calm down and speak slowly.

'I . . . I want to report a break-in and assault.'

'And the address?'

Reassured by the woman's homely voice, she gave the address. The woman assured her that a constable would be around in five minutes and, holding back her tears and thanking the woman, Maria replaced the receiver.

155

She wanted to talk to Donald, to hear his no-nonsense Midlands accent. The castle's phone number was back at her apartment, so she rang the operator and asked to be put through to Major Gordon of Loch Corraig Castle, Glenross, Inverness-shire – only to be told that the line to the Highlands was cut off due to bad weather.

She sat back on the sofa, then jumped up and raced to the front door. They had left it open. She slammed it shut, then shot the bolts at the top and bottom of the door.

She moved to the back of the house, into the bathroom, and discovered how the thugs had gained entry. The bottom right-hand window pane, above the bath, had been covered with gaffer tape and then smashed, creating a gap large enough to crawl through from the fire escape.

She hurried from the bathroom, fetched a carving knife from the kitchen in the unlikely event of the thugs returning and moved to Donald's study.

She went through his desk until she found the address book, then returned to the living room and paced back and forth for fifteen minutes until the police arrived.

Thirteen

'Of course,' Professor Hardwick said as they descended to the cellar, 'ninety-nine per cent of all reported sightings of ghosts and allied phenomena turn out, upon rigorous examination, to be instances of either erroneous perception or hoaxes. I find it amazing, in my many years of psychical investigation, that the human mind can persuade itself that it has seen something which, in fact, is not there – and also that there are so many people out there willing to perpetrate tricks in order to deceive the general public, which is why I take my research deadly seriously and admit only the most rigorous of my findings to the review of my peers.'

'And the opinion of your peers?' Langham asked, strolling along the dank corridor with the professor and Ryland. He wondered how many of these august personages there might be in the presumably limited field of psychical research.

The professor beamed. 'I am pleased to say that in five years of study I have presented eight cases which eminent minds in psychical research find beyond their ability to explain.'

They passed from the armoury – a dingy chamber arrayed with metal pegs hammered into the walls on which, in days of yore, weapons such as muskets and blunderbusses were hung – into a long, arch-ceilinged room which the professor announced was the cellar.

'It was probably used for the storage of perishable foodstuffs,' he explained. 'The flight of stairs, over there, leads to the kitchen.'

Langham hugged himself and wished he'd thought to wear his overcoat. It was freezing in this unheated, subterranean chamber, though the professor, garbed only in a threadbare cardigan and baggy corduroy trousers, seemed oblivious of the cold. The only illumination was provided by a naked bulb suspended from the ceiling on a brown flex.

Professor Hardwick moved to a bulky camera on a wooden tripod and fiddled with a black box affixed to its side. 'I'll switch it off for the moment. I've designed this apparatus myself,' he went on. 'It's motion sensitive – that is, the slightest movement down here will set the camera turning and so, hopefully, capture whatever phenomenon occasioned the activation.'

'And has it filmed anything so far?' Ryland asked.

'Only a rat,' the professor admitted, crestfallen.

Langham hid his smile and indicated the camera. 'And this is the only one in the castle?'

'One of two,' Hardwick said. 'The other is in the south wing.'

'And this cellar is where the serving girl was strangled?' Ryland asked.

Professor Hardwick crossed the chamber, pointed to the flagstone and said, 'Upon this very spot, as good authority has it. The story goes that the laird had a soldier in his employ follow the girl down here late at night and strangle the poor creature. He dumped the body in the loch but, just days later, her shade entered this very room through the door to the loch just over there . . .' he pointed, and Langham and Ryland stared at the door like tourists being favoured with a glimpse of a holy shrine, '. . . climbed the stairs to the laird's bedchamber and there accused him.

It is said that, soon after, the laird lost his mind and died a raving madman.'

'That's quite some story,' Langham allowed, and refrained from asking why a ghost should have entered the cellar by way of a door and not simply walked through the wall.

'Melodramatic,' the professor said, 'but all documented by a local scribe not twenty years after the event.'

Then it must be true, Langham thought.

'But come. It's getting a trifle chilly down here. I'll show you some auditory apparatus on one of the occupied floors.'

They retraced their steps; Professor Hardwick reactivated the camera and then ushered them from the chamber.

For the next hour the professor showed them around three rooms on the ground floor, each one laid out with tangles of flex and silver mesh microphones that resembled the compound eyes of giant insects. 'I switch these on only at night,' he explained, 'when the residents are abed.'

'And have you had any results?' Ryland asked.

The benign professor held a finger aloft like a saint indicating Heaven, smiled his satisfaction and ushered them along a corridor to a large bedchamber. He crossed the room to a bank of recording apparatus on a Victorian chest of drawers.

His bony fingers danced over the controls of a huge reel-to-reel recorder, and the great spools, laced with magnetic tape, began turning.

'Now listen carefully, gentlemen.'

159

Langham and Ryland bent to listen.

At first, all that could be heard was a faint hiss, and then more loudly came the unmistakable sound of heavy breathing – it sounded laboured, as if the person caught on the recording were asthmatic or carrying a heavy weight. It continued for about a minute and ended in a loud sigh.

Hardwick flicked the switch with a flourish. 'This was timed at three thirty on Thursday morning. Only the major and myself, Elspeth, Renata and the Fergussons were present that night. And no one, gentlemen, entered this room. It was locked, you see.'

'No one,' Ryland said in hushed tones, 'other than the spook who was caught on tape.'

'My reasoning exactly, my friend!'

Ryland rubbed his hands together. 'I think this calls for a hot cuppa and crumpets, Professor.'

'Capital idea,' said Hardwick.

They descended to the Stewart room, ordered tea and crumpets from Mrs F and warmed themselves before the fire.

The conversation soon moved on to the reason for Langham and Ryland's presence at the castle.

'I must admit,' Professor Hardwick said between sips of tea, 'that I find this beastly business hard to understand.'

'Understand?' Langham repeated.

'Who might conceivably want to do either of the men harm? It's beyond my comprehension. The major is the most amenable of men and not the sort to make enemies or to have skeletons

160

rattling in his cupboard. The same goes for Hans Vermeulen.'

Ryland bit into his buttered crumpet. 'You've known the major for a long time, right?'

'From school, Mr Ryland. Getting on for seventy years, would you believe? We saw a lot of each other before the war – my late wife and I would often holiday at the major's place beyond Glenross. We lost contact during the war but he got in touch again in 'forty-seven when he returned from India. And when he bought this place and told me that it was said to be haunted . . .' He beamed. 'Well, it was as if all my Christmases had come at once.'

'And the major was agreeable to having you conduct your research?'

'My good fellow, it was at the major's suggestion that I came and set up the project. I think, partly, that it was because he was a tad lonely with only Elspeth and the Fergussons for company. He missed someone of his own age about the place, you see. I insisted on not only paying the going rate as a guest but a little over and above to make up for the inconvenience of having all my apparatus cluttering the place. And when I got wind that the place wasn't doing as well as I thought . . .' He trailed off, staring into the flames.

Langham glanced at Ryland. 'Yes?'

'I was speaking to Mr Vermeulen a while back and he happened to mention the major's financial straits. I buttonholed the major and suggested I doubled what I was paying him already – I am not without means, gentlemen.'

'And what did the major say?'

'He wasn't having any of it. He bridled at the idea. Hurt pride and all that. He rather lost his rag, if truth be told. Tore me off a strip and stormed out.'

Langham recalled Gabriel's mention of his father and the professor's contretemps.

'I must say I was rather taken aback,' the professor continued. 'We made it up, though. The old man apologised and we set things straight over a whisky or two. No hard feelings. Water under the bridge, you understand.'

'That's good to know,' Langham said, finishing his crumpet and taking a mouthful of tea. 'And you aren't aware of the major's having words with any of his other guests?'

Hardwick shook his head. 'As I said, he's the most amenable of men. The perfect gentleman, I'd say, and a fine host. Which is why, my friends, I find this talk of someone wishing to do him harm all rather distressing.'

Langham was about to move the conversation on to a less disagreeable topic when the door from the kitchen opened and Elspeth Stuart appeared, swaying.

Langham stood up quickly, spilling what little remained of his tea. Elspeth took a step into the room, her face even paler than usual. She raised her hands to her face, pressing her cheeks, then sobbed, 'Mr Langham, come quickly . . . I found him. He's in the cellar and I think he's dead.'

She fainted, fell against the oak-panelled wall and slipped to the floor.

Ryland jumped to his feet and knelt beside the

girl, arranging her limbs. 'Get Mrs Fergusson,' he said to the professor. 'See if she has any smelling salts. Then give her a tot of brandy.'

Trembling, the professor nodded and stumbled off towards the kitchen.

Langham and Ryland hurried from the Stewart room.

Fourteen

Langham found himself shaking with shock as he followed Ryland to the cellar.

At the bottom of the steps the detective switched on the light, its naked bulb casting a dim light over the dank chamber. At the far end, before the door, a body sprawled on the flagstones, face down and arms outstretched.

He followed Ryland to the end of the chamber and stopped in his tracks.

'Jesus Christ . . . It's Vermeulen,' Ryland said.

Langham leaned against the wall, his stomach heaving. Someone had beaten Vermeulen about the head, many times. The back of his skull was a pulverized mess of bone and grey matter in a lagoon of blood. A single dark rivulet, as tawny as old port, trickled from the slick and ran in a straight line between the flagstones.

'Probably didn't know a thing about it,' Ryland murmured.

'He was hit more than once,' Langham said.

Ryland nodded. 'The first blow would have

sent him sprawling. My guess is that he was dead before he hit the ground, or certainly unconscious. And then the killer wanted to make sure and hit him again and again.' He pointed to something on the floor a few yards away.

The murder weapon lay on the flagstones where it had been discarded, a medieval mace – a spiked metal head on a timber shaft – matted with hair and clotted with blood.

'So,' Langham said, 'the shooting . . . Vermeulen was the target.'

'Looks that way.' Ryland reached out and touched the Dutchman's outflung left wrist, then dipped a forefinger in the blood. He placed his thumb and forefinger together, as if testing the blood for stickiness.

'Ralph?'

'Just checking something. Instinct tells me that the blood is pretty fresh. My hunch is that this happened within the last five or ten minutes.' He looked at his watch. 'It's three minutes past eleven now.'

Langham moved to the solid timber door, took out his handkerchief and, wrapping it around the great metal handle, eased the door open. He peered out. The snow had drifted up against the door, creating a vertical plane three feet deep. The pathway leading to the pontoon was unmarked. No one had entered the cellar from that direction.

'There's a heck of a lot of blood,' Ryland was saying. 'Chances are the murderer was covered. We'll have to check on that.'

They heard a commotion from the far end of

the chamber and turned to see the major, followed by Professor Hardwick, descend the stone stairs.

The major's face was slack with horror, his eyes wide as he took in the corpse. A film of tears glittered in the old man's eyes.

'Good God,' he murmured.

Professor Hardwick laid a hand on his friend's shoulder, his long face ashen.

'Poor Hans,' the major said. 'Poor, poor Hans . . . He was a good man, Langham. He didn't deserve . . . My God, if I find out who did this . . .'

Kneeling beside the corpse, Ryland looked up and said, 'There are a few things we need to do. Major, could you get Mrs F to rustle up a mortar and pestle, some talcum powder and see if she can lay her hands on a vial of perfume – but it's essential that it's one of those spray devices. Oh, and I'll need a shaving brush.'

'Mortar and pestle, talc, spray perfume and a shaving brush. But what on earth . . .?'

Ryland pointed to the mace. 'I don't suppose the killer was stupid enough to leave his dabs on the shaft, but you never know. We're cut off and God knows how long it'll be before the police get here, so I'll have to look for fingerprints myself.'

The major nodded and limped off up the stairs.

'While he's fetching that stuff . . .' Ryland went on: 'Professor, if you'd kindly come with me, we'll check every outside door to see if anyone entered this morning. Then we'll go from room to room to find out where each and every guest is at the moment. Don, could you stay here and guard the fort? I won't be long.'

Ryland and Hardwick hurried off, leaving Langham alone with the body.

He hugged himself against the cold and looked around the cellar.

It *was* possible that the killer came in from outside, he told himself, through another door – it wasn't necessarily someone already resident in the castle. Try as he might, he found it hard to conceive that someone he knew could have killed Vermeulen in cold blood, and in such a gruesome fashion. Far better if the killer were an outsider.

But a small, cold voice of reason whispered that he was deluding himself.

He looked along the length of the cellar and his heart kicked as he saw the camera on its tripod, its dark lens directed at him.

He crossed to it quickly, his heart thumping. If the killer had come in from outside, then the chances were that they would have been unaware of the motion-activated camera.

His hopes were dashed, however, when he saw that the bakelite housing of the camera was open and the film case that should have filled the chamber was missing.

It was another object that Ryland, with his jerry-rigged fingerprint kit, would have to attend to. Though as the detective had said, the killer would hardly have been stupid enough to leave his prints.

Footfalls sounded on the stairs. Ryland appeared, followed by the professor. The detective shook his head. 'The only tracks leading to and from the castle were made by Mr Fergusson when he hiked up to Fraser's place first thing.'

Langham indicated the camera. 'Whoever did it was clued up about the surveillance. They took the film.'

'Which suggests,' Ryland said, 'that the killer is resident in the castle.'

Langham nodded. 'It certainly looks that way.'

'Oh, my word!' Professor Hardwick exclaimed.

'We went around all the rooms,' Ryland said. 'Everyone was present and correct. I said nothing about the attack, but asked 'em all to gather in the dining hall as soon as possible.'

'Where was everyone?' Langham asked.

Ryland ticked off the list on his fingers. 'Gabriel in his pit, like a bear with a sore head at being disturbed. Renata was in her room, taking a bath and more than a little indignant at our intrusion. Meyer was on the battlements, "admiring the view", he said. The Fergussons were in the kitchen. Elspeth, accounted for. I asked the major and he said he was in his library until summoned by Mrs F when she'd ministered to Elspeth.'

'How is the girl?'

'Coming round, but shocked. As I said, we'll see everyone in the dining hall. I don't fancy making the announcement.'

'I'll do that,' Langham said.

Ryland nodded. 'And I'll gauge the reaction. Then I think it'll be a good idea if we interviewed everyone one by one. It might be wise to send Mr F out to get PC Ross down here.'

'It'd be a damned sight easier if it wasn't for the snow, Ralph.'

The detective laughed but with little humour. 'This is like one of your whodunits. Guests captive in a lonely castle and a murderer on the loose . . .'

Langham said grimly, 'But in a book, I'd make sure the first murder was followed by a second, to ratchet up the tension.'

'Don't tell that to the guests, Don. I don't want them getting ideas.'

'This is a nightmare . . .' the professor said.

Langham turned as the major limped down the stairs, clutching a small cardboard box containing the items Ryland had requested.

'Good man,' Ryland said, taking the box. 'And even the perfume. Excellent. We'd be stymied without it.'

They crossed the cellar to the bloody mace. Ryland knelt, watched closely by Langham, Hardwick and the major, and took the perfume from the box. 'First thing to do is apply a fine, sticky film. While I do that, Don, be a pal and grind a little talc in the mortar. It'll be fine already but I want it as fine as you can damn well make it.'

Langham sprinkled half an inch of talcum powder into the mortar, took the pestle and ground it into the talc.

Ryland held the vial about a foot away from the haft of the mace and sprayed three puffs of perfume on to the handle, explaining as he did so, 'I don't want to get too close to the thing in case the perfume comes out too thick and washes off any prints that might be there. That should do it. Now, that talc nice and powdery?'

Langham passed him the mortar and watched as the detective took the shaving brush, dipped its bristles in the powder then lightly dabbed at the handle of the mace. A fine film of talc adhered to the smooth timber haft.

'Not ideal, and the forensic boys would laugh themselves silly – but needs must.'

When the entire length of the handle was coated in a dusting of talcum, Ryland set aside the shaving brush and took something from the inner pocket of his suit jacket. He opened the case and pulled out a pair of glasses. 'Reading specs,' he said. He got down on all fours and used the lens as a magnifying glass to examine the handle of the mace.

He swore pithily and pulled a face.

'Nothing?' Langham asked.

'Not a ruddy thing. Whoever it was wiped it clean – or wore gloves.' He looked up at the major and pointed at the mace. 'Do you know where this came from?'

The major chewed at his moustache. 'There's one in the Stewart room, in the hand of one of the suits of armour, and another hanging on the wall by the front entrance. It could be either.'

'We need to check that,' Ryland said, gathering up his fingerprint kit and crossing to the camera.

Five minutes later, after going through the same application process on the housing of the camera, he shook his head. 'Not a thing. Wiped clean.'

'I wonder where they dumped the film case?' Langham said.

'Probably destroyed the film first,' Ryland said. 'We need to institute a search pretty damned quick. We'll tell everyone when we have them gathered in the dining hall. And I want them to stay there till the search is over. Major, Professor Hardwick, could you go and see if everyone is in the dining hall?'

The major nodded, then pointed across to the body. 'What do you suggest we do with poor Hans?'

'Best thing is for the body to remain where it is until the rozzers can get here. It's cold enough down here, so we don't have to worry on that score. Can the cellar be locked?'

The major nodded.

'If you could make sure it's secured as soon as possible . . .'

'I'll do it straight away,' the major said.

'Right, Don,' Ryland said as the major and Professor Hardwick moved off up the stairs. 'This is where it gets interesting.'

Langham followed the detective from the cellar.

Fifteen

Langham was in the Stewart room, and about to move into the dining hall, when the major entered from the corridor. 'That's the cellar secured, Langham. I've locked the outside door, the door from the corridor, and the one at the top of the steps from the kitchen.' He jangled a set of keys

170

and slipped them into his pocket. 'And I'll keep these about me person till we can get the police in.'

'Good man. I was wondering . . . Was Vermeulen in the habit of going out to the pontoon via the cellar? He *was* going out to the pontoon, I take it?'

The major nodded. 'He always went through the cellar. It's a shortcut, you see, rather than going the long way round through the door in the southern tower and along the side of the castle.'

'In that case, what about the professor's camera?'

'Vermeulen switched it off every time he passed through, then turned it on again when he came back.'

Ryland, in the process of tapping a Woodbine on the back of his hand, stopped and looked up. 'That's interesting.'

Langham nodded. 'It means that whoever killed Vermeulen didn't know that he switched off the camera every time – or else why did they take out the film?'

'Unless,' Ryland pointed out, 'they took the film as a precaution. Maybe they thought they couldn't be certain that Vermeulen *had* turned off the camera this time, so took the film just in case?'

'Which further suggests that it's an inside job, as an outsider wouldn't have known about the camera.' Langham turned to the major. 'Did you find out where the mace . . .?'

'Over there.' They crossed to a suit of armour

171

and the major indicated the right gauntlet, its thumb and fingers shaped to grip the appropriated mace.

Ryland said, 'Anyone might have filched the mace when they came through here after breakfast.'

'Or what about last night, after dinner?' Langham said. 'Would anyone notice that it was missing?'

The major pulled at his moustache. 'Very much doubt it, Langham.'

'It obviously wasn't a spur of the moment thing,' Langham said. 'Whoever did it knew of Vermeulen's movements. The killer couldn't have come down the kitchen stairs, as Mrs F and Elspeth were in there this morning. So . . .'

Ryland lit up his cigarette and slotted it into the side of his mouth. 'So they followed Vermeulen along the corridor, down the cellar stairs and struck as he was approaching the outside door. Or,' he went on, 'if they knew of Vermeulen's routine, they could always have been lying in wait for him.'

Langham gestured to the corridor leading to the dining hall. 'Shall we go through?'

Everyone was seated around the long dining table when Langham, Ryland and the major entered the room. Elspeth sat between the stout, grey-haired forms of Mr and Mrs F, the latter gripping Elspeth's hand and murmuring consoling words. The girl blotted her cheeks with a lace kerchief and smiled bravely when Langham caught her eye.

Renata Káldor sat on the far side of the table, from time to time glancing at Elspeth with ill-disguised curiosity. She was smoking a cigarette in an elegant holder and looked overdressed in a navy blue trouser suit.

At the head of the table, Gabriel Gordon achieved the feat of sprawling on his dining chair as if it were a chaise longue. He wore a white silk shirt with cavalier cuffs, and with his posture and five o'clock shadow emanated an air of wilful irreverence.

By contrast, Ulrich Meyer sat severely upright on his dining chair as if it were an implement of torture and he was suffering accordingly. His long face wore a pained expression and Langham wondered which of his many injuries was upper-most now.

Professor Hardwick was hunched over in his chair, absently cleaning his glasses; the major took a seat beside him, grim-faced.

Langham stood before the fire, waiting for the major to settle himself and for Ryland to take up his position leaning against the window embrasure before he began.

In the event, he was pre-empted by Gabriel Gordon.

'Now that we're all here, Langham, I hope this will be entertaining. I for one don't like being dragged out of bed—'

'That all depends,' Langham interrupted, 'if you're of a mind to find murder entertaining.'

He switched his gaze from Gabriel to Renata and on to Meyer, in order to gauge their reaction.

The poet's protests were halted; he sat open-mouthed, and at least had the good grace to look abashed. Renata looked blank, her long, elegant face expressionless. She blinked, once, then took a long draw on her cigarette. Meyer sat forward, his one good eye wide as it fixed on Langham.

It was Gabriel who found his voice first. 'Murder? What do you mean, murder?'

'I'm sorry to have to inform you that one of our fellow guests was brutally killed this morning.'

'But who . . .?' Renata began, and looked frantically around the gathering. 'Hans Vermeulen?' she said. 'Where is Vermeulen?'

Langham watched her as he said, 'I'm afraid that it was Hans who was murdered.'

She reacted as if slapped in the face, jerking her head back.

Gabriel was shaking his head. 'Vermeulen?' he said, as if he couldn't bring himself to believe what Langham had said.

'How?' Meyer asked. 'When exactly did this happen?'

'We think a little before eleven o'clock, about forty minutes ago. He was beaten over the head in the cellar.' He looked around the room. 'I've gathered you together to apprise you of what happened and to explain one or two things. The situation is this: we are effectively stranded in the castle. The only road to Glenross and the outer world is impassable. Added to that, the telephone line is down and we can't get word out to inform the authorities of what's taken place. I want everyone to remain here, in this room, for

174

the time being, and come through one at a time to the Stewart room where Ralph Ryland and I will conduct interviews. Afterwards, if you would return here and wait, we will conduct a thorough search of your rooms.'

'Our rooms?' Gabriel bridled. 'Looking for what?'

'I'm afraid I'm not at liberty to disclose that at the moment.'

'It sounds to me,' Gabriel said, 'as if you suspect one of us of murdering Vermeulen.'

Langham stared at him. 'Unfortunately, as no one from outside entered the castle this morning, that is the only conclusion to be drawn.'

'But that's ridiculous!' Renata exclaimed, staring around the table. 'One of us? But who would do such a thing?'

Meyer said, 'That, my dear, is what Herr Langham and Herr Ryland intend to find out, and it behoves us to assist them in their investigations.'

'But on whose authority . . .?' Renata began.

The major said, 'On my authority, m'dear. I brought Ryland and Langham in, and until the police can get here I suggest we rely on their experience on such matters.'

Gabriel said, half-laughing, 'But no one here would kill Vermeulen! Someone came in from outside, some maniac . . . This is preposterous!'

'For pity's sake, listen to what Langham is telling you,' the major said. 'Hans was killed by someone in this room, and that's a dashed fact. No getting away from it. We've checked every approach to the castle, every blessed entrance and pathway, and I'm telling you that the snow was undisturbed all around the castle other than where Mr F set out this morning for Fraser's place.'

Langham said, 'The only conclusion we can draw, however unpalatable it might be, is that someone in this room wanted Hans dead, and this morning they achieved that aim.'

He looked around the gathering. 'Right, there's just one or two further things I'd like to add while we're all together. Needless to say, there will necessarily be a restriction on our movements. I would like no one to leave the castle until further notice. To this end, Mr Fergusson, will you ensure that all the outer doors are locked and the keys in the possession of the major?'

Mr Fergusson nodded. 'And there's locks on all the windows. I'll go round and check that they're all secure.'

'Good man,' Langham said. 'Also, in the circumstances, I think it would be a wise precaution when we're alone in our rooms, and again when we retire this evening, to ensure that we lock our doors. I'm sorry I have to say this, but I think you'll see the necessity.'

He looked around the group; the professor and the major nodded. Gabriel was staring through the window with brooding intensity. Renata Káldor eyed Langham neutrally, her expression unreadable.

'That makes eminent sense, Herr Langham,' Meyer said.

'Right,' Langham went on, 'we'll start seeing people in the Stewart room straight away. I'm sorry for the inconvenience but I'm sure you'll understand that it's absolutely necessary if we're to get to the bottom of all this. Ralph?'

The detective pushed himself away from the wall and said, 'Elspeth, if you could come through in a minute, we'll get this over and done with.' He looked around at the guests. 'We'll tell the person we've just interviewed who we'd like to see next.'

Langham and Ryland moved along the corridor to the Stewart room. 'Thanks for that, Don. Nicely done.'

'What did you make of Gabriel, Meyer and Renata's reactions?' Langham asked as he arranged three armchairs before the fire, a single chair facing those he and Ryland would be occupying.

The detective shrugged. 'They seemed genuine enough to me. Either that or they're bloody good actors.'

Langham pulled out his notebook and a biro. 'Here comes Elspeth.'

Elspeth Stuart slipped into the room. Langham's earlier notion of her as resembling a church mouse seemed apposite on this occasion: she crept around the edge of the room as if fearful that a predatory tomcat might pounce at any moment. She sat in the armchair, its great wing-back dwarfing her, and twisted a handkerchief as she faced her interrogators.

Langham gestured to Ryland that he had the floor.

'We're sorry we have to drag you in here and go through all this rigmarole,' the detective said.

'Just a few questions and then it'll be done. Won't keep you long.'

She glanced at Langham and he thought she was about to burst into tears again. She said in a tiny voice, 'Isn't it strange, Mr Langham, but just this morning we were talking about whodunits and I was reading your novel until it was time to help Mrs F in the kitchen. And then something like this happens and you . . . you realize that it isn't really a game, is it? It's not a cosy puzzle but real, horrible life.' And then she did break down and weep into her handkerchief.

'I'm sorry,' she said, sniffing. 'I'm sorry, but it was such a shock.'

Ryland waited until she had gathered herself, then said, 'What I'd like to ask you, Elspeth, is how you came to find Mr Vermeulen? Did you go down to the cellar on some errand?'

She shook her head. 'No, I never go down there, sir. This morning I was at the top of the steps that lead down to the cellar, putting pots away in the pantry, and I heard something.'

'Something?'

'I heard someone speaking. Well, I presume there were two people down there, but I only heard one voice: Mr Vermeulen's. Seconds later I heard a cry. A sort of . . . it's hard to describe . . . but a kind of grunt.'

'And nothing more?'

'Nothing.'

'And you went straight down?'

'Not *straight* down, sir. I was putting the pots away, you see, and I had them in both hands. It took me a minute, or perhaps not that long, to

178

find the hooks in the shadows. Then I went down and . . . and saw . . .'

Ryland nodded. 'But you didn't see the second person? The person Vermeulen had been speaking to?'

She shook her head. 'No. There was no one else down there, sir. They . . . they must have left up the other stairs just before I . . .' She shook her head, her eyes wide at the thought of missing the killer by mere seconds.

'And then you came straight back up to the kitchen and into the dining hall where we saw you?'

She nodded. 'That's right. You see, when I came back up I couldn't find Mrs F. I know it sounds strange but I panicked and ran into the dining hall.'

'Do you know where Mrs F was at the time?'

Elspeth smiled sheepishly. 'I was silly. She was in the scullery on the other side of the kitchen, putting the meat away. But at the time . . .'

'I understand,' Ryland said. 'I presume you saw no one loitering in the corridor outside the kitchen or nearby before or after you made the discovery?'

She shook her head. 'Not a soul, sir.'

'Right. Well, I think that's all, unless you can think of anything else, Don?'

Langham shook his head. 'No, I think that covers everything.'

'If you could tell Mrs F to come through, please?' Ryland said.

Elspeth dipped her head in assent and slipped from the room.

179

'Well,' Ryland said, blowing out his cheeks, 'that's not what I was expecting.'

'You mean the fact that Vermeulen spoke to his killer?'

'Exactly. So the killer follows him down, the bloody great mace concealed behind his back, engages Vermeulen in conversation then waits till he turns to the door and coshes him over the head . . .'

'In the half-light down there, the fact that someone was concealing something behind his back wouldn't be so apparent,' Langham pointed out. 'And Vermeulen wouldn't be expecting whoever he was speaking to be carrying the mace.'

The door opened and Mrs Fergusson entered the room and took the vacant armchair. The interview was conducted within minutes. Mrs F confirmed that she had been in the kitchen and the scullery from seven that morning until the time, around eleven o'clock, when Professor Hardwick rushed into the kitchen requesting her assistance with Elspeth.

Ryland asked her how long she had been in the major's employ, which turned out to be twenty years: three at the castle and the remainder at his previous house in Glenross. She had no idea who might bear a grudge against Vermeulen, who she said was a polite and considerate guest. Needless to say, she had been too busy in the kitchen to notice anyone passing along the corridor in the vicinity of the cellar steps. She said that her husband had been in the kitchen most of the morning, helping with the breakfast first thing, and then mounting a cupboard in the scullery.

Ryland thanked Mrs Fergusson and asked her to send in her husband.

Langham scribbled a few notes and looked up as Mr Fergusson entered the room.

He confirmed that he'd been in the kitchen and scullery all morning, and no, he'd seen no one in the corridor. When asked if he'd seen Vermeulen arguing with anyone over the course of the past few weeks, he considered the question and then shook his head. Vermeulen kept himself to himself, he said, though the engineer was in constant communication with the major about the reclamation project.

Ryland said, 'I wonder if you could slip up to PC Ross's croft and ask him to come down?'

'I'll do that, sir, but I doubt he'll be home. He has a lady friend over in Glenross, and as Sunday's his day off he often drives across to see her in the evening. If he did so yesterday, then the likelihood is that he's still over there, snowed in.'

Langham nodded. 'Would you ask Renata Káldor if she'd care to come through, please?'

Mr Fergusson left the room.

Ryland said, 'How should we go about this, Don? Do we say anything about her and Gabriel?'

'I don't know what that might achieve or what relevance it might have to the murder. We could ask her about her dealings with Gabriel and see how she reacts.'

'There was certainly no love lost between her and Vermeulen,' Ryland said. He paused. 'Would

181

you like to do the honours with this one, Don? Give you some experience for when you join the agency. I'll just sit back and watch.'

Renata strode into the room, took the proffered armchair and crossed her legs. After the down-to-earth homeliness of the Fergussons, the Hungarian's elegance and poise was a striking contrast. Her ivory cigarette holder was empty, but she nevertheless held it between her long fingers like an actress with a prop.

She regarded Langham and Ryland with her characteristic hauteur, and Langham wondered how she managed to invest her immobile features with such iciness and disdain.

'First of all,' Langham said, 'I'm sorry we have to go through all this unpleasant business. I hope you understand?'

'I suppose you have a certain duty to perform, under the circumstances,' she allowed. 'Though I for one will be relieved when the police can be summoned.'

'Your relief will be matched by our own. We're not exactly delighted to find ourselves conducting a murder investigation. Now, I understand you were in your room from after breakfast until summoned by Ralph at around eleven twenty?'

'That is correct.'

'At what time did you leave the dining hall following breakfast?'

'That would be soon after I saw you, gentlemen. Perhaps ten minutes later, say nine thirty.'

'And you went straight to your room?'

'I did.'

'And what did you do there?'

'I cannot see what relevance—'

'Please, if you would answer the question.'

'If you must know, I read for a while and then drew myself a bath. I had just stepped from the bath when I was interrupted.'

'And you didn't leave your room between nine thirty and eleven twenty?'

'I've already told you that.'

Langham paused and wrote in his notebook, more to give himself a space in which to formulate his next question.

'You've been at the castle, as a guest of the major, for about a month now. In that time have you noticed anything . . . anything at all unusual, untoward?'

'Untoward? In what way, Mr Langham?'

'In the relationships, say, between certain individuals?'

She arched an elegant eyebrow and regarded him cynically. Her reply surprised him. 'I find most human relationships unusual, if you must know, if not untoward. You British try to maintain unruffled personal relations – one could almost say you prefer to maintain relations on a *superficial* level – but under the surface there are many interesting psychological factors at play.'

'Are you speaking of specific instances?'

She fitted a cigarette into the holder, lit it with a silver lighter, and blew out a cockade of fragrant smoke. She wafted it away with a lazy hand. 'Where to start? For instance, I find interesting the major's splenetic regard of his son, merely because Gabriel does not to conform to the major's conception of what a man should be. He is a sensitive poet, not a man of action, and this rankles with the old man. I say this merely as an observation – I am quite attached to the major. Also of interest is the girl, Elspeth, and her insipid and rather pathetic adoration of Gabriel – the result of a sheltered upbringing and inadequate socialization. She is conflicted in her relationship with the major, too; for while she is grateful for all he has done for her, at the same time she resents his interference in her affair with his son.'

Langham stared at her. 'You know about this?'

'Her affair with Gabriel?' She smiled at him. 'Gabriel told me, of course.'

'Told you?' Langham said. 'And what are your feelings on the matter?'

She considered her response, then said, 'A part of me feels sorry for the fool of a girl, while another part thinks she deserves what she gets for being so naïve. Uncharitable of me, I admit.'

Beside him, Ryland tapped a Woodbine on the back of his hand and lit up, leaned back and stretched out his legs. Langham gained the impression that the detective was enjoying the interview.

'"Deserves what she gets"?' Langham repeated. 'And what might that be?'

'Come, Mr Langham. You're a man of the world. You know what Gabriel is.'

'What is he, Renata?'

'Gabriel is an animal, albeit a sensitive animal . . . or should I say sensitive to his own feelings and desires? To him, other people are . . .

184

merely objects to use for his own ends. And when I say "people", I refer principally to women. He conforms to a description of a man I once read in a cheap novel as a "serial philanderer" – the consequences, I think, of an insecure personality.'

Langham stared at her and wrote in his notebook: *Serial philanderer. And how does she feel about being used by the poet? Or am I mistaken? Is it she who is using Gabriel?*

He said, 'And Gabriel's relationship with Hans Vermeulen?'

Renata smiled. 'Gabriel loathed the man.'

'For what reason?'

'They are, to use that very British expression, like chalk and cheese. Gabriel is uninhibited, unrepressed; he embraces life to the full, takes what he can and never regrets. He is a creative soul with insight and passion.'

Beside him, Ryland snorted quietly.

Renata went on: 'Whereas Vermeulen is – *was* – a literal-minded engineer who had little or no insight into human beings and their psychological struggles. He understood diagrams and blueprints but not people. And what he didn't understand, he resented, which is why he reviled Gabriel so and why he never missed an opportunity to poke jibes at him.'

Langham nodded and made further notes. 'And do you think Gabriel Gordon loathed Vermeulen sufficiently to attack him?'

She placed her right elbow on her knee, drew on her cigarette and smiled at him. 'I think Gabriel is too sensitive a soul to attack anyone.'

185

'And how would you describe your own dealings with Hans Vermeulen?'

She lifted her shoulders in a nonchalant shrug. 'They were, on my part, cordial and non-confrontational.'

'On your part? And on Vermeulen's?'

'Let's say that we had certain differences of opinion. He harboured ridiculous political ideals, ruled by his heart and not his head.'

'You mean he was of the Left?'

She smiled. 'He was of the Left. What he failed to take into consideration in his espousal of communist ideals was that you cannot fit a political template upon the human race which is, at base, motivated by greed.'

Langham said, 'That depends whether you feel that by changing the political environment you can change the collective psychological condition of society.'

'Oh, but I forgot – you, too, share Hans's naïve political assumptions.'

'I think we're straying from the point,' Langham said, angered despite himself. 'I was asking you about your dealings with Hans Vermeulen. You said you had differences of opinion, but no more?'

'Do you mean by that, did I have reason to wish the man dead?' She smiled. 'I said we had differences of opinion. I cannot say I liked the man that much, but I certainly did not dislike him sufficiently to kill him. And anyway,' she went on, smiling icily from Langham to Ryland, 'if I had killed him, I would certainly not have bashed him over the head but shot him through the heart.'

186

Langham inclined his head. 'That's good to know, if ever I find myself in a serious political argument with you.'

She stabbed out her cigarette in an ashtray. 'Will that be all, gentlemen? If we really must suffer enforced imprisonment in the dining hall while you search our rooms – an exercise in futility, in my opinion – then I would like a little drink.'

Langham glanced at Ryland. 'Anything else, Ralph?'

The detective sat back and took a long draw on his Woodbine. He shook his head. 'No, Don. I've heard enough.'

'Could you ask Gabriel to join us, please?' Langham asked as she rose and moved to the door. 'But not for a minute.'

She left the room and Langham blew out a long breath. 'Well, what did you make of that?'

Ryland regarded the glowing tip of his cigarette. 'You want the truth, Don – she gives me the heebie-jeebies.'

'Her cynicism?'

'Her intelligence. She's calculating, cold. But I must admit that her analysis of the various guests was perceptive.'

'She certainly has Gabriel's measure.'

'And yet he's giving her a bit of the old "how's your father". Or using her, as she'd say.'

Langham shook his head. 'I rather think that nobody uses Renata Káldor. If anything it's the other way round. As you say, she's calculating and strong. She knows what she wants and goes for it.'

187

He was interrupted by the door opening and Gabriel Gordon striding into the room with a tumbler half full of whisky. He sat down, stretched his legs towards the fire and crossed them at the ankles.

He glared from Ryland to Langham. 'Very well, gentlemen, I'll come clean. I admit it, there was no love lost between Hans Vermeulen and myself. I detested the man. He was everything I dislike in a human being.'

Langham eased himself back in his chair and regarded the poet. 'Isn't that going a bit far?'

'I suspect the reason for these interviews,' the poet said, 'is so you can assess how we all regarded the deceased. Well, I'm telling you candidly what I thought of him so that we can get all this over and done with.'

'Very well . . .' Langham took his time as he perused his notes. 'First of all, I'd like to know why you disliked Hans Vermeulen as you did? He seemed to me a perfectly likeable man.'

'Vermeulen was boorish and crass. Did you ever try to talk to him about anything other than his precious engineering? Oh, what he didn't know about stress analysis wasn't worth knowing, but come on!'

Langham smiled. 'I would have thought, as a poet, you'd be more open to the infinite variety of character that goes to make up—'

'Life's too short to listen to the kind of monotonous drivel Vermeulen spouted. Also . . .'

'Go on.'

Gabriel hesitated, looking from Ryland to Langham. 'I found him propositioning Elspeth a

188

while back. She was clearly uncomfortable and I told Vermeulen to watch himself in no uncertain terms.'

Langham said, 'Elspeth mentioned nothing of this just now.'

The poet shrugged. 'She clearly didn't think it relevant. And also,' Gabriel went on, 'there was the fact that Vermeulen was bleeding my father dry.'

Langham leaned forward, relishing what he had to say next. 'Were you aware, Gabriel, that he was charging your father absolutely nothing for his services?'

'I was at dinner last night when he said he wasn't charging the old man while he was sitting on his backside doing nothing, yes. But as for the rest of the time—'

Langham shook his head. 'He wasn't charging your father *anything* for the reclamation work. He was doing it all gratis. Granted, he hoped to gain from the publicity when the plane was eventually raised but he knew of your father's financial situation, was interested in the project on a personal level and consented to perform the salvage operation free of charge.'

For a moment, the poet was lost for words. Then he gathered himself and said, 'I find that hard to believe, I must say.'

'Then I suggest you go and ask your father.'

'And what's all this about the old man's "financial situation"? You make it sound as if he's on his uppers.'

'Well, perhaps that's another thing you can ask your father about, isn't it? But to get back to

189

Vermeulen and your dealings with him.' Langham paused. 'Given that you mistakenly assumed the engineer was, in your words, bleeding your father dry . . . this would appear to give you a pretty strong motive for wanting Vermeulen out of the way, wouldn't you say?'

'As I said, I didn't like the man, and I thought – and still think, until I'm proved wrong – that he was taking my father for a ride. But that doesn't mean to say I'd kill him.'

'Of all the people in the castle,' Langham went on, 'it does appear that you have the strongest motive.' He turned to Ryland. 'Wouldn't you agree, Ralph?'

The detective grinned around his tab end. 'Too bleeding true it does. The rozzers would whip him straight into custody for a good old chinwag.'

Gabriel looked from Ryland to Langham. 'You can think what you like, gentlemen, but I didn't lay a finger on Vermeulen and you can't prove that I did.'

'Where were you between around ten thirty and eleven this morning?'

'In bed.'

'Didn't you come down for breakfast?'

'I'd partaken a little too much of the grape last night, if you recall.'

'Can anyone corroborate your story?'

Gabriel smiled sweetly. 'You were all there at the dinner table to witness my inebriation—'

'I mean,' Langham said, 'can anyone corroborate that you were in bed all morning?'

'Unfortunately, on this occasion, I was alone.'

'And your room is directly above the corridor with the staircase leading to the cellar. In fact, there's a narrow flight of stairs just along from your room, leading directly down to the corridor. It would have taken you a matter of a minute or two to have slipped from your room, descended the stairs and followed Vermeulen down into the cellar.'

'I concede the point. I could have been down there, coshed him over the head and got back to my room in around . . . oh, say, forty-five seconds, all things being equal – *in theory*. In actuality, I did nothing of the kind.'

Ryland commented, 'We have only your word for that.'

'Your little scenario presumes that I *knew* that Vermeulen would be descending to the cellar when he did so.'

'Or that you arranged to meet him down there beforehand.' Langham smiled.

'Touché,' Gabriel said.

'Aside from Vermeulen, how would you characterize your relations with the other guests?'

'I don't see what that has got to do with anything, or how it might help in your investigations.'

'I'm trying to build the larger picture of social dynamics within the castle. It helps to know how various people relate to each other. Now, what about Renata Káldor?'

'What about her?'

'I'd like to hear your opinion of her. I seem to recall that, in the car on the way to the castle, you called her somewhat remote, icy. Is that still your opinion of the woman?'

The poet narrowed his eyes as he regarded Langham. 'Why shouldn't it be?'

Langham shrugged. 'Oh, I thought perhaps that you might have reason to revise your opinion of Káldor in light of recent events.'

'Recent events?' Gabriel repeated, arching an eyebrow.

Ryland leaned forward and nipped the tab end from his mouth. 'Like the fact that you're knocking her off.'

Gabriel flung back his head and laughed. 'Oh, I see what you mean – Langham was being rather coy. But why should I revise my opinion of the woman merely because we've enjoyed carnal relations?'

'It occurred to me that you said what you did about Káldor in order to disguise the fact of your affair.'

'I'd hardly grace our union with the sobriquet of an affair, Mr Langham. But who told you about us?'

'No one. I saw you leave her room in the early hours.'

'And I thought I was being discreet.' He regarded his empty glass as if wishing it were full. 'But not a word of this to Elspeth, OK?'

Ryland said, 'I'm surprised you care about her feelings, Gordon.'

Langham watched the poet as he gazed through the window. Gabriel drew a deep sigh, then looked at Langham and said, 'You might find this hard to believe, but I do care about the girl. I care deeply.'

'But not enough that you don't mind going behind her back and making love to Renata?'

The poet looked genuinely pained. What he said next surprised Langham. 'Have you ever loved a woman?'

'I don't see—'

'Please, answer the question.'

'Very well.' Langham nodded. 'Yes, of course I have.'

'Have you ever loved someone, and then met someone for whom you feel very strongly – it might not be love, but call it affection? And that person possesses a certain fatal attraction which you can't withstand . . .'

'No. No, I haven't.' Langham regarded the young man. 'But you're saying that that's how you regard Renata?'

'I'm saying that . . . that what I feel for her is complex. She's a very strong woman, Langham, and I've never met anyone like her before. She understands me, and . . . yes, I do find her incredibly attractive.' He waved. 'Of course, I don't expect you to understand. But despite everything, I do feel for Elspeth, and I don't want her to be hurt.'

'Then I suggest,' Ryland said cuttingly, 'that you do nothing to hurt her.'

Gabriel whispered to himself, 'If only it were that easy.'

Langham sighed. 'I think that'll be all for now; if you'd care to return to the dining hall and remain there until further notice. And would you ask Meyer if he'd be kind enough to come through?'

Gabriel rose, nodded to Langham and left the room.

'Christ, I'd like to lay one on the bastard,' the detective said.

'He's an odd one,' Langham said. 'I honestly don't know what to make of him. But I don't think he killed Vermeulen.'

'He has the only motive we've come across so far.'

'Even so, I don't think he'd be so brazen in his avowal of disliking the man if he was responsible for Vermeulen's death.'

'Unless he's a bloody good actor and he's playing a game of double bluff.'

The door opened and Ulrich Meyer limped into the room. Langham glanced at Ryland. 'Would you care to . . .?'

'No, he's all yours, Don. You're doing well.'

Meyer walked around the armchair, stood before it then slowly lowered himself, wincing as he did so.

His bright blue eye moved from Ryland to Langham. 'I am totally at your disposal, gentlemen, and will assist you in any way possible to clear up this deplorable incident.'

'We appreciate that,' Langham said. 'I'd like to ask a few questions.'

'Certainly.'

'First of all, how long have you known Hans Vermeulen?'

'I met him for the first time perhaps six weeks ago when I came to the castle at the major's invitation. We struck up an immediate rapport, having certain topics of interest in common, not least of which was the salvage operation. When the bad weather began, with severe frost in

November delaying the lifting of the plane, I decided to continue on my touring holiday of Scotland.'

Ryland asked, 'Sightseeing?'

'That is correct.'

'Have you been to Scotland before, Herr Meyer?'

'Only once, to visit the major in Glenross before he purchased the castle.'

Langham asked, 'In your relations with Hans Vermeulen, did you notice anything at all remarkable or noteworthy in his dealings with any of the other guests?'

Meyer ran a finger around the lower edge of his eyepatch. 'I must say that Hans was an entirely inoffensive person. He was cordial with everyone he met, in my experience. However, in certain instances, other people did not reciprocate with cordiality.'

'These people being?' Langham asked.

'Gabriel Gordon, for some reason, treated Hans with untoward animosity. That might not be so remarkable, as the young man exhibits a rather intolerant, not to say disrespectful, attitude to many people. But he seemed to regard Hans with a particular dislike.'

'Have you any idea why this might have been?'

The German shrugged. 'I found it hard to understand. They were of different temperaments and ages, and perhaps their politics varied. But I put it down simply to the young man's . . . how do you say? . . . bloody-mindedness.'

'And the other person who took against Mr Vermeulen?'

'His relationship with Renata Káldor was rather . . . frosty, shall we say? Now in this case I think their politics were at odds, as I think you are aware. And Renata is a somewhat – you English have that wonderful phrase – cold fish.'

Langham made a note. 'I hope you don't mind my asking where you were at a little before eleven o'clock this morning?'

'Not at all. At ten thirty I decided to take a turn around the battlements of the eastern wall.'

'And how did you reach the battlements? I understand that the snow outside the exits was undisturbed?'

Meyer said, 'Opposite the entrance to the cellar is a small door which leads, via a spiral stairway, to the battlements. After breakfast I decided that I needed some fresh air, and I was enjoying the rather spectacular view when Herr Ryland found me and summoned me to the Stewart room.'

'Isn't the footing up there rather treacherous, particularly at this time of year?'

Meyer inclined his head. 'Indeed it is. I proceeded with utmost care, especially as, with my injuries, I sometimes find walking a little difficult.'

'I don't think there's much else to ask, for now,' Langham said. 'Thank you for your time. Could you ask Professor Hardwick to come through, please?'

Herr Meyer stood, inclined his head towards the two men and limped from the room.

'Well?' Langham asked when they were alone again.

196

'He said himself that the door to the battlements was right opposite the cellar steps . . .'

'Go on.'

'Well, he was in a prime position to slip down, cross the corridor and follow Vermeulen into the cellar.'

Langham gave the detective a dubious look. '"Slip down"? You've seen how he walks? He's almost a cripple. He couldn't move at speed if he tried.'

Ryland pointed at him. 'Ah, but we've only got his word for that, haven't we?'

Langham looked up as the door opened and Professor Hardwick entered rather diffidently.

'This is just a formality, Professor,' Langham said. 'As you were with us when the murder was committed, I think that puts you out of the running.'

'I'm relieved to hear that, Mr Langham. I am one of those unfortunate souls who cannot but feel guilty even when I know myself to be perfectly innocent! The mere sight of a policeman brings about the desire to confess!'

Langham smiled. 'I'd just like to ask if you'd noticed, during your stay here, whether Vermeulen was involved in any altercations or disagreements with other guests? Can you recall anything at all that might have a bearing on what happened in the cellar this morning?'

The professor considered the question. 'To be perfectly honest, gentlemen, I cannot. I'm sorry but my mind is a blank in that department. I recall Mr Vermeulen with nothing but fondness. We had one or two rather stimulating

197

conversations on the subject of the salvage, and to the best of my knowledge the other guests got on well with him, too, though he and Renata exchanged differences of opinion from time to time.'

Langham thanked the professor and asked him to send in the major.

'Going on the assumption that Vermeulen was the gunman's intended target all along,' Langham said, 'does that mean the major's no longer in danger?'

Ryland pointed at him with an unlit Woodbine. 'That's a risky assumption, Don. *If* the killer is out to get the salvage shut down, then surely he'd want the major out of the way too? I think it'd be safest if we assume the major is still in danger.'

Langham thought about it. 'In that case, I have an idea.'

He outlined his plan to Ryland, who nodded in agreement.

The major entered the room and took his seat before the fire, looking drawn and tired. He nodded to the two men. 'Well, I hope you're getting somewhere with your investigations, gentlemen. I must admit I'm at me wits' end thinking about poor Hans.'

'You were in the library when it happened, Major?'

'Locked in with me gun to hand, Langham. Mrs F's pounding on the door nearly gave me a heart attack.'

'Have you any idea who might have wanted Vermeulen dead?'

'Not a ruddy clue, Langham.'

'But what about a motive?'

'To get the project closed down, I'd say.'

Ryland said, 'If that's so, Major, then it means that you're still in danger. We've been mulling it over, and here's what we think you should do . . .'

Five minutes later they moved through to the dining hall. The guests looked up, expectantly, as they filed in.

Langham stood by the fire and addressed the gathering. 'Thank you for your cooperation.'

He noticed Gabriel turn away and refill his glass from a crystal decanter on the table. 'All that remains now is for Mr Ryland and me to make a thorough search of all the occupied bedrooms, as well as the rest of the castle. Can I ask if any of you have locked your rooms?'

Of the eight people present in the room, excepting Langham and Ryland, only Renata Káldor had taken the precaution of locking her room.

'Then if I might ask you for the key?'

She hesitated – reluctant, it appeared, to acquiesce to his request. At last, she rummaged in her tiny handbag and pushed a key across the table.

'We'll be as quick as we possibly can,' Langham said. 'As for the dining arrangements this evening . . . We see no reason why dinner should not go ahead, communally, as usual. We would be grateful if everyone were present.'

He thanked them again and followed Ryland from the room.

For the next three hours he and Ryland traversed the various floors of the castle, starting with the bedrooms then moving on to the unoccupied

199

bedrooms and the other rooms in the rambling edifice. Ryland told Langham at the outset that he held out little hope of finding the film; the search was less about that, he said, than turning up anything amongst the personal possessions of the guests that might shed light on the murder or prove otherwise incriminating – including blood-stained clothing.

Gabriel Gordon's room was a sybaritic shambles. Empty wine and whisky bottles littered every available flat surface, competing for space with tottering piles of contemporary poetry. The bed was an unmade tangle of sheets, replete with dirty dinner plates and the remains of half-eaten toast. Clothing lay discarded on the carpet, alongside old newspapers and magazines. 'Would you believe it,' Ryland said at one point. 'Have a gander at this, Don.'

The detective was flipping through a volume of Victorian pornography. 'Didn't know they got up to this kind of thing back then.'

From the poet's room they moved down the corridor to that of Renata Káldor. In contrast to Gordon's, Renata's room was almost obsessively orderly. Not an item was out of place, and all her clothing neatly occupied a wardrobe and a chest of drawers. Only a range of toiletries in the en suite, and three books on the bedside table, suggested occupancy. Two of the books were texts in what he presumed was Hungarian, while the third was Camus' *The Plague*, in French. Langham went through the drawers of the bedside table looking for an address book or personal papers, but found nothing.

Meyer's bedroom was so neat and tidy that it appeared, as first glance, as if no one was occupying the room. The German's only possessions, other than clothing and toiletries, appeared to be a pile of books on a writing desk and a scroll of what turned out to be blueprints for a Dornier aircraft.

They moved on to Professor Hardwick's room across the corridor and gave it a cursory once-over, then took a quick look around the major's bedroom in the southern tower. Elspeth Stuart's bedroom, in the truncated south wing, was a clutter of personal possessions dating back to her childhood, dolls and teddy bears and a painted rocking horse, together with more grown-up, feminine accoutrements like a sewing machine and tailor's dummy; it appeared that Elspeth made many of her own clothes.

The Fergussons' set of rooms, beyond the kitchen, were the last on the list, by which time Langham was weary and in need of a drink. They progressed through the castle's unoccupied rooms with little enthusiasm for the search but fascinated by the variety of nooks and crannies they came across: an ancient kitchen and a grain store, a dungeon and a primeval toilet – a tiny cantilevered cubby with an opening in the floor giving direct access to the loch far below.

At the end of the abortive search, Langham sent Ryland to tell the captive guests that they were free to leave the dining hall, then retired to his own room and attempted to concentrate on the book he was reading for review.

* * *

Dinner that evening was a subdued affair, as befitted the circumstances.

Langham was pleased to see that all the guests were present. The seating arrangements were as they had been on the previous evening, though with Renata Káldor returned to the end of the table and Ulrich Meyer taking Hans Vermeulen's place.

Langham looked around the table; he was aware of others casting covert glances at their fellow diners; all of them but one, he thought, harbouring suspicions, or fears, apropos the identity of the killer in their midst.

The conversation consisted of hushed small talk between neighbours; the major regaled Ryland with a tale of tiger-hunting in India; Elspeth asked Langham what he was working on at the moment and he outlined the plot of the thriller he'd just finished. Gabriel ate in silence, other than when he addressed one or two comments to the professor. The latter, for the most part, discussed something in lowered tones with Meyer. At the far end of the table, opposite the major, Renata Káldor consumed her meal in regal silence, as if conversation were beneath her dignity.

An hour into the meal, as Mrs Fergusson was clearing away the remains of the main course, the major rapped on the table with a serving spoon. The time had come to make the announcement he'd agreed with Langham and Ryland earlier.

'I've been thinking about poor old Hans,' he said, 'and mulling everything over. I know it's not what he would have wanted, but to be honest all this business has knocked the stuffing from me. I've decided, after thinking about it long and hard, to pack in the ruddy salvage operation. What with poor Hans dead, I can't bring myself to continue. It'd always remind me of Hans, y'see.' He terminated his announcement with a hefty draught of wine.

Langham glanced around the table, judging the reaction to the old man's words.

Meyer looked shocked. He lowered his spoon to his bowl and stared at the major. 'But I find this hard to believe, my friend. Surely you should give yourself a little time before making such a decision?'

'I've thought about it long and hard,' the major said, 'and I've made me decision.'

Gabriel said, 'That's eminently sensible. Always thought it a hare-brained project.'

'You're wrong on that score,' the old man responded. 'With Hans at the helm it was far from "hare-brained", as you say. But enough's enough.'

Renata Káldor set aside her spoon. 'Are you absolutely sure about this, Major? You have been working on the project for almost a year, after all. You talk about little else.' She smiled across at him. 'I think Herr Meyer is correct: you should take a little more time to think about it. After all, perhaps you owe it to the memory of Hans to continue with the project?'

The major shook his head, defiant. 'I've made me decision, Renata, and I'm sticking to it. The project has come to an end and I'll hear no more on the subject, y'understand?'

The Hungarian opened her mouth as if to protest, thought better of it and continued her dessert.

Professor Hardwick blinked around the table. 'Well, for my part, I think the decision rests entirely with the major. It was, after all, his project.'

Conversation resumed between neighbours, and a little later the guests departed for bed one by one. The major buttonholed Langham and Ryland as they rose from the table. 'Word in your ears, m'boys. How about a swift nightcap?'

They repaired to the Stewart room and the major splashed a generous measure of single malt into their glasses.

'Well, I certainly hope that does the trick,' he said.

'It was the sensible thing to announce in the circumstances,' Langham said. 'Not that you should relax your vigilance. It's possible that Hans was killed for reasons that had nothing to do with the project, but you never know.'

Ryland said, 'What did you make of how your decision went down?'

The major grunted and shook his head.

Langham said, 'I'm not sure we should read too much into how people responded. We're dealing with a devious mind; he or she would have checked their reactions against what was expected of them.'

'Dammit, Langham. Look here, I just can't bring myself to believe that *anyone* around the table tonight would have killed Hans – or would want me dead, for that matter. Gabriel's me own flesh and blood, for God's sake, even though the boy's a ne'er-do-well. And I've known Renata for years; we're close. As for Hardwick, preposterous! Known the fellow since I was five. Ulrich I consider a good friend and he's committed to the project. The Fergussons have been with me for twenty years! And I defy you to think wee Elspeth could have . . .'

'I know,' Langham said. 'I'm with you in finding it hard to believe that any one of them might be responsible. But the fact remains . . .'

The major imbibed his whisky. 'You don't think it possible, remotely possible, that someone did get into the castle, somehow, and did for poor old Hans?'

'I honestly don't see how they might have managed it, Major. We checked all the approaches. The castle's surrounded by a few feet of snow. We'd have seen tracks if anyone had entered.'

'But what about if they slipped in days ago and concealed themselves?'

Langham shook his head. 'I think we're entering into the realms of fantasy there, Major.' He paused, then smiled across at the old man. 'But we won't dismiss the possibility out of hand, OK?'

The major stared into his glass and nodded abstractedly.

'Oh, by the way,' the old man said a little later as they drained their glasses and prepared to retire, 'Mr F was right. PC Ross must've skedaddled over to his fiancée's place in Glenross yesterday and got snowed in. He wasn't at home and his car was gone.'

205

'Pity,' Ryland said. 'It'd help to have him down here.'

Langham recalled something the major had told him yesterday evening about Renata Káldor. 'There's one other thing before we turn in,' he said. 'You said something yesterday about Renata's "condition"?'

The major pursed his lips, considering. 'That's right, Langham. I did.' He shuttled a glance between Langham and Ryland, then said, 'Look, this is between thee and me, understood? On no account must the fact that I've told you get back to Renata.'

Langham nodded. 'Very well.'

The old man sighed. 'She told me this summer. Hell of a shock. Knocked the wind from me sails, I'll tell you. Life is cruel, Langham . . .'

He fell silent, staring into his empty glass.

'Major?' Langham prompted.

'Hell!' the major said. He swallowed, keeping a tight rein on his emotions. 'Renata's ill, gentlemen. Six months ago she was diagnosed with leukaemia. It's terminal. They gave her a year.' He shook his head. 'She's taking it with remarkable fortitude. She's accepted the inevitable and is coming to terms with her fate. But, dammit, it's harder for her friends to do the same. I mean, for God's sake, she's so ruddy young – not yet forty-five . . .'

'I'm sorry,' Langham murmured.

The major slapped his thigh. 'Well, that's life, I suppose: a bloody tragic mess most of the time.' He sighed. 'It's late. I really must be turning in. I'll see you in the morning.'

He climbed wearily to his feet and limped from the room.

'The poor bloody woman . . .' Ryland said. 'You don't think it has any bearing on what's happened, do you?'

Langham shrugged. 'Impossible to say,' he said. 'But it's a bit of a shocker.'

They left the room and filed up the creaking staircase.

In his bedroom, Langham lifted the phone on the off-chance of finding the line reconnected, but the receiver was silent.

Before he went to bed, he drew the curtain aside and stared out into the moonlit night.

The snow was still falling with a vengeance.

He lay awake, his head full of Renata Káldor and her fate, and that night sleep was a long time coming.

Sixteen

Maria spent the evening alone in her Kensington apartment, opened a bottle of white wine and ate two slices of melted cheese on toast – a 'delicacy' to which Donald had introduced her.

She had gone over and over the events in Donald's flat that morning, each time reassuring herself that she had done the right thing in admitting to the thugs that Ralph Ryland was a private detective and in divulging the whereabouts of his office. If she had stubbornly refused to tell them what they wanted, then she had little doubt that they would have make good their threats to harm her.

She suspected that the thugs' desire to know about Donald and Ryland was linked in some way to the affair in the Highlands. But if she were right, then how might they be involved?

The thought of Donald, so far away, was like a physical pain.

The police, when they had arrived at Donald's flat a little after midday, had been efficient, consolatory and reassuring. She had given a long statement describing exactly what had happened from her entering the flat to the thugs making their getaway – and the sergeant had commended her on her decision to divulge Ryland's profession and the whereabouts of his office. She had mentioned the affair in the Highlands, but the sergeant had been non-committal on whether in his opinion the break-in was related. Maria had accompanied the policeman to Kensington station, where a police artist had sketched a very good likeness of both Scarface and the knifeman.

Maria finished her cheese on toast and, at eight, listened to the news broadcast on the Third Programme. The inclement weather featured prominently: snowstorms were inundating the north of England and much of northern Scotland was cut off. In some outlying Highland areas the snow had fallen to a depth of five feet.

She thought of Donald, sequestered in the castle with a potential killer on the loose.

At eight thirty the telephone bell shrilled,

making her jump. It could be Donald, she told herself, the phone lines having been repaired.

She snatched up the receiver and said expectantly, 'Yes?'

A male voice said, 'Miss Dupré? Maria Dupré?'

'Yes?' Her heart thumped. 'Who is it?'

'I'm sorry to bother you at this hour. We have met before. I'm a friend of Donald's – Detective Inspector Mallory. Jeff Mallory. We met briefly back in the summer.'

'I remember,' she said, her relief tempered by concern. 'Donald hasn't contacted you, has he?'

'Donald? No . . . I was called into Kensington station today by a colleague. I was working on a case recently involving one of the men suspected of the break-in at Donald's flat today. I know it's late, but I was wondering if I might pop round for a quick word?'

'By all means. Yes, do. I think I need to talk to someone about everything. Donald isn't here at the moment—'

'The sergeant explained the situation, Maria. Right. If you'll give me ten minutes.'

'I'll see you then.'

She moved to the kitchen, put the kettle on and prepared a pot of tea. She recalled that Mallory liked his tea strong and sweet.

A little over ten minutes later the intercom buzzed and Maria let the detective inspector up to the first floor. She opened the door to her apartment and he removed his hat and ducked in. Mallory was a tall South African who looked more like a Springbok prop-forward than a police

209

detective: a burly man, running to fat, with thinning blond hair and boyish features.

'Tea?'

'Marvellous.'

'Strong and two sugars, if I recall?'

He smiled. 'Two it is. I know I should cut down.' He patted his paunch. 'But you know how it is.'

She showed him into the sitting room, fetched the tray from the kitchen and poured two cups. She noticed that he was carrying a manila envelope.

'Now what's all this about Donald haring off up to Scotland on the trail of a suspected murderer?' Mallory asked as he sat back on the sofa with his tea. 'The sergeant you saw today gave me the outlines, but if you wouldn't mind I'd like to hear the details.'

Maria told Mallory about the situation at Loch Corraig Castle. She said that she'd last heard from Donald yesterday afternoon but had been cut off since then. 'He asked me to check on a few people. I was at Donald's flat this morning, looking for his address book, when I disturbed the intruders.'

Mallory opened the manila envelope. 'The description you gave – and the artist's sketch of one of the men – matched a certain individual we have on our records.'

He pulled the artist's impression of the scar-faced thug from the envelope and laid it on the sofa, then withdrew a black-and-white photograph of the same man and showed it to Maria.

'This the fellow?'

She took the photograph. He looked a little younger in the picture, but it was definitely the same man. 'Yes. Yes, that was him.'

He nodded. 'These are from Dutch police files, three years old.' He tapped the photograph with a fat forefinger. 'I was working on a case recently and interviewed the chap – a criminal by the name of Patrick Vermeulen.'

He stopped as he saw Maria's expression.

She said, '*Vermeulen?*'

'That's right. Patrick Vermeulen. Dutch national.' He narrowed his eyes. 'The name means something to you?'

She nodded. 'Yes, yes, it does.' She gathered her thoughts. 'When I spoke to Donald yesterday someone called Vermeulen was one of the people he wanted me to check up on. But he was called *Hans* Vermeulen.'

Mallory nodded. 'According to our records, Patrick has a brother called Hans, an engineer based here in London.'

'That's right. He's staying at the castle.'

'Do you know what Hans Vermeulen is doing there?'

She told him about the salvage operation of the German plane the major was funding, and how Vermeulen's company was undertaking the work.

She broke off and stared at him. 'But surely it can't be a coincidence, can it? The fact that Hans Vermeulen is at the castle and that his brother Patrick broke into Donald's flat – wanting to know who Donald and Ryland were? You see, they suspected Donald and Ryland were detectives.'

Mallory nodded. 'It sounds to me as if they were put up to finding out who Donald and Ryland were by Hans Vermeulen. Donald's obviously been nosing around, and Vermeulen became suspicious.'

Maria gripped her cup. 'But . . . but does that mean Donald and Ralph are in danger?'

'I wouldn't jump to that conclusion immediately,' Mallory reassured her. 'I'll get on to my colleagues in Inverness, but the weather up there being as it is . . .'

'You said you'd interviewed Patrick Vermeulen recently.'

'For suspected involvement in a bank robbery in Mayfair. He's a known criminal in his home town of Rotterdam. According to my Dutch colleagues, he collaborated with German occupying forces during the war, as well as running small criminal operations. After the war Patrick stepped up a gear and got into money laundering, drugs and the prostitution racket.'

'But the other brother, Hans – he runs an engineering company. He isn't a known criminal?' she finished hopefully.

'That's the odd thing, Maria. You see, Hans Vermeulen worked for the resistance in Rotterdam during the war. He and his brother were on opposing sides, if you like. After the war he took an engineering degree in London and set up a company here. However, he came on to my radar earlier this year when I investigated Patrick Vermeulen. I suspect that Hans Vermeulen's company is being used as a front to launder stolen money. I don't know if Hans entered

212

willingly into this or whether he was coerced by Patrick.'

Maria sat in silence for a while, contemplating her tea. She looked up. 'I wonder . . .'

'Go on.'

She shook her head. 'Might it be possible that Major Gordon has got wind of Hans Vermeulen's illegal activities, which is why Hans is . . .'

'Trying to bump the major off?' Mallory finished. 'It's a possibility, I suppose. One thing for certain is that Patrick Vermeulen is not a particularly savoury character.'

She shivered. 'And to think he broke into Donald's flat today . . .' She looked up. 'The other man, the one with the knife?'

Mallory withdrew a second photograph showing a younger version of the knifeman, his bulldog jowls unshaven. 'Kurt Dreyer, a thug who's served time in Dutch gaols for assault and manslaughter.'

He returned the photographs to the envelope. 'But rest assured, we've got an alert out for them. If Donald does manage to get through, could you tell him to give me a ring? I'd like to know more about what Hans Vermeulen is up to in the Highlands.'

'Of course.' She finished her tea and asked Mallory if he'd care for a refill. He looked at his watch, told her he'd been on the go since seven that morning and thanked her for her time.

'Oh,' he said as she showed him to the door. 'I hear congratulations are in order. When's the big day?'

She told him, and felt a reassuring warmth at

the thought of the wedding as she locked the door behind the detective. She made herself another cup of tea, curled up on the sofa and considered the situation in the Highlands.

What Mallory had said about the police being on to the thugs was reassuring. But, at the same time, the thought of one of the Vermeulen brothers abiding in the same castle as Donald . . .

If only she could get through to Donald and warn him.

She sat for an hour, going over her options, and by the time she went to bed she had come to a decision.

Seventeen

Langham awoke at nine the following morning and lay in bed for ten minutes. Had he caught the train as planned last night, by now he would be in London with Maria and welcoming Charles from gaol. He hoped Maria would put his silence down to the bad weather rather than thoughtlessness on his part or, worse, assume that he'd fallen foul of the criminal in their midst.

His enforced sequestration up here wouldn't be so bad if he could have phoned Maria, heard her voice and reassured her that all was well. It occurred to him that, as Glenross was only four miles away, he should strike out later today, hike to the town and kill two birds with one stone:

inform the police of the killing of Hans Vermeulen and ring Maria. It was certainly an idea he'd discuss later with Ralph.

He tried the phone again, but the line was still dead.

He ran himself a bath and soaked for thirty minutes. At one point he thought he heard a tap on the bedroom door, but as there was no follow-up knock he assumed he'd been mistaken and closed his eyes.

He'd lain awake for an age last night, going over the events of the day. He knew that it might be rash to discount the least likely suspects in the case, but he thought it unlikely that Elspeth Stuart or the Fergussons could be considered as suspects. Likewise the major. He'd served under him for five years and trusted the man implicitly; and anyway, there was no way he could have staged the shooting on the pontoon. Also, Professor Hardwick was out of the frame, with the cast-iron alibi of being with Langham and Ryland when the murder was committed.

Which left only three possible suspects.

Gabriel Gordon, Renata Káldor and Ulrich Meyer.

His last thought before falling asleep had been the news of Renata's terminal illness, and he'd wondered if her icy disdain of all around her was a result of the diagnosis or if it had always been a part of her character.

He heard his bedroom door open and expected to hear Ryland's cockney tones asking if he was coming down for breakfast. When he heard the door shut again, seconds later, he thought it odd and quickly climbed from the bath and dried himself. Pulling on his dressing gown, he moved into the bedroom and looked around. On the carpet before the door was a folded sheet of paper.

He picked it up, sat on the bed and read the scrawled note.

> *Dear Mr Langham,*
> *I need to speak to you on an urgent matter. Would you meet me in the morning room at ten?*
> *R. P. Hardwick.*

He looked at his watch. It was almost nine forty. An 'urgent matter'? He wondered if the professor had seen or heard something pertaining to the killing . . .

He stepped from his room and crossed the corridor to Professor Hardwick's room. He tapped on the door. 'Professor Hardwick? Hello?' He waited ten seconds and tried again. 'Professor?'

He returned to his room, dressed quickly and made his way downstairs to the morning room, expecting to find the professor awaiting him. The room was empty; Langham swore to himself and hurried along the corridor to the dining hall.

Elspeth Stuart and Renata Káldor were seated at the table, the latter reading Camus, eating toast and pointedly ignoring the girl. Gabriel Gordon was loading his plate with scrambled egg.

Ulrich Meyer stood before the window, cup and saucer in hand, in conversation with the major.

'Has anyone seen Professor Hardwick this morning?' Langham asked.

Renata looked up from her novel. 'Why? Is he missing?'

'Ah . . . No,' Langham temporized. 'He mentioned that he had a recording he wanted me to listen to.'

Renata laid aside her novel. 'I really find it hard to believe that anyone with an ounce of intelligence could waste their time chasing ghosts.'

Meyer said, 'Each to their own, as I think the saying goes.'

The Hungarian cast Meyer a withering glance, which the German failed to notice.

'I find a belief in such phenomena sickening,' Renata went on. 'Cannot people accept that there is no afterlife of any kind – that this life is the one and only existence we have – and *appreciate* that?'

Langham looked across at the Hungarian and experienced a sensation of vicarious despair.

Meyer set his empty cup on the table, murmured to the diners and limped from the room.

'Herr Meyer was very quiet this morning,' Renata observed.

Gabriel said, 'Probably a bit miffed about the old man putting the kibosh on the salvage operation.'

'Not a bit of it,' the major said. 'I was discussing it with him just now. He understands perfectly.'

Langham left the room. He turned along the corridor towards the morning room and almost

217

collided with Ryland as the latter came down the stairs.

'Just the man, Ralph,' he said. 'Look at this.'

He passed the detective Hardwick's note. Ryland read it and looked up. 'An "urgent matter".'

Langham looked at his watch. It was just after nine forty-five. 'Come on.' He ushered Ryland along the corridor towards the southern tower.

They came to the morning room, Langham half expecting to be met by Professor Hardwick. He was disappointed, yet again, to find the room empty.

'With a bit of luck,' Langham said as they seated themselves in armchairs on either side of the unlit hearth, 'this just might be the break we've been waiting for.'

'God knows, we deserve a bit of luck. We've had bugger all to go on so far.'

As they waited, Langham regaled Ryland with his thoughts regarding the principal suspects: Gabriel Gordon, Káldor and Meyer.

'Well, the only one with a motive is Gabriel,' Ryland said. 'He thought Vermeulen was bleeding his father dry, mistakenly as it turns out.'

Langham nodded, staring out through the window. The snow had abated and he could see beyond the loch to the snow-clad hillside and the tiny, muffled shapes of half-a-dozen crofts. It was a bleak prospect, and he wondered at the hardy souls who made a living in this inhospitable landscape.

'Let's go back a bit,' he said, 'to when we said the German plane might be at the bottom of all this. We wondered if whoever wanted the major or Vermeulen dead did so to halt the salvage operation. Now the question is who stands to gain if the operation is halted? Gabriel Gordon? He might have thought he'd save money if the project was ended, but we pretty much agree that it's a damned thin reason for committing murder. Meyer? As far as we know he's fully behind the salvage and has something to gain if he writes that monograph he's been going on about. Káldor?' He shook his head. 'What might she possibly gain from not having the wreck resurrected?'

'And she was against the major's announcement last night that he was halting the operation.'

'Might always have been a bluff,' Langham said. 'It's impossible to tell.'

He pulled out his pipe, filled it from his pouch of Navy Cut and went about the business of lighting up while considering his next words. 'Yesterday we wondered if the reason someone didn't want the wreck raised was because it contained incriminating information concerning high-ups in the British establishment. I must admit that I thought that scenario a bit unlikely. But what else might account for someone not wanting the plane salvaged?'

'It flew from Germany towards the end of the war, early 'forty-five,' Ryland said. 'By then the Nazis knew the game was up. Already some of 'em were making their escape plans. What if the plane was carrying some Krauts bent on escape?'

Langham looked at him dubiously. 'To Britain?'

219

Ryland shrugged. 'Why not? What if these people weren't high-ups in the Nazi regime? What if they were just people wanting out before the allies invaded?'

'But why would they "want out" if they weren't high-up Nazis? They'd have nothing to fear.' Langham stopped there and stared at the detective. 'Just a sec. How about this: they weren't high-ups, just common or garden, rank-and-file Nazis who wanted away from a country about to face defeat and occupation – and they had something they didn't want to fall into allied hands.'

'*Something*, Don?'

'Stolen goods, perhaps.'

'Valuables?' Ryland sat up. 'Gold and the like?'

'Gold, art treasures, jewellery, whatever. They got hold of a plane and escaped. They didn't necessarily make for Scotland; they might have been heading for anywhere in Britain. Whatever, they hit difficulties over the North Sea and came in over the Highlands, crash-landing in the loch.'

'And one or more of them survived?'

'They managed to get out of the plane but were unable to take the valuables with them.'

Ryland leaned forward, animated. 'Hold on – the murder of the crofter Ross told us about . . . What if they took refuge in his place, stole food – and the crofter objected and was killed for his troubles?'

Langham nodded. 'It's a working hypothesis, Ralph. Then the survivors left the area, fled south and took up new identities in Britain. Maybe they had contacts, people who could issue them with papers, passports . . . so they could disappear into society.'

'And all along the valuables were lying untouched at the bottom of the loch and only the survivors were aware of the fact.'

Langham experienced a surge of elation similar to when, during the writing of a novel, a particular knotty problem regarding the plot resolved itself. He pointed at Ryland with the stem of his pipe. 'And Vermeulen gets to hear about the crashed plane and contacts the major, who decides to go about salvaging it. And the survivors, when they get wind of this, are horrified – and do all they can to stop the plane from being raised.'

'It fits, Don. They want to stop the salvage operation so that they . . .' He stopped, his eyes wide. 'Bloody hell, Don – the Morris Commercial PC Ross saw last week, the boat . . .'

'It was the survivors,' Langham said, 'making a recce on the pontoon. They were taking advantage of Vermeulen obligingly locating the precise whereabouts of the wreck for them, and in the dead of night they rowed across to the pontoon to retrieve the valuables?'

'Christ, Don – but what if they got the stuff last week?' He stopped. 'No, they *can't* have got what they wanted last week, or why would they have killed Vermeulen yesterday?'

Langham thought about it. 'Listen, there must be at least two of them – one working in the castle, and another, or more than one, in charge of the boat and the diving operation. Perhaps

221

last week was just a preliminary dive, to see what the conditions were like at the bottom of the loch and to see if they could access the plane.'

'And whoever was in the castle killed Vermeulen – to halt the salvage. Or perhaps he'd got wind of what was going on?'

They sat in silence for a minute, Ryland pulling on a Woodbine and Langham his pipe.

'So who, amongst our suspects,' Langham said at last, 'is the most likely candidate?'

'We can rule Gabriel Gordon out straight away. He was . . . what? . . . a young teenager in 'forty-five.'

'Renata Káldor?'

'According to her, she was already in Britain during the war,' Ryland said. 'Of course, we only have her word for it.'

'Ulrich Meyer?' Langham said. 'On his own admission he was in Germany during the war, *and* he worked at a Nazi airfield. He would have had access to a plane – even if he was unable to pilot it himself.'

'He's the favourite,' Ryland said. 'But I wouldn't rule out anyone. We're making a mistake if we assume that whoever killed Vermeulen was a survivor from the plane – what if the survivors merely promised someone a share of the spoils if they'd work for them on the inside?'

Langham nodded. 'That's a possibility. So . . . how do we go about this?'

'Perhaps we should wait until we hear what the professor has to say, and see if he did see something that ties in with all our theorizing.'

222

Ryland looked at his watch. 'It's almost ten past ten.' He looked up. 'What do you think that "urgent matter" might be, Don?'

Langham considered the possibilities. 'He could have recalled hearing something someone said, or . . . or perhaps we're in luck and he saw someone trying to get rid of the film?'

They waited another two minutes, and then Ryland jumped up. 'I've had enough. I'll pop up to his room and see what's keeping him. Back in a jiffy.'

He slipped from the room and closed the door after him.

Langham relit his pipe, which had gone out through neglect, and moved to the window. A watery sun was trying to force its way through the pewter caul of cloud; momentarily it succeeded, sending a brilliant searchlight slanting across the hillside and illuminating the waters of the loch. It was as if it were indicating the position of the German plane; an omen, perhaps, of the affair's imminent culmination. Langham smiled to himself. He didn't believe in omens, though he hoped fervently that the case would soon come to a close.

He turned as the door opened and Ryland looked in. He knew immediately, from the immobility of the detective's expression, that something was wrong.

'Ralph?'

'The professor's room is locked. I looked through the keyhole.'

'And?'

'You'd better come,' Ryland said ominously. 'I

223

found the major and asked him to fetch a spare key.'

Langham stood and followed the detective from the room.

Eighteen

Maria pulled up before the main gates of Wormwood Scrubs, her Sunbeam the only car parked on the slush-covered road. The occasional vehicle sluiced by, a coal lorry or milk float, and such scant signs of activity served only to make the scene more desolate. It was approaching eight thirty and dawn was lightening the skies over London; street lights flickered off one by one, making the grey dawn appear even greyer.

The grim aspect of the gaol perfectly matched her mood. What should have been a happy occasion, a cause for celebration, would now be nothing of the kind. She had planned to greet Charles with the news that she was taking him somewhere exclusive for lunch, but now she would have to break it to him that, after she had dropped him off at his flat in Pimlico, she would be taking a train to Scotland. He would feign understanding, being the magnanimous kind of man he was, but she knew he would be upset.

She looked at her watch. It was twenty-five minutes past eight. Charles was due for release at eight thirty, and she suspected that Her Majesty's Prison Service would run to a punctilious timetable. She climbed from the car and stood on the pavement beside an arched metal gate into which was set a small hatch.

Fortunately the snow had ceased and the wind had dropped; it was still bitterly cold, but Maria was belted into her thick Burberry overcoat and her feet were clad in fur-lined boots.

She glanced at her watch again. It was eight thirty-two.

An old woman pushing a shopping basket through the slush shook her head at Maria and muttered, 'They ain't worth it, dearie, believe me.'

Maria smiled.

'Oh, it'll be all lovey-dovey for a week or so, before he falls in again wi' 'is mates. Then where'll you be? All that waiting up the spout! Take me advice and go home and warm yourself with a cuppa.' The woman looked her up and down. 'An' you look a nice girl, too. Believe me, he don't deserve you.'

The wisdom of her years dispensed, the old lady shuffled on.

Maria heard the report of bolts being drawn and turned to see the hatch swing open. The aperture was small and the man who squeezed through it gargantuan – and his smiling emergence into the free world melted Maria's heart.

'Maria!' he cried.

They embraced and Maria kissed his cheeks, three times, French fashion.

'My girl! But you look more beautiful every

225

time I see you! Oh, freedom!' He looked up into the grey sky, his piggy eyes brimming with tears. 'How I have waited for this day, Maria. How I have dreamed!'

She felt like weeping at what she had to tell him.

'You look well, Charles.'

He laughed. 'But just look at how my suit sags on this undernourished frame! I have lost almost a stone, my dear!'

'Well, we'll soon put that right,' she said.

He peered into the Sunbeam. 'But no Donald? He isn't ill?'

'It's a long story, Charles. Climb in and I'll tell you.'

He stowed a case on the back seat and squeezed into the passenger seat while Maria rounded the car and slipped in behind the wheel. She switched on the engine in order to run the heater but made no move to start the car.

He gripped her hand. 'Maria? Is something wrong? Donald's absence?' He looked suddenly aghast. 'You two are still . . .?'

'Of course we are!' she reassured him, laughing. 'He did plan to return in time but he's stranded in a castle in the Scottish Highlands.'

The fleshy acres of Charles's face registered open-mouthed alarm. 'Stranded? Scotland? But what on earth, my dear, is he doing in the Highlands?'

'Thereby hangs a tale, Charles, as you're so fond of saying.' She recounted Ralph Ryland's invitation to Donald to accompany him to Scotland, and the affair at the castle.

226

'But then the snow came down and stranded him there – he had intended to get the sleeper last night and be here to celebrate your release. But what is worse is that the telephone line is down so I cannot even speak to him.'

'And you mentioned a potential murderer?'

'Not only that, but yesterday I was threatened by a man with a knife at Donald's flat.'

'Slow down, slow down, child!' He pressed his palms to his cheeks, his eyes wide in comical alarm. 'But what was a man with a knife doing in Donald's flat?'

She recounted the incident, and the visit last night of Detective Inspector Mallory, and the fact that the man was a Dutch criminal by the name of Vermeulen, whose brother was the engineer working to raise the German plane.

'So you see, Charles,' she went on, with a heavy heart, 'Donald is in danger and . . . and while I would have loved to take you to lunch and celebrate . . .' She gripped his hand. 'You do understand that I must make my way to Scotland to warn Donald, don't you?'

'But Maria, my word.' He was rendered, for a moment, uncharacteristically speechless. 'When is your train?'

She looked at her watch. 'Nine forty-five. I've packed a bag.' She indicated the case on the back seat. 'I'll have enough time to drive you to Pimlico, drop you off and go on to the station.'

'You will do nothing of the kind, my girl—'

'But . . .'

'I mean, you will not drop me off at my flat.

Or rather, you will come in with me and wait a second until I pack my case.'

'Charles?'

He regarded her like a kindly uncle. 'You do not think for one minute, do you, that I would let you tear off into the unknown, facing who knows what danger to life and limb at the hands of sadistic knifemen? You do not think that I could allow you to sally forth alone? I am coming with you, my dear, and I will countenance no arguments!'

'But Charles,' she said, her heart swelling.

'But me no buts, Maria! Engage the engine of this chariot and make speed to Pimlico. Time is of the essence! Away we go!'

Sniffing back her tears, she started the car and pulled into the road.

'But if the castle is snowed in,' Charles began as they sped westwards, 'how do you hope to reach your imperilled beau?'

'I rang through to Inverness last night,' she explained, 'and managed to contact a garage. I've hired a vehicle – a Land Rover – and it has snow chains. The man I spoke to assured me that if anything can get through to Glenross, then the Land Rover can.'

She glanced at Charles. 'I hope you don't think me silly, but I felt so useless – and so terribly *frightened*. I just want to be with Donald, you see. Even if he isn't in danger, then at least I will *know* that. Down here, so far away . . . it is the not knowing that I find intolerable.'

He patted her hand. 'I understand completely, my child. I would do the same in your situation. But can you imagine the expression on his face when we emerge through the snow – like a cavalry of two, no less! – and come to his aid?'

She laughed. 'He'll probably call me a ninny for worrying and claim that he had everything under control.' She sighed. The thought of being in Donald's arms again made her heart flutter. 'Am I a love-struck fool, Charles?'

'You're a wonderful woman in love with a fine man, and the fact brings tears to this old romantic's eyes!' He smiled at her. 'And on that front, my girl, I have news. But not yet – Pimlico approaches. Tell Molly that we must dash on a most important business matter. Can she hold the reins for a day or so?'

'She's proved more than competent so far,' she assured him.

'Excellent! I should pack, and I will need a stout pair of hiking boots – for one must go for at least one brisk turn when in the Highlands!'

She turned into Cambridge Street and parked outside the agency.

Charles paused on the pavement at the bottom of the steps, staring up at the navy blue front door and the brass plaque beside it, bearing the legend: Elder and Dupré Literary Agency. 'My word, but I have dreamed of this very day for months. Would that I had known.'

They hurried up the steps and into the office.

'Charles!' Molly exclaimed, looking up from her typewriter.

'I have but time to kiss your hand!' Charles declared, and suited action to the words before charging up the stairs to his flat like a hippopotamus in grey flannel.

Maria explained, 'We're dashing for the nine forty-five from King's Cross. We have business in Scotland. Be an angel and fend off indigent authors and impatient editors, would you?'

Charles trundled down the steps minutes later with two bulging pigskin cases. 'You deserve a bonus, Molly,' he said in passing, 'if everything Maria says about you is true! A bonus – and a haggis from bonny Scotland on our return!'

Maria winked at the bemused girl and followed Charles from the premises.

She drove through the snow-silent, empty streets with as much speed as she dared, and made it across the city to King's Cross without mishap.

She parked on a side street off the main road and hurried, with just five minutes to spare before their train departed, into the echoing, vaulted chamber of the station. Maria bought two tickets, willing the doddering clerk to greater haste, thanked him and ran, with Charles in exhausted pursuit, from the ticket office and across the footbridge to platform seven.

Their train steamed and chuntered like an impatient beast, and all along its length carriage doors slammed with resounding finality. She heard a whistle shrill and a guard shout something incomprehensible. She came to the first carriage, tossed her case through the open door and looked back along the platform for Charles.

He was lumbering in pursuit, perhaps twenty yards away. She hurried to him, relieved him

230

of an overstuffed case and ran towards the train.

A whistle sounded again and the guard called out in admonition. Maria jumped on to the train and reached behind her to haul Charles aboard.

Seconds later the carriage bucked and the train pulled from the platform.

They found an empty compartment and collapsed into their seats, Maria laughing with relief and Charles mopping his beaded brow with a red bandana.

'And to think,' he declared like a Shakespearian player, 'that just two hours ago I was sleeping the sleep of the blameless 'neath the Scrubs' finest linen.'

Maria opened her suitcase and withdrew two small packages. 'For you,' she said. 'A little something to celebrate your release.'

'But you shouldn't have,' he said, tearing off the wrapping paper. He then declared, 'But how exquisite. I shall wear it now!' He affixed the pin to his navy-and-silver diagonally striped tie, then opened the Belgian chocolates. His eyes watered. 'But my dear! Oh, the finest! And all I ate by way of chocolate in the Scrubs was Fry's, and considered myself fortunate!'

Maria beamed. 'And in a little while I shall treat you to lunch,' she said. 'I've heard that the dining car does a very passable steak and kidney pie.'

She reached out and took his hand as the train raced north to Scotland.

Nineteen

Langham and Ryland came to the staircase and ascended. The detective led the way to the professor's room, ensured that there was no one else in the corridor, then pointed to the keyhole. 'Take a look.'

Langham knelt and applied his eye to the keyhole. He made out a tipped chair, a scatter of books across the floor and a counterpane dragged from the bed.

The major arrived with a door key, his face ashen. Langham stood aside as the old man fumbled with the key, turned the handle and led the way into the room.

Ryland eased the door shut. The major crossed the room and stopped dead. 'My God!'

Heart pounding, Langham moved around the bed and stood beside him.

Professor Hardwick lay face down in the narrow space between the bed and the window, one arm outstretched above his head, the other trapped uncomfortably beneath his torso. Uncomfortably? Langham thought. The professor was beyond such concerns as bodily comfort now.

The hilt of a long dirk protruded from between his shoulder blades and his cardigan was caked with blood.

The major slumped on to the bed and hung his head. He looked defeated, and Langham had the urge to sit beside the old man and attempt, in some way, to comfort him.

In the event, he merely murmured, 'I'm sorry.' He moved away so that the body was out of sight, and sat down heavily in a straight-backed chair.

'There was obviously a struggle,' Ryland said, indicating the tipped chair, the books on the floor and the counterpane dragged halfway off the bed. 'My guess is that the killer entered the room and confronted the professor. They fought, skittling the chair. The professor turned and the assailant stabbed him in the back. Then the killer slipped from the room, locking the door behind him. There's no sign of the key.'

'Perhaps I was right when I surmised that he'd seen something,' Langham said. 'Maybe he saw Vermeulen's killer getting rid of the film – and the killer knew that Hardwick had seen him.'

The major shook his head. 'Old Reggie Hardwick. Knew him since I was this high. Lovely, lovely man . . .' He took a deep breath, struggling to regain his composure.

Ryland said, 'Do you recognize the murder weapon?'

The major nodded. 'Again, it's from the Stewart room. It was on the wall near the door, one of two.'

'Easy enough to filch and conceal up one's sleeve,' Langham said.

'I'm not going to bother with the malarkey over prints,' Ryland said. 'The killer's no fool. He'd've wiped the hilt clean, and the same with anything else he might've touched in the room. The police

233

can look for prints when they get here, whenever that might be.'

Langham stared through the window. It had started to snow again, an intense flurry which obscured the loch. If the snowfall continued like this, he thought, then it would soon be impossible to leave the castle, even on foot. He looked down at the body, briefly, and came to a decision.

'Speaking of which . . .' he said, '. . . I was thinking earlier that it'd be wise if I hiked over to Glenross and alerted the police, and in light of what's happened to the professor . . .'

The major glanced through the window, then looked at him. 'Sure you're up to it?'

Langham was back in India again, being asked by the major if he was the man for a tricky mission. 'Of course, sir. I reckon it shouldn't take me much above four or five hours, even in this weather.'

Ryland said, 'How do you think we should play this, Don?'

'You mean, should we tell the others about the professor?' Langham looked from the detective to the major. 'I'm not sure. What do you think?'

The major chewed at the overhang of his moustache. 'I'm all for keeping the ghastly thing quiet. Elspeth's frightened enough, poor gal, what with finding Vermeulen as she did. I don't want to scare her even more.'

Ryland nodded. 'Fine. We'll keep mum.'

The major said, 'But what if the guests ask where the professor is – and you, come to that?'

'Perhaps say we're not well,' Langham said. 'Make some excuse, anyway, if anyone enquires.'

'Will do.' The major looked out at the falling snow. 'Look here, if you're setting off in this weather, it'd be wise to go well provisioned. I'll get Elspeth to pack you a thermos and a flask of brandy.'

'Capital,' Langham said. 'Can't say I'm looking forward to the trek.'

'I'll go and see Elspeth now,' the major said. He handed the key to Ryland and slipped from the room.

'I know you probably don't feel up to a feed,' Ryland said, 'but it'd be a good idea to get some food inside you before you set off.'

'You're right. I don't feel like eating a thing, but I'd be a fool to go out in that on an empty stomach.'

'Let's go see what Mrs F can rustle up,' Ryland said. 'Some of the others might still be hanging around. I wouldn't mind having a quiet chat with 'em.' He glanced at the professor's body. 'Poor old blighter . . .'

He crossed to the window, opened it to admit an icy wind and turned off the radiator. 'Soon be as cold as a morgue in here,' he said.

They moved out into the corridor and Ryland locked the room behind them.

Gabriel Gordon and Ulrich Meyer were absorbed in a game of chess in the Stewart room when Langham and Ryland passed through to the dining hall. At the other end of the Stewart room, Renata was seated before the open fire, reading her novel.

Mrs Fergusson was clearing the table as they

entered. 'Not too late for a quick bite?' Ryland asked.

'Not at all, sir. What would you be wanting? I've a few devilled kidneys left and a wee bit of liver.'

The very thought turned Langham's stomach, though Ryland's was made of sterner stuff. 'Just the thing, Mrs F,' the detective said.

'Just scrambled egg and toast for me, please,' Langham said.

As they ate, the major came in from the direction of the kitchen and joined them at the table. He sat down heavily and sighed. 'Elspeth's getting you a few things together, Langham.'

'I'll set off just as soon as I've finished this,' he said. 'I should make it to Glenross by five, easily, even in this weather. Chances are we'll be back by ten or so.'

'I'll keep a watch on everyone,' Ryland said. 'I'd like to think the killing's over, but . . .'

The major gave him a despairing glance; he looked like a melancholic bulldog that had been kicked by its owner. 'Oh, Renata was asking where Professor Hardwick was. She said It was unlike him to miss breakfast. I said he wasn't feeling a hundred per cent . . .'

'What was her reaction?'

The major shrugged. 'She just said she hoped it was nothing serious.'

Langham finished his egg and toast and refilled his tea cup. 'I'll take this through to the Stewart room. I wouldn't mind a word with Gabriel and Ulrich.'

The major nodded. Langham carried his cup

through to the adjacent room, followed by Ryland.

Langham crossed the room and paused beside the chess players. He looked from Gabriel to Meyer as he said, 'Professor Hardwick challenged me to a game the other day. Apparently he's rather good. We could have a tournament – take our mind off things . . .'

Gabriel looked up and smiled. 'Capital idea. Why not? It'd certainly while away a few hours.'

His reaction, Langham thought, seemed entirely natural. The poet went on, 'I should really have brought more books with me. I've finished what I did have, and – no hard feelings and all that, Langham – but Elspeth's whodunits are not my cup of tea.'

Meyer said, 'I thought you were working on an epic poem, Gabriel?'

'I was, but conditions are hardly conducive to prolonged concentration, old boy.'

'Quite,' Meyer said. He nodded at Langham. 'But a chess tournament would be most welcome, Herr Langham.'

Langham looked across the room and said, 'Do you play, Renata?'

She looked up from her Camus. 'I do not,' she said, and returned to her novel.

Ryland said, 'I'll talk to Professor Hardwick and we'll arrange a round-robin.'

The chess players merely nodded abstractedly, giving nothing away – if they had anything to give away, that was.

The door from the dining hall opened and Elspeth hurried through, carrying a knapsack.

'Here we are, Mr Langham. Tea and a hip flask of brandy. And I've packed you some sandwiches and a torch.'

Renata looked up. 'Are you going somewhere, Mr Langham?'

Before he could stop her, Elspeth said, 'Mr Langham's setting off to Glenross.'

Meyer sat back and looked at Langham. 'A very good idea. It is about time the police were brought in.'

Langham took the knapsack and smiled at Elspeth. 'Thank you. I'll need the brandy . . .'

From before the fire, Renata said, 'Well, ensure that you take care. It's freezing out there, Langham, and the last thing we want is a second death on our hands.' Smiling to herself, she turned her face to her book.

The major entered the room and crossed to Langham. 'I'll see you out.'

Langham nodded to Ryland and left the room, followed by the major.

'I keep a load of spare hiking boots for guests,' the old man said. 'You'll need them with all that snow. What size do you take?'

'Good idea. Size nine.' They moved to the entrance hall and the major fetched Langham's overcoat from the cloakroom along with a pair of stout boots. Langham slipped them on, declared them a good fit, then bundled himself up in his coat, pulled on his hat and slung the knapsack over his shoulder.

'Take care,' the major said.

'I'll be fine. Elspeth even packed me some sandwiches and a torch.'

'That girl thinks of everything,' the major said as he hauled open the oak door.

Langham saluted and marched out into the freezing cold, considering the fact that the killer knew that he was heading to Glenross and the police station. He would rather have kept it to himself, ideally, and surprised the culprit when he arrived back that evening with the constabulary in tow: now *that* might have put the wind up the killer.

He passed under the gatehouse archway and emerged into the open.

It was just after midday, but the louring cloud cover gave the air the aspect of dusk. A rapier wind whistled around the walls of the castle, and even here, in the lee of the southern tower, the snow was two feet deep. Out in the open, where the snow would have drifted with the wind, he expected to find it considerably deeper.

The wind descended, blasting him full on, and he bent his head against its force. Snow fell incessantly, and he cursed it and wished the wind would drop. He turned left along the road, his steps compacting the fresh snow with a series of pressurized creaks.

The loch was a dull scimitar blade curving away to his left, its margins frozen and covered in snow. Directly ahead, the road passed the woods – though it appeared less like a road than a slight depression in the snow that blanketed the undulating landscape. If he soldiered on at this pace, he estimated he would be in Glenross by around four o'clock, five at the latest. He wound his scarf more tightly around his lower face, pulled his hat down and paused to look back at the castle.

The edifice stood, dark and broodingly menacing, two hundred yards away. A couple of lighted windows showed along its eastern wall, welcoming in the gloom. He turned and tramped on.

The wind raged across the loch and piled snow in a great drift to his right. Ahead, on the section of road above the woods, the snow was comparatively shallow, perhaps only eighteen inches deep. Even so, he was forced to adopt an awkward, galumphing high step that soon had his calf muscles aching in protest.

He wondered what Maria was doing now. Charles had been due for release at eight thirty that morning, and Langham imagined Maria treating her boss to his first good meal in months. He wondered where they might be dining – the Moulin Bleu, one of Maria's favourites? He thought of the restaurant's French onion soup and realized that he was almost salivating.

He heard a sharp report and saw a puff of snow dance up before him.

He had no time to wonder what it might have been before something whistled by his head. As if from a great distance he heard the report of a rifle. Without thinking he threw himself to the ground, rolled into the cover of a tree, then picked himself up and ran. He heard another report. The shot missed him and kicked up a plume of snow a few yards ahead. He sprinted – or tried to, his progress impeded by the snow. If his assailant was shooting at him with a two-bore hunting rifle then he was due another shot before he reloaded.

Anticipating the shot that might end his life, Langham darted to his left, heading for the cover of the woods. He slipped and fell, crying out in alarm as he rolled down the icy incline.

His head hit something hard – whether timber or stone he had no idea – and he passed out instantly.

Twenty

On the way to Edinburgh, Maria and Charles discussed the affair at Loch Corraig Castle.

'So you see why I'm so afraid of what might happen, Charles? Now that this Vermeulen and Dreyer know Ryland is a private detective, the danger is that they will communicate this to the engineer, Hans Vermeulen, at the castle.'

Charles had attempted to reassure her on that score. 'And how might they do that, my dear? By pigeon post, perchance? The castle is incommunicado.'

'I know. But I feared the telephone might be restored at any moment. That was why I *had* to make the journey. '

'And I would have done the same, my dear.'

'My other fear is that we'll fail to reach the castle this evening. If the snow continues, and the road is still impassable, then not even the Land Rover will be able to get through.'

'As the wise man says, we shall cross that bridge when we come to it. But I have every confidence in our achieving our destination – even if we have to walk the last leg of the journey. And if we cannot reach the castle, then the Dutch thugs will be unable to do so, too.'

She smiled at his reassurance and squeezed his hand.

They changed trains at Edinburgh and caught the express to Inverness.

For the first hour they shared a compartment with an elderly parson who was immersed in a book on bee-keeping, and a middle-aged Women's Institute-type who insisted on instructing Maria on how to bake the perfect Victoria sponge. Both parties alighted at Perth, and Maria was able to ask Charles about the special 'friend' he had made in Wormwood Scrubs.

As the train raced through the snow-covered Perthshire countryside, Maria leaned forward and murmured, 'And now, Charles, tell me about this friend you made on the "inside", please.'

He leaned back and stretched out his short legs. Donald had once described Charles as having a 'brandy glass' physique, and he was perfectly correct. Charles's torso was rather globular, while his legs were proportionally stem-like.

He laced his plump fingers over his bulging waistcoat and his porcine features, topped with a snowy peak of hair, took on the dreamy aspect of happy reminiscence.

'His name is Albert and he is not yet twenty-five. A scallywag, I might add, but a scally of the first order. He would do anything for me. He is quite devoted. We were made for each other; indeed, our meeting seemed destined.'

Maria smiled. 'Tell me.'

'I was in the recreation room during the first week of my incarceration, and as a "new boy" I was suffering the perusal of the old lags. They like to size one up, you see, for future reference. A quite nasty piece of work, going under the somewhat melodramatic appellation of the Camden Crusher, took against the cut of my jib and set out to make my life a misery. When the Crusher demanded that I hand over my weekly ration of cigarettes – "yer ciggies or I'll mash yer queenly phisog" is, I believe, a reasonably accurate quotation – a strapping young fellow stepped between us and had a quiet word in the Crusher's cauliflower ear. The upshot was that the Crusher dealt the young man an upper-cut, or rather tried to. He acted in ignorance of Albert's pugilistic expertise. Young Albert danced on his toes and, with a swift right-left-right combination, laid out the Crusher with a bloody nose. He bothered me no more.'

'Bravo for Albert!' Maria said, clapping.

'My sentiments exactly,' Charles said. 'And when Albert turned to me and gave a most winning smile, I do not mind admitting that I felt quite weak at the knees. Needless to say, Albert and I became fast friends.'

'And why was Albert behind bars?' she asked.

'A tale of treachery and woe,' Charles said. 'He was "done" for receiving stolen goods – a clear miscarriage of justice. Albert was on his uppers and was merely looking after certain "items" for a friend. A gesture of goodwill, no more, for which the law came down on him with rather excessive force. I don't mind admitting, Maria, that I miss him dearly.'

'When will he be released?'

'He has a week of his sentence to run, after which . . .' Charles beamed.

'Tell me!'

'After which, Albert will become my chauffeur-cum-handyman. I have it all arranged. You know how I deplore driving in the city, and while I am up in London I shall require a driver – taxis are so expensive these days – and when I am down at my place in Suffolk I shall need the services of a general factotum. Albert, needless to say, is overjoyed at the prospect of a proper job and the opportunity to "go straight".'

Maria said, 'But "go straight", I take it, only in a manner of speaking?'

'Oh, my dear – your wit outshines even my sparkling repartee. Wait until I tell Albert of your little *mot juste*! Quite priceless!'

'I'm looking forward to meeting Albert,' she said.

'And I cannot wait to introduce him. You will invite him to your nuptials, of course?'

'Of course.'

She stared through the window and wondered what Donald was doing now. She imagined him ensconced before a blazing fire, sharing a whisky and reminiscences of India with Ralph and the major. She hoped that, when she and Charles arrived at the castle, it would be to find everything in order and her fears unfounded. And yet a niggling, sneaking voice in her subconscious told her she was being optimistic.

She looked across at Charles, who was reading an omnibus volume of Wilde's plays. 'I would like a cup of tea. For you too, Charles?'

'Why not, indeed? I doubt they will serve lapsang souchong so whatever emerges from the spigot will suffice. One sugar, my dear.'

Maria slid open the door of the compartment and made her way along the corridor to the buffet car, rocking back and forth with the motion of the train.

She moved to the next carriage – the buffet car being at the very rear of the train – and glanced into each compartment as she passed. She was surprised at how quiet the service was – compared to London trains, that was. Many compartments were empty and others were occupied by only one or two passengers. As she passed the last compartment before she reached the communicating door to the next carriage, she glanced to her left.

She almost halted in her tracks – which would have been a serious error of judgement. She hurried on, came to the door leading to the next carriage and leaned against it, her heart pounding. She tried to order her thoughts and work out if somehow she had been mistaken.

Seated in the compartment she had just passed, staring out of the window, was the scar-faced man, Patrick Vermeulen. He had not been alone, and though she had been unable to identify the man seated opposite, she suspected that his companion was Dreyer.

She was in danger, dithering here like this, if either Vermeulen or Dreyer were to step from the compartment.

245

She turned and looked back along the corridor. If she passed their compartment at a brisk walk, with her collar turned up . . . She arranged the collar of her coat, adjusted her hat so that it sat on the right side of her head, not the left, squared her shoulders and hurried past the compartment occupied by the Dutch thugs. Her heart pounded and she expected to hear the door slide open and a guttural command ordering her to stop.

She made it to the end of the carriage and hurried into the next one.

Charles looked up when she entered the compartment and sat down quickly.

'Maria?'

'They're here! I've seen them . . .'

'What?'

'Vermeulen and the other thug. In the next carriage.'

He stared at her. 'Are you absolutely sure?'

'I'm sure. I saw the scar-faced man, Vermeulen. It was only a glimpse, but . . .' She shook her head. 'They can only be heading for the castle, Charles! They know Ralph is a detective and they're going to warn Hans Vermeulen.'

'That does make eminent sense,' he allowed. He pulled down the blinds on the windows to the corridor. 'As soon as we reach Inverness I'll find the police station and inform them. You said Mallory had an alert out for the pair?'

'That's right. But is there anything we can do before we reach Inverness?'

Charles glanced up at the communications cord. 'Like stop the train?' He shook his head. 'And then what? Inform the ticket collector that two

246

wanted men are aboard his train? And what would he be able to do? If the thugs got wind that you were aboard . . .' He shuddered at the notion. 'As Inverness is the next stop, we'll wait until then.'

She thought desperately. 'But how long will it take to find the police station? If they have a car waiting, then they might be away before the police have time to give chase. I don't want them reaching the castle before us.'

He looked at his watch. 'We should arrive in a little less than an hour. At least we have the advantage of knowing where they're heading. It will be simplicity itself for us to follow them.'

'Follow? Wouldn't it be better if we tried to reach the castle *before* them, to warn Donald and Ralph? And forget about notifying the police . . .'

Charles chewed his pendulous lower lip. 'Perhaps it would be best if we consider our options when we reach Inverness,' he said. 'Do you know the location of the garage from which you're hiring the Land Rover?'

'It's almost next door to the station.'

'There is always the possibility that they won't head off immediately, of course. As far as they're concerned, there will be no need for haste. At any rate, we need to pick up our vehicle as quickly as we can. Perhaps you're right. Perhaps our priority should be to reach the castle and inform Donald.'

Maria sat with her hands clasped before her face, as if in prayer, biting the tips of her thumbs.

He smiled at her. 'Now if Albert were on hand, he'd have them sorted out in no time.'

The next fifty minutes seemed to expand to fill an aeon. Every time she glanced nervously at her watch, only a minute or two had passed. She expected the door to the compartment to fly open and the thugs to barge in at any second. She knew the notion was wholly irrational, but this did nothing at all to diminish her fear.

And if she and Charles were in danger now, then what about when the time came to disembark and they had to follow the pair?

Charles said, interrupting her thoughts, 'I'm going to take a stroll to the next carriage and peek in at our friends. I'd like to know what they look like if I need to describe them to the police, or for that matter if it comes to following them.'

'They are in the last compartment, Charles. Be careful.'

He patted her hand. 'They don't know me from Adam, my dear. I'll be back in a jiffy.'

He slipped from the compartment and disappeared along the corridor.

Maria stared out of the window at the passing landscape, hills bristling with plantations of snow-laden pine, interspersed with the occasional sloping field dotted with sheep which appeared grey against the dazzling white snow.

Dusk was approaching and soon it would be dark; she was not looking forward to the long drive across the country to the castle – always assuming, of course, that the roads were navigable.

The sliding door rattled open, startling her, and Charles slipped in nimbly on his size eight, two-tone brogues. She looked up. 'I wasn't imagining them, was I?' she asked forlornly.

'Unfortunately not, my dear. They're there – the ugly-looking brute with a scarred face and his swarthy friend in one of those nasty workmen's coats with the orange back panel.'

She smiled. 'They're called donkey jackets, for some reason.'

'Are they, indeed?' He looked at his watch. 'We should be arriving in a little over five minutes. We'll wait until they alight, and then I shall follow them at a safe distance. I think it would be wise if you left the train only when they've disappeared from sight.'

He took her hand. 'Maria, don't look so downcast. At least we are here to warn Donald and Ralph about the pair. And even if we weren't, I'm sure they would be well able to look after themselves. Smile, Maria, for me.'

She put on a brave face and stared through the window as the train slowed. Small, dark stone houses slid into view, dim in the falling twilight. Charles pulled down their cases from the overhead rack. 'When we stop, Maria, I'll move along to the next carriage and follow our friends from the station.'

She stood and gripped her suitcase, her nervousness increasing tenfold.

The train drew into the station and jerked to a halt. Charles pointed through the window. 'Wait beside the newspaper kiosk, Maria, and I shall be back in no time at all.'

He left the compartment and disappeared along the corridor.

Maria heard the multiple reports of doors banging open. She stepped into the corridor, moved to the exit and peered through the window. Further along the platform she saw the Dutch pair alight and cross towards the exit; with their woollen caps and duffel bags they looked like merchant seamen on shore leave. Charles was ten yards behind them, marked out from the other passengers by his huge girth and silver-grey worsted overcoat.

One by one they submitted their tickets to the inspector at the exit and filed from the station. Maria watched as the thugs passed from view, followed by Charles, and only then did she reach through the window and open the door.

She crossed to the newspaper kiosk and stood out of the wind. Station staff had shovelled snow into great mounds against the walls and gritted the platform. She glanced at the newspapers stacked on the counter, then scanned the paperbacks out of professional interest to see if any of her authors were represented. Coincidentally enough, one of Donald's early thrillers, bought by Pan last year, was prominently displayed.

She saw a rack of maps and bought a roadmap of Inverness-shire, slipped it into her coat pocket and glanced at her wristwatch.

It was almost four. Charles had been away for a matter of minutes but it seemed far longer. She willed him to return with the news that the Dutch pair had booked into a hotel for the night but knew she was deluding herself. She paced up and down, hunched in her coat against the wind. At least the snow had stopped falling.

She looked at her watch again. It was approaching ten past four. What *could* he be doing? Her heart jumped as it came to her that, somehow, he'd fallen foul of the thugs. She told herself that that was impossible; as Charles himself had said, they didn't know him from Adam. But what if, she thought, they had become suspicious of the conspicuous fat man tailing them and decided to do something about it?

Her fears were allayed, a minute later, when Charles hurried into the station and crossed over to her. 'They had a van waiting and drove off immediately,' he reported. 'The police station is just along the road, but would you jolly well believe it, it's closed! Four o'clock on Tuesday evening and the constabulary lock up shop and go home.'

'I thought you were gone an age,' she said.

'That was because I popped into the garage, paid the deposit on the Land Rover and asked the mechanic to get it ready *post-haste*.'

'Good thinking.'

He looked red-faced and exhausted from the exertion of hauling his cases through the town. 'I thought to pack a hip flask of Courvoisier,' he said. 'Once we're under way I shall sit back and imbibe. You will take the wheel for the first leg of the journey, my dear?'

'Of course.' She pulled the roadmap from her pocket and passed it to Charles. 'You can navigate.'

They hurried from the station and along the street to the garage. The Land Rover stood in the road, the mechanic beside it with the keys which he passed to Charles with a volley of instructions in an accent Maria had no hope of comprehending.

She stowed their cases in the back of the vehicle and climbed into the driving seat just as a new fall of snow was feathering down from the darkening sky. Charles thanked the mechanic and eased his bulk into the passenger seat.

'I told the young fellow we were heading for Glenross,' he said as Maria familiarized herself with the controls. 'And he obviously thought we were out of our minds. He instructed us to continue ahead until we come to the main road, then turn left and follow the signs to Glenross. I think he said it couldn't be simpler.'

Maria started the engine and the Land Rover bucked into life. 'You understood him?'

Charles laughed. 'Or perhaps he said we were simpletons! But the good news, Maria, is that a snow plough set off for Glenross at midday, so our four-wheel drive equipped with snow chains should see us triumph!'

Maria accelerated along the street and turned left on to the main road; only one other vehicle was in sight, a single-decker omnibus coming in the opposite direction. 'Did you notice what kind of van the Dutch pair were driving?'

'It was pale green, my dear. I admit it; vehicle identification is not my forte. But I am pretty sure that it did not have snow chains.'

'Good. I hope the thugs have a nasty accident

252

and freeze to death on the way, or veer off the road and drown in an icy loch.'

Charles unscrewed his flask and took a nip of brandy. 'Maria, my dear, you exhibit a sadistic side of your nature you have hitherto concealed from me.'

She smiled. 'You'd discover *your* inner sadist, Charles, if they'd threatened you at knifepoint.'

'Touché,' he said.

'Now, are you going to let me have a sip of that, or are you going to hog it all to yourself?'

He laughed and passed her the flask, and she took a mouthful and hunched over the wheel.

They left the outskirts of town and in minutes were bowling through darkened countryside.

Twenty-One

Langham was brought to his senses by the bone-gnawing cold.

He groaned and tried to move. His head throbbed and he felt like a frozen corpse, his limbs stiff and unmoving. He opened his eyes and blinked. To his surprise he found himself in a sheltered hollow, out of the wind and padded with a mulch of dead leaves. Darkness had descended and he stared up through a shifting latticework of bare branches at a brilliant full moon.

He was freezing, but it could have been worse. Had he lost consciousness in the open, prone to the depredations of the wind, the chances were that he would be dead by now.

He wondered how long he had been unconscious. The moon was riding high, its luminance punching a halo through the racing cloud cover. He pushed up his sleeve and peered at his watch but couldn't make out its face. Then he recalled that Elspeth had packed him a torch.

He sat up, his head pounding, shrugged the knapsack from his shoulders and rummaged in it until he found the torch. He also came across the hip flask of brandy. He unscrewed the cap and drank, gasping as the alcohol burned down his throat. He took another mouthful, then stowed the flask away and switched on the torch. He directed it at his watch and was surprised to find that it was just after half past six. So he had lain, dead to the world, for over six hours. So much for reaching Glenross by five o'clock.

He reached up and touched the side of his head. His fingers came away sticky with blood. The wound had stopped bleeding, which was reassuring, even if his brain pulsed with a migraine. His hat was missing, and he reflected on the odd fact that he felt more put out by its loss than by the fact that someone had tried to kill him. Maria had bought him the hat just last week, declaring that his old one was hardly fit for a scarecrow.

He pulled out the thermos of tea, poured out a cup and drank gratefully.

So someone had shot at him with the intention of preventing his trek to Glenross. Someone wanted him dead, obviously fearing that the professor had informed him of the identity of the killer.

Clearly, then, Professor Hardwick *had* witnessed the killer disposing of the film, and perhaps the killer had seen the professor leaving the note in his room and assumed that the note vouchsafed the killer's identity.

Then the killer had murdered the professor and bided his time until he could make an attempt on his, Langham's, life . . .

Had the killer followed him from the castle? He dismissed the idea as all the doors were securely locked. Someone had obviously hastened to a window on the eastern wall of the castle and taken a potshot from there.

He wondered if the shots had been heard in the castle, and if Ryland had been quick enough to apprehend the gunman. But the castle was a big place and the shooting had been over in a matter of seconds. It wouldn't have taken the killer long to conceal the weapon and leave his vantage point.

The gunman must have seen him run for the woods, so he would know that his assassination attempt had failed. Would he be expecting him to continue his trek to Glenross or to return to the castle, his tail between his legs?

He took another mouthful of tea, followed by a brandy chaser.

The idea of continuing on to Glenross was ludicrous. He was frozen to the bone and had suffered concussion. He would be a fool to soldier on. The sensible course of action would be to beat a retreat to the castle and consult with Ryland and the major about what to do next.

And what might that be? Until the snow thawed and the telephone line was restored, the fact was that he was in danger. The sensible thing to do, as far as he could see, would be to insist that the prime suspects were locked in their rooms in the interim.

He stowed the torch in the knapsack, along with the thermos and the hip flask, and eased himself to his feet. His legs trembled and his head swirled, his vision blurring. He reached out to a nearby tree for support and rested against it for a minute.

He was about to turn and climb up the banking to the road when he heard a sound.

It came from further down the slope, towards the loch, and as he stared in the direction of the noise he made out the flicker of distant torchlight. The sound came again and he knew what it was – the scrape of timber on shingle, accompanied by voices. He couldn't be far away from where he and Ryland had located the tyre tracks the other day, and the furrow made by the keel of a rowing boat.

So they were back, and they were making another trip across to the pontoon.

Cautiously, moving from tree to tree, he made his way down the incline towards the shore. He came to a vehicle on his right – not a Morris Commercial this time but a green Austin K8, parked in exactly the same position beneath the overhanging trees. Ten yards away, on the foreshore, he made out two dark shapes pushing a rowing boat into the ice-laced shallows.

One of the men was garbed from head to foot in a jet-black frog suit; the other wore a donkey jacket, dark trousers and high rubber waders. The boat was piled with bulky equipment – air tanks and other diving paraphernalia. As he watched, his pulse racing, the men climbed into the boat one after the other, rattled the oars in the rowlocks and skulled off across the loch. The pair could have only one thing in mind: the recovery of whatever the German plane might be harbouring.

As the boat disappeared into the mist, Langham turned and hurried up the banking.

He came to the road and stopped, smiling at the object he'd spotted in the snow. He reached down and retrieved his trilby. Maria would have been furious had he left it in the Highlands.

The snowfall had resumed, obliterating his earlier footprints. The moon passed from behind a cloud, silvering the landscape. With the snow-decked castle in the distance and the dark loch alongside, it was a scene that would have changed very little over the centuries.

He marched along the road, his footsteps compressing the snow. To his right the loch was in darkness, shrouded in mist, and he was unable to make out the progress of the boat. He bent against the wind, tightening his scarf around his mouth and nose and hurrying on.

The castle loomed a hundred yards away, lights burning in the east wing. He imagined the guests enjoying a pre-dinner drink in the Stewart room

– or perhaps *not* enjoying a drink in each other's suspect company. He hurried through the arch, past the gate house and ran the last twenty yards to the castle.

He had been in half a mind to tackle the pair in the boat himself before realizing the madness of that plan. Ryland had brought his old service revolver; he'd requisition a rifle from the major and only then pursue the pair.

He came to the oak door and yanked on the bell pull, stamping his feet against the cold. Half a minute elapsed and he wondered if Mr and Mrs F were too busy preparing dinner. He cursed aloud and hauled on the bell pull again.

Just as he was beginning to give up hope that his summons would be answered, he heard bolts being shot and the door creaked open.

Mrs F peered out cautiously; her eyes widened at the sight of him.

'But Mr Langham, I never! You're all covered wi' blood!'

He eased his way in and took her hand. 'This is vitally important, Mrs F. Go and fetch the major and Mr Ryland. And tell Ryland to bring his pistol, quickly now!'

'Aye, sir – I'll away and do that.' She turned and hurried off. Langham leaned against the wall, his head pounding. He remembered the hip flask in the knapsack, pulled it out and took a long swallow of brandy.

The major arrived moments later. 'Good God, Langham! I hardly believed Mrs F when she said you'd turned up. What in God's name happened, man?'

'Long story which I'll bore you with later. For now, we have visitors.' And he recounted his sighting of the divers and the rowing boat.

'I'll get me rifle!' the major said and hurried off along the passageway.

Langham called out, 'And bring one for me while you're at it!'

Ryland came into sight at the end of the corridor, pulling on his coat. He clutched his service revolver in his right hand and scowled at Langham's bloody head. 'What happened?'

'The rowing boat's back and they're heading for the pontoon. There are two of them and one's a diver.'

Ryland indicated Langham's head wound. 'They did that?'

'They don't know we're on to them, Ralph. I was shot at earlier – just after I set out. I ran like hell and slipped – banged the old head on something. I've been unconscious ever since. You didn't hear the shots?'

'Not a thing, but then I was at the other end of the castle.' Ryland examined his head. 'It's a nasty cut. We'll get you cleaned up.'

'That can wait till we've sorted out the blessed divers,' Langham said. 'Here comes the major.'

The old soldier limped along the corridor, carrying two rifles. 'Loaded 'em both,' he said, passing one to Langham.

He gripped the rifle, overcome by an odd sensation. This was the first time he'd held a rifle since the war, and it brought back memories of the landing in Madagascar and how he'd shot a Vichy

259

French soldier in order to save Ryland's life. He had no desire to take another life tonight.

'How're we going to go about this, men?' the major asked.

'I thought just Ralph and I should go—' Langham began.

'Like ruddy hell, Captain!' the major retorted. 'I'm not missing out on the fun. I'll bag the blighters if I have to do it meself!'

'They've more than likely landed on the pontoon by now, coming in from the east,' Langham said. 'We'll approach slowly. I'll lead the way. Major, you bring up the rear, covering us.'

The old man nibbled at his moustache, clearly put out at the relegation. 'Very well.'

'We should wait till the diver's underwater,' Langham said, 'then nab the other one. At least we'll have the element of surprise on our side. Then we wait till the diver resurfaces and grab him.'

'Good God,' Ryland said, 'this is just like Madagascar.'

'Is it?' Langham said, staring at him. 'I can't recall being this scared, truth to tell.'

'Wouldn't be a man if y'didn't feel a little fear, don't y'know!' the major barked. 'Right, gentlemen, shall we advance?'

Langham opened the door and led the way out into the night.

Twenty-Two

It was almost seven o'clock by the time Maria and Charles reached Glenross.

The plough might have burrowed a passage through the snow but the new fall had done its best to fill in the channel. That, together with a high wind that drifted snow back across the road, had made the journey from Inverness not only tediously slow but treacherous.

And it hadn't helped matters that they had taken a wrong turning and lost, Maria estimated, at least an hour.

The thought filled her with despair.

Almost three hours after setting out from Inverness, Maria espied a collection of distant lights, then a collection of buildings huddling in the snow, and at last a sign reading, Glenross.

'How far away is the castle?' she asked as she forced the Land Rover up the incline towards the town.

'Perhaps five miles, according to the map,' Charles said. 'I'll take over the wheel when we reach the Glenross.'

'And not a sign of the thugs!' she cried. 'If only I hadn't taken that turning . . .'

'Do not castigate yourself on that score, Maria. I was reading the map, after all. Or rather, I was supposed to be.'

'They'll certainly have reached the castle,

261

Charles. And there I was, hoping we might have passed them by now or found their van broken down in a ditch.'

She was warmed by the fact that Donald was only a few miles away, but the rosy glow was doused by the thought of the Dutch pair arriving at the castle.

'Charles, didn't the mechanic say that the snow plough had "set off for Glenross"?'

'That's right.'

She swore in French.

'What?'

'But Charles,' she exclaimed, 'what if the plough *stops* at Glenross? What if it goes no further? What then?'

Charles frowned. 'In that eventuality, my dear, we shall have to trust the snow chains to get us through.'

'If we could get even part of the way, then walk . . .'

He looked alarmed. 'In this? My dear, we would be risking life and limb through frostbite if we set out in these conditions.'

'Then if we're stranded and the Land Rover can't make it any further, *I* shall walk alone.'

'You will go nowhere alone, my girl. Fortified by brandy, we shall battle through like Trojans.'

She eyed him dubiously. 'I think you're a little drunk, Charles.'

'Just a little, my dear. Sufficient to allow me to view our predicament through rose-tinted spectacles. I perceive a happy ending in the distance. A reunion of loved ones and friends. Whiskies around a blazing hearth and a resolution to the mystery.'

Maria laughed. 'I hope you're sober enough to drive,' she said, 'and that you've saved some brandy for me.'

'A wee dram still resides,' he said, hoisting the flask. 'But can one have a dram of brandy?'

'A *petit verre* would be more appropriate,' Maria said.

They drove along the main street of Glenross for a hundred yards before Charles said, 'Stop here, my dear, and I shall take the wheel.'

Maria braked, jumped from the driving seat and rounded the cab, gasping in the cold air. Charles shuffled his bulk behind the steering wheel and applied himself to the controls while Maria took charge of the hip flask and the map.

He started the engine and drove from the town. Maria pointed to a gap in the bank of snow to the right.

'We are in luck, my dear,' Charles said. 'It appears that the plough ventured beyond the town.'

She nodded, biting her lip. 'Which helps the thugs as well as us . . .'

Charles turned the vehicle and gunned the engine as they climbed through the high-sided cutting in the snow.

Maria glanced at the speedometer. They were averaging around ten miles an hour. The road before them forged through the snow, with banks of the stuff piled five feet high on either side. The moon shed a waxy light over a still and silent landscape.

She sat with the roadmap folded on her lap,

from time to time switching on the overhead light to chart their progress. She made out the fish-shaped loch on the map, with the symbol of the castle on its southern shore.

They drove on for another five minutes, then Charles slowed the vehicle and braked on the crest of the road. They sat in silence and stared down on an enchanting moonlit scene. The land fell away in great white swathes with nothing but the distant smudge of woodland to mar the snowfall's domination.

'And look!' Charles exclaimed, pointing ahead.

She made out the silver glint of the loch like the blade of a knife.

'Almost there,' she said to herself.

Charles slipped the Land Rover into gear and eased it down the incline.

They bucked back and forth. She looked at Charles as he fought with the steering wheel; this was a side of her friend she had never witnessed before, and she had to admit that he looked more than a little out of place in the driving seat. She was more accustomed to watching him steer his epicurean way through a lavish five-course banquet.

'Is that what I think it is, my girl?' Charles said a little later.

'The castle!'

Perhaps a mile away, an inky outline on the shore of the loch, Maria made out the round towers and crenellated battlements of the Loch Corraig Castle. It presented such a romantic image that she wished she had seen it first in circumstances other than these.

'They *must* have reached the castle by now,' she murmured.

'They are hardly fearsome invaders with trebuchet and Greek fire!' Charles said. 'I have every faith that Donald and Ralph will be equal to them.'

They descended, coming down the hillside and skirting the loch; the snow had drifted to their left and was piled six feet high. Charles steered to the right of the road, their progress still painfully slow.

'Maria . . . if I am not mistaken – are those tyre tracks directly ahead?'

Her heart skipping, she leaned forward and peered out. She saw nothing at first, just the milky whiteness in the moonlight, and then, as her eyes adjusted, she made out faint parallel runnels in the snow.

Charles surprised her by laughing aloud. 'And look!'

She followed the direction of his sausage-like finger, indicating the tyre tracks that veered off the road and entered the margins of woodland on the shore of the loch. Fifty yards to their right, sheltered under an overhang of foliage, was a green van.

'But why have they left it there?' she asked.

'For the same reason,' he said, 'that I fear we too must abandon our trusty steed and continue the journey on foot. Look. The plough did its job but the snow has had the last word!'

He pointed through the windscreen at a drift of snow blocking the road ahead.

He braked the vehicle and cut the engine, and

an absolute silence reigned until, breaking it, Charles said, 'We must proceed with utmost caution. I think a little brandy might be in order.'

She passed him the flask and he tipped it back swiftly.

They climbed from the Land Rover into the teeth of the wind, and hand in hand marched resolutely towards the drift and the distant castle.

Twenty-Three

Langham, Ryland and the major crept down the path that ran alongside the loch.

Langham reached the end of the low wall and ducked, peering around the corner. The gangway to the pontoon was twenty yards away. In the light of the moon, the timber deck was oddly transformed, the flat raft bloated with heaped snow. He tried to make out the diver and his companion, but the bulk of the lifting rig hid the men and their boat from view.

He signalled for Ryland and the major to follow him and crept, doubled-up, towards the pontoon. Snow crunched underfoot as he stepped on to the timber gangway, Ryland and the major following him across.

He came to the gate, paused and peered through the metal mesh. He still could not see the men but he could hear them, their voices carrying on the wind. He guessed they were lifting something from the boat as he heard a grunt and the sound of metal scraping across timber.

He turned to Ryland, put his mouth to the detective's ear and breathed, 'We'll cross to the rig and see what they're doing.'

He reached out and eased the gate open. When the gap was wide enough to admit him, he slipped through and crossed to the lifting rig. He hunkered down beside it and peered across the great square of water to the far deck of the 'picture-frame' pontoon.

The pair had moored the boat on the outer edge of the pontoon. The diver was sitting on the inner lip, facing Langham. The second man was lifting a pair of air tanks on to his colleague's back. The diver strapped them into place, tightened the straps, then fitted the mouthpiece and lowered the face mask.

He signalled to the other man, who patted him on the back. The diver slipped feet-first into the icy water with hardly a splash.

A bulky device sat on the snow-covered boards, and Langham was wondering what it might be when the second man picked it up and lowered it into the loch after the diver. An eerie luminescence appeared beneath the surface of the loch as the diver turned on the underwater light, the glow diminishing as the diver descended.

The second man stood on the edge of the pontoon. He was short, squat and looked even bulkier in his donkey jacket. He lit a cigarette and stared into the water, a solitary figure bathed in moonlight.

Langham turned to Ryland and whispered, 'We

267

have him trapped. If one of us heads right, the other left . . . He might see us but there's nowhere he can go – other than jumping into the water.'

'And if he does see us?' Ryland said.

'Then we aim our weapons and tell him to put his hands up. Even if he is armed, he'd be foolish to risk firing when there are two of us.' Langham looked at the major. 'If you'd remain here, covering us . . .'

'Will do.'

'You go to the right, Ralph. I'll head left. On the count of three. One, two, three – go.'

Langham rose and stepped from the cover of the rig, moving left. He came to the first corner of the pontoon's 'frame', his progress so far hidden from the smoker by the bulk of the rig. When he turned the corner, however, he would be in plain sight. And if the smoker were armed . . .

He gripped his rifle, crept out from behind the rig and turned the corner.

Each side of the 'frame' was forty yards long, and as Langham stalked through the snow, doubled up, he thought that never had forty yards seemed so far. If the smoker should happen to look up and glance his way now . . .

Across the pontoon, directly opposite Langham, he saw Ryland creeping along like a shadow. So far the smoker had failed to see either man. His gaze was intent on the dim halo of light in the depths of the loch.

Langham moved silently over the snow-covered boards.

Then the man looked up and saw Ryland. He turned, flung his cigarette into the water and pulled something from his pocket. Langham feared it might be a gun, then breathed with relief when he saw the glint of a knife blade in the man's hand.

Realizing that he'd been seen, Ryland approached the man at a brisk walk, his revolver held out before him.

Langham hurried through the snow. With the man's attention focused on Ryland, he could approach unseen on his blindside. He came to the second corner of the pontoon and turned, approaching from behind.

Ten feet from the man, Langham raised his shotgun and aimed at his back, only then realizing that his hands were trembling.

Ryland had slowed his approach. He was perhaps ten yards from the man and speaking to him. 'Now do the sensible thing, matey, and drop the knife.'

Instead of obeying Ryland's instructions, the man dropped into a crouch and faced the detective.

'Don't be a fool! Drop the knife or I'll shoot.'

Langham was aware of his heart thudding deafeningly as he approached the knifeman. He was ten feet away, then five . . .

Ryland halted, smiling. He raised his revolver, aimed at the man's chest and said, 'I said drop the bloody knife!'

Langham reversed his grip on the rifle, took the last three steps towards the man, raised his improvised club and brought the butt down with

269

all the force he could muster. The man hit the snow-covered deck with a grunt.

Ryland knelt beside the prone form. 'Good work.'

Panic gripped Langham. 'He's not dead?'

The detective felt for a pulse. 'Just out for the count.' He searched the man's pockets. 'No gun, Don. Just this.' He picked up the knife from where it had fallen in the snow.

The major joined them. 'Good work, men. What about the other chappie?'

Langham moved to the edge of the pontoon. A rope was tied to one of a dozen metal rings positioned along the raised timber lip; it disappeared over the edge of the deck and into the loch, its other end connected to the diver.

Langham could see, far below, the dim, rippling luminescence of the diver's light like a reflection of the full moon.

Ryland grinned. 'A couple of quick tugs on the rope should get his attention.' He looked from Langham to the major. 'When he surfaces, grab his arms before he realizes what's happening. I'll cut the rope and use it to tie him up.'

Langham nodded.

Ryland knelt, took a grip on the rope and yanked it twice.

Seconds later the rope slackened and Ryland said, 'He's on his way up.' He took the rope and sliced through the braided cords, then wrapped the severed rope around his left wrist, stood up and backed off as the diver rose.

Langham and the major set aside their rifles and knelt at the edge of the deck.

270

Ryland walked backward step by step, the rope in one hand, his revolver poised in the other.

The ball of light expanded and Langham made out the dark, shimmering shape of the diver. He broke the surface in a surge of churned water and Langham and the major reached out, grabbed the man's rubber-clad shoulders and hauled him on to the deck. The diver released his grip on the light and it went tumbling back into the depths.

He sprawled, spitting out his mouthpiece and gasping like a landed fish.

Langham took up his rifle and stood over the diver as he rolled on to his back, staring up in bewilderment through his face mask.

'Don't even think about moving!' the major barked, aiming his rifle.

Disoriented, the diver put up no resistance as Ryland bound him hand and foot with the rope, leaving enough slack between his ankles so that the man could hobble. He pulled off the diver's flippers and face mask and levelled the revolver at his head.

Langham stood ready, his rifle poised. The diver appeared to be in his forties, a short, swarthy man with a jagged scar running down the left side of his face.

'Kurt?' he said in accented English. 'Where is Kurt?'

'Your friend's taking a little kip. Now up you get and off we go.' Ryland hauled the diver to his feet, none too gently, and pushed him in the direction of the gate.

'What should we do with . . .?' the major asked, indicating the unconscious Kurt.

271

'We'll come back for him later,' Ryland said. Langham took the remaining length of rope and bound the second man.

They moved off around the pontoon, Ryland prodding the driver ahead of him.

'When we get you into the castle, matey, we'll have a little question-and-answer session,' Ryland said. 'I think the police'll be very interested in what you're up to.'

'We were doing nothing,' the diver said, his teeth chattering.

Ryland laughed. 'Yeah, right. We'll let the police decide on that.' He prodded the diver in the small of the back with his revolver. 'Move it.'

The diver hobbled along the snow-covered deck, shaking with cold. Langham, even in his overcoat and hat, was frozen to the marrow; he almost felt sorry for the man.

They left the pontoon and took the path around the castle. The major unlocked the door and Ryland prodded their captive inside.

'Where now?' the detective asked.

'The only place for the blighter,' the major said. 'The dungeon. He can sweat down there, or rather freeze, until the police get here. This way.'

The major led the way along the corridor and down a flight of stone steps, switching on a naked bulb that bathed the stairwell in buttery light. Ryland followed, still prodding the diver in the small of the back, and Langham brought up the rear.

At the bottom the major indicated a cell and Ryland gestured the diver inside. The man shuffled into the cell and sat on his haunches against the far wall, shivering.

Langham, the major and Ryland conferred in whispers. 'I doubt he'll tell us who their collaborator is,' Langham said.

Ryland looked at the diver. 'The geezer looks perished. Offer him a few blankets and some hot soup and see if he'll blab.'

Langham leaned against the stonework of the door. 'We know what you're doing here,' he said. 'And we know you have help on the inside. I think you'll benefit by telling us who that person is.' He looked around the bare, freezing cell. 'It'll get even colder in here but we could supply a few blankets and food. Now, who helped you?'

The man looked up. 'Go to hell!'

Langham smiled. 'It's only a matter of time before the police investigate and find out the truth. Now, why don't you help yourself and tell us?'

The diver stared up at him, fury making his face even uglier. 'I don't know what the hell you're talking about.' His English was excellent, but with the harsh intonation of what Langham thought was German.

'If you don't spill,' Ryland chipped in, 'we'll leave your friend out there to freeze to death.'

The man merely laughed. 'Let the bastard die, for all I care.'

Langham pushed himself from the stonework. He was about to move from the cell when he was struck by a thought. He turned to the man. 'And the police will be very interested when they

273

find out that you, or one of your cohorts, was responsible for the murder all those years ago.'

Did the man tense slightly at the sound of Langham's words?

'You don't recall the farmer you killed?' he went on. 'February, 'forty-five. Your plane came down in the loch. You got out and swam ashore. You took refuge in the croft, surprising the farmer. And you killed him – beat him to death.'

The man stared up at Langham, hatred in his eyes. 'I did nothing,' he said in a small, defeated voice.

Langham smiled and left the cell. The major closed the timber door and shot the bolts.

'Nice touch about the murder, Langham,' the major said. 'You think he did it?'

'Or one of his cronies.'

'We'd better fetch the other geezer,' Ryland said as they climbed back up the staircase, 'before he really does freeze to death.'

Langham and Ryland hurried from the castle and made their way to the pontoon. The man in the donkey jacket was still unconscious, face down in the snow. They eased him over on to his back and Langham took his legs while Ryland gripped him under the arms. On the count of three they lifted him, grunting with the effort, and made their slow, shuffling way off the pontoon and back to the castle.

Langham was sweating by the time they'd manoeuvred the man down the narrow staircase and into a second cell. The major bolted the door and led the way up the stairs.

'Now how about we warm ourselves in front

274

of the fire with a peg or two?' the major asked.

'That sounds like the best idea I've heard all evening,' Langham said.

They were making their way along the corridor when a frantic pounding sounded at the door, followed by the more orderly summons of the bell pull.

'Now who the bally hell can that be at this time of night?' the major said, and retraced his steps along the hallway.

Langham and Ryland turned and faced the door.

Twenty-Four

Maria pounded on the door. The longer her frantic summons went unanswered, the more time she had to dwell on the consequences of the Dutch pair having arrived at the castle before them. She imagined Donald and Ralph lying dead in pools of blood, the other guests cowering petrified at gunpoint.

Charles hauled on the bell pull. 'Patience, my dear. Please believe me, all will be well.'

She was about to start banging on the door again when she heard the rattle of bolts. If anything, her impatience increased. The door swung open to reveal a small, bald-headed man with a huge moustache and copious side whiskers.

'Is Donald—?' she began.

'Maria?'

In the long perspective of the hallway she made out, rushing towards her, Donald's over-coated figure, followed by Ralph Ryland. Maria's heart skipped and she felt suddenly faint with relief.

The major stood aside as Maria ran into Donald's arms. 'You're in danger! The Dutch pair! They . . .'

She pulled away and stared at him. He looked totally bemused. She gasped when she saw the gash on his temple and the caked blood covering the side of his face.

'Donald, did they—?'

He held her and she never wanted him to let go. 'Maria . . . How on earth?' he began. He was laughing now, totally mystified by her sudden appearance. He looked up and his eyes widened, incredulous. 'Charles! My word, what a reunion!'

'My boy! How relieved we are to see you in the land of the living!'

'On the train from Edinburgh,' Maria said, 'we saw the Dutch pair. We raced here as fast as we could—'

'They're Dutch?' Donald said.

The major said, 'Get yourselves in here, d'you hear me! Come on, we can't be standing in the hall like this! I'll get Mrs F to fetch some tea and coffee, and how about a whisky while we're at it! Mr F will get a fire going. You both look frozen to the bone!'

'My man!' Charles declared. 'Never more welcome words spoken!'

Donald introduced Charles and Maria to Major Gordon, then took Maria by the arm and led her into a side room. He sat beside her on a sofa while Ralph pulled up an armchair for Charles, who inserted himself into it with a sigh.

Donald gripped her hand. 'Now what's all this about a Dutch pair? How on earth do you know about them?'

'They broke into your flat yesterday, Donald. They . . . I was there. I disturbed them.'

His eyes widened in sudden alarm.

'It's OK,' she said. 'They . . . they just questioned me. They wanted to know who you were, and Ralph too. They had a knife, and . . . Oh, Donald – I had to tell them that Ralph was a detective.'

'But they didn't harm you?'

She shook her head. 'They left and I called the police. But I was so worried. I had to come here and warn you.'

'You said they were Dutch. How did you know—?'

'I spoke to Jeff Mallory last night. They were known thugs – Dutch, he said – so you see why I was so worried about you?'

'And when Maria collected me,' Charles declared, 'she was about to hare off hither all by herself! I couldn't have that, of course, and offered my services.'

A middle-aged couple bustled into the room and set a tray on a small table. The man busied himself making a fire while the major poured stiff whiskies all round.

Mrs F had brought a first-aid kit and attended to the gash on Donald's forehead while he listened to Maria's story.

'And on the train,' she said between sips of Scotch, 'I saw the pair. We tried to follow them here but we took a wrong turning . . .'

Charles said, 'We saw their van parked in the woods, Donald, and feared the worst.'

Maria reached up and touched his cheek. Mrs F dabbed antiseptic on to the wound and declared, 'There you go. It's not as bad as I feared. You won't be needing stitches.'

Donald smiled. 'That's a relief, Mrs F.'

'But what happened?' Maria said. 'The Dutch pair?'

He stopped her, holding her hand tight as he said, 'I set off earlier to Glenross to summon the police. On the way I . . . Well, I fell and . . .' He indicated his forehead. 'When I came round I saw their van in the woods, so I raced back to the castle and alerted Ralph and the major.'

'And between us,' Major Gordon put in, 'we apprehended the blighters at gunpoint on the pontoon, and Donald here whacked one of 'em over the head. Upshot: they're both where they damned well belong – in the dungeon!'

Maria shook her head. It was her turn to be mystified. 'On the pontoon? But what were they doing there?'

'We're pretty sure they were after valuables in the German plane,' Ralph explained. 'One of the geezers was a diver.'

Charles called out, 'Skulduggery and intrigue in a Scottish castle! But, Donald, you must write about this one day!'

Donald made a wry face. 'Skulduggery, intrigue *and* murder,' he said.

278

Maria's heart skipped. 'Murder?'

'Someone,' the major said, standing before the roaring fire with a whisky glass clutched in his hand, 'killed me engineer, Hans Vermeulen, and then did for me good friend Professor Hardwick.'

'Which is why I was trying to reach the police this afternoon,' Donald added.

Maria stared from the major to Donald, shaking her head in mystification. 'But who would have done that?' she asked.

'That's the big question,' Ralph said.

Donald shook his head. 'We don't know. We think the Dutch pair – though we didn't know they were Dutch – might have been aboard the plane back in 'forty-five, transporting a valuable cargo from Germany . . . only they came down in the loch.'

'We think a couple of 'em survived,' Ralph went on, 'got out of the plane before it went down and skedaddled. Years later, when Vermeulen locates the plane, up they come like wasps around a jam pot and do their damnedest to get the haul.'

Maria looked from the detective to Donald. 'But who would want Hans Vermeulen dead?' she asked.

'The way we look at it,' Donald said, 'is that one of the guests is working with the Dutch pair. They wanted to stymie the salvage operation to buy themselves time to dive and retrieve the valuables, and what better way to do that than kill the chief engineer?'

Maria stared at the whisky clutched in her right

hand. She shook her head, her thoughts confused, as she looked around the gathering and finally at Donald.

'No,' she said at last. 'No, that doesn't work.'

He stared at her. 'What?'

'No,' she said. 'You see, Hans Vermeulen was working for the Dutch pair.'

Donald blinked comically, then laughed. '*What?*' he said again.

'Jeff Mallory told me last night. One of the Dutch pair was *Patrick* Vermeulen, Hans's brother. Jeff had a photo of him, so I could identify Patrick Vermeulen – which wasn't hard. He has a nasty scar running down the left hand side of his face.'

'The diver,' Donald murmured.

'You see,' Maria went on, 'the Vermeulen brothers were working together. Jeff suspects that Hans had laundered money through his company for Patrick – money gained through drugs and racketeering, apparently. Jeff said that Hans must have contacted his brother when you turned up here, Donald, and asked Patrick to find out about you and Ralph, which is why they broke into your flat, wanting to know if you were police.'

The major slumped into an armchair. 'My God!' he gasped. 'Hans? I never thought . . .'

Donald looked across at Ralph. 'So the whole salvage operation was a cover for retrieving the valuables, which the Dutch pair *had* to do before the wreck was lifted.' He shook his head. 'This puts an entirely different complexion on things, Ralph.'

'You're not kidding,' the detective said. 'Like, why the ruddy hell did someone bash Vermeulen over the head? Why did they want him out of the way? Did someone suspect what he was up to?'

Maria looked up, her thoughts racing. She considered what Donald had said about the Dutch pair having help on the inside, someone in the castle.

'What about this . . . .?' she began tentatively.

Donald squeezed her hand. 'Go on.'

'The Dutch pair *did* have someone in the castle, working with them. Someone who got close to the major and kept an eye on things, ensuring that no one might suspect what was really going on.'

Donald looked frustrated. 'That's all very well, but who, and why, would someone murder Hans?'

'That same person – the insider – might have murdered him,' she said.

'But *why*?' he asked, looking exasperated. 'They were working *with* him, after all.'

As far as Maria could make out, there was only one credible reason.

'Why else?' she said. 'Greed, Donald. The four – the Vermeulen brothers, Kurt Dreyer and the insider – would have agreed on taking a split on the proceeds from the German plane, no? But what if the insider decided he wanted more – wanted Hans's share? He killed the engineer and later, when Vermeulen retrieved the valuables, they would divide the spoils. The killer could claim that someone in the castle found out about

281

the scheme and murdered Hans. They would split the proceeds three ways and off the murderer goes.'

'Well, blow me down,' Donald said. He looked at Ralph. 'It's a possibility.'

The detective was pacing back and forth, pulling furiously on a Woodbine.

'But who the bally hell was the insider?' the major cried.

Ralph stopped and pointed at Donald with his cigarette. 'There's one way to find out . . .' He resumed his pacing again, then stopped and stared around the gathering. 'Supposin' Maria's right – and it sounds pretty plausible to me. Someone in the castle got greedy and killed Vermeulen. Now there's two people in the dungeons right now who bloody well know the identity of that person, right?'

'That's right . . .' Donald said, draining his Scotch.

'So how about this. We let Patrick Vermeulen know that his brother is dead, killed by their colleague. How do you think he'll feel about that, eh? Pretty hacked off, I'd have thought.'

'But hacked off enough to reveal the identity of his accomplice?' Donald asked.

Maria lowered her head. It occurred to her that the ploy was cruel, and she almost spoke up and objected. Then she saw Patrick Vermeulen's sadistic smile as Dreyer had threatened her with the knife yesterday and held her tongue.

Ralph said, 'OK, so what if he *doesn't* tell us? He keeps mum, thinking he can bluff his way out of the mess, even when the rozzers turn up.

He's done nothing wrong, technically, other than a little trespass. But let's see how he reacts when we drag him up in front of the suspects, eh? Let's see if he gives the killer away.'

'Or,' Donald said, 'see how our *suspects* react when we introduce Mr Vermeulen to the gathering.'

'Good God!' the major said. 'We'd better have our wits about us and make sure Vermeulen is restrained.'

'If it comes to trooping him before the guests, I'll keep the ropes around his ankles,' Ralph said. 'I'll go down and break the news to Vermeulen now. You coming, Don?'

Donald squeezed Maria's hand. 'I'll be back in two minutes, darling.'

'Be careful,' she said.

Donald stood and followed the detective from the room.

Maria smiled across at the major. 'It is a pity we couldn't have met in less fraught circumstances, Major. Donald has told me a lot about you and your times together in India.'

'And he told me he was about to wed the most beautiful woman in London, m'dear – and he's not wrong.'

'Hear, hear!' Charles sang.

Maria finished her whisky, feeling a little light-headed. She smiled across at Charles. 'And there I was, imagining Donald and Ralph lying dead.'

The major harrumphed. 'Not that pair, m'girl! You should have seen 'em deal with the Dutch blighters. It was as if we were back in Madagascar again. But you've finished your drink. How about a top up?'

She laughed. 'I've had quite enough for now, but I would love some tea.'

The major was pouring Earl Grey into a china cup when the door opened and Donald entered, followed by Ralph. Maria looked up. 'What happened?'

Donald shook his head. The detective said, 'Geezer was having none of it. Didn't believe me when I said his brother'd bought it, murdered by their accomplice in the castle. He thought we were bluffing. Gave us a right mouthful, he did.'

'So what, pray, did you do?' Charles asked.

'Only thing we could do, in the circumstances – we took the geezer along to the cellar and showed him Hans Vermeulen's body.'

Donald looked across at her and gave a shrug. 'He just stared,' he said, 'and wouldn't say a word. We took him back to the cell.'

'So what now?' the major asked.

Donald said, 'Major, could you get the guests together in the Stewart room, if they're not already there? Ralph, give us ten minutes and then bring Vermeulen up. I'm pretty sure the suspect will react at the sight of him, even if Vermeulen doesn't spill the beans.'

Ralph drew his revolver and slipped from the room. The major and Charles left after him.

Maria restrained Donald on the threshold. 'It's so good to see you,' she murmured. 'You have no idea how worried I've been.'

He stroked her cheek. 'If I'd known what you'd

gone through at the flat . . .' He hesitated. 'I didn't like the business of showing Vermeulen his brother's corpse, you know? Wasn't exactly cricket. Then I thought of what he'd put you through . . .'

'Donald,' she said, silencing him with a finger against his lips. 'Thank you.'

They hurried along the corridor hand in hand.

Twenty-Five

They paused in the corridor beside a window overlooking the moon-silvered loch.

'The guests won't be expecting me back so soon,' Langham said, then briefly explained the circumstances of Professor Hardwick's murder and the attempt on his own life.

'Two murders!' Maria exclaimed, her eyes wide. 'But I had every right to worry myself sick over your safety!'

'Anyway, the killer assumes I know his identity – he took a shot at me because he thinks the professor told me who the killer was. So when he sees me now, with a little luck he might react. And, if not then, then surely when we parade Patrick Vermeulen before everyone.'

He indicated the door to the Stewart room, opened it and followed her in.

His pulse quickened as he ushered Maria over to a settee against the far wall. Charles was already seated, occupying an armchair and chatting to Elspeth, who sat beside the fire. 'Mr Langham!' she exclaimed when she saw him.

Renata Káldor, perched upon a chair beside the door leading to the dining hall, looked up as they entered. 'Mr Langham, you're back. But what happened to your head?'

She appeared surprised to see him, but not shocked. He touched the patch on his forehead. 'A little fall, nothing serious.'

'Did you reach Glenross?' Elspeth asked.

'Unfortunately not. After the fall I thought it wise to turn back.'

He glanced around the room. Gabriel Gordon and Ulrich Meyer had yet to arrive, along with the major. 'Renata, Elspeth, allow me to introduce my fiancée, Maria Dupré, and my good friend, Charles Elder. Maria, Charles – Elspeth Stuart and Renata Káldor.'

They exchanged greetings and Renata expressed her surprise that Maria and Charles had managed to make it through the snow.

'A plough eased our passage for most of the way,' Charles said, 'or we might still be in Inverness.'

The door opened and Ulrich Meyer limped into the room, leaning heavily on his stick. 'I was summoned by the major,' he said, 'as was everyone else, I see. Most extraordinary.' His left eye widened in surprise as he took in Langham.

Langham introduced Meyer to Maria and Charles, and the German exchanged formal greetings and lowered himself carefully on to a straight-backed chair.

286

'But I thought you were in Glenross,' the German said, eyeing Langham.

He explained his fall and his decision to return to the castle.

'Do I thereby take it that the police have not been informed of the situation here, Herr Langham?'

'That's correct,' Langham said, 'though the authorities in London are aware of the situation. It shouldn't be long before the police arrive.'

He glanced from Meyer to Káldor as he said this, but neither took the bait nor looked unduly perturbed.

Mrs F bustled in just as a tense silence came down on the group and her sudden presence – along with her enquiry as to what everyone was drinking – leavened the atmosphere.

Langham asked for Earl Grey, wanting to keep a clear head for the imminent proceedings; Maria requested the same, while Charles asked for whisky. 'For me, nothing, thank you,' Meyer said.

Renata Káldor ordered a gin and tonic and Mrs F returned in due course and dispensed the drinks.

Maria murmured to Langham, 'Just Gabriel Gordon to come.'

He whispered, 'That's right. It'll be interesting to watch his reaction when he sees me.'

'I am intrigued, Donald, to see this Casanova in the flesh. So far I have seen only naked representations of him on canvas.'

'I'll be interested to hear what you make of him. He has an amazing ability to put people's backs up. Speak of the devil.'

287

The door swung open and Gabriel Gordon sauntered in, followed by his father.

Gabriel dropped himself into an armchair and reached for the whisky decanter.

The major hurried across to Langham and whispered, 'Ralph's waiting outside with Vermeulen. Just give the word and I'll tell him to come in.'

'Give me a couple of minutes. I'll signal when it's time.'

'Understood,' the major said, and stationed himself beside the door.

It was a few seconds before Gabriel looked up and registered Langham's presence. 'Good God. What happened? I thought . . .' He slurred his words. 'I mean, didn't you set off for Glenross?'

For the umpteenth time that evening, Langham found himself explaining his fall and his return to the castle.

He squeezed Maria's hand, cleared his throat and rose to his feet. He moved to the fire and stood with his back to the blaze, aware that all eyes were focused on him as he gazed around the gathering.

He had contemplated his words while waiting for everyone to arrive, and now he was surprised to find himself feeling more than a little anxious.

'As I mentioned earlier to one or two of you, there have been certain developments in the matter concerning the killing of Hans Vermeulen. For one thing, I regret to inform you that the killer struck for a second time this morning. Professor Hardwick was stabbed to death in his room.'

Meyer remained stony-faced. Renata shook her head as if in disbelief, her eyes wide. Elspeth gave a small, frightened cry and began weeping, comforted by Charles who took her hand.

Gabriel said, 'The professor? Dead?'

'He was killed by the same person who murdered Hans Vermeulen, because the professor saw the killer dispense with vital evidence—'

Gabriel interrupted. 'Out with it, Langham. Do you know who the killer was?'

'The question I asked myself,' Langham said, 'was *why* was Hans Vermeulen killed? What was he, and his cohorts, really up to with the salvaging of the German plane? We think the wreck contains something of great worth – or of great value, anyway, to certain people who would do anything to get theirs hands on it. We suspect that Hans Vermeulen was killed by someone he trusted, someone who wanted his share of the spoils.'

'What are you talking about!' Gabriel called out. 'Who killed Hans and the professor?'

Langham ignored him. He was watching Ulrich Meyer closely as he said, 'One person in this room knows very well what I'm talking about.'

'But who?' Elspeth gasped.

Langham tuned to the major and nodded.

The old soldier opened the door and signalled to the waiting Ryland.

All eyes turned to the door as the detective prodded Patrick Vermeulen into the room. The man shuffled in, his legs hobbled, hunched beneath a ragged blanket.

Langham looked from Meyer to Káldor to

Gabriel Gordon. Meyer blinked once at the new arrival, then returned his gaze to Langham.

Renata sat back and regarded Vermeulen as if he were a particularly loathsome species of insect. Gabriel merely gazed at the Dutchman with seeming incomprehension and knocked back his Scotch.

Langham looked across at Vermeulen and said, 'Who was your collaborator, Patrick? Who killed your brother?'

Amid the exclamations that met Langham's words, Vermeulen yelled out loud and evaded Ryland. Either the rope binding his ankles snapped or he'd loosened it while in the cell – but he managed to dodge the detective's lunge and dive across the room. At first Langham thought he was heading for Ulrich Meyer, then realized that the enraged Dutchman's intended target was not the German but himself.

Salvation arrived from the improbable quarter of Charles Elder, who leaped up nimbly and stuck out a well-judged foot as Vermeulen came within a yard of his intended target. The Dutchman tripped and hit the carpet with a thud as Langham moved aside.

Cries and shouts followed, and much movement as startled guests jumped to their feet and Ryland, revolver drawn, ran across the room and apprehended the Dutchman.

Langham looked up, his heart racing. In the melee that had followed Vermeulen's outburst, one person had taken the opportunity to slip from the room.

He brushed past Ryland, who was manhandling

290

the Dutchman to his feet, and hurried from the room and along the corridor. He passed through the dining hall and saw that the door leading to the kitchen was swinging shut. He crossed the hall, pulled open the door and sped along the corridor. His first thought was that his quarry had taken the steps leading down into the cellar; then he noticed that the narrow timber door leading up to the battlements was ajar.

Taking a breath, he pulled the door open and followed.

The corkscrew staircase was narrow, the stone cold to the touch as he took the steps two at a time. He heard footfalls above him, then the sound of another door opening. Seconds later he came to the open door. A freezing wind pounced, taking his breath away.

He stepped out on to the battlements and saw a line of footsteps, like so many exclamation marks in the snow, leading from the doorway and across to the crenellated wall. A dark figure stood with its back to him, leaning against the stonework.

Langham stepped forward and approached the figure.

They were high up and the wind raged. The moon illuminated the scene like a floodlight and the wind whipped at the figure's hair.

Langham said, 'Why don't you do the sensible thing and come with me? There's no way down from here.'

The figure remained immobile, head hanging, arms apart and braced against the icy stone blocks.

Gabriel turned around and stared at Langham. 'It's a hell of a mess,' he said.

'What is?'

'Life . . . Everything.' The poet fell back against the battlements, and for a second Langham thought he was about to tip backwards and fall to his death. He steadied himself, swaying, and laughed drunkenly.

'Why is everything a mess, Gabriel?'

'It's all right for you, Langham, with your success as a writer and your posh fiancée—'

Langham took a small step towards the poet. 'You don't do too badly in that department yourself, Gabriel.'

The young man laughed derisively. 'You understand nothing! As if I'm bothered about the kind of bitch who throws herself at me! They're ten-a-penny . . .'

Langham began, 'I wouldn't say Elspeth is—'

Gabriel interrupted. 'She's different! Elspeth is . . . She's naïve, inexperienced.'

'And neither,' Langham said, 'would I call Renata ten-a-penny.'

'Again . . . Renata is different. She'd didn't throw herself at me. The ice maiden, that's what I called her. So aloof, so cool, so *disdainful*. No, she wouldn't throw herself at me.'

'Is that why you're so . . . so fascinated by her? Because she resisted you, was strong, resourceful, independent?'

Gabriel gestured. 'Perhaps . . . Yes, perhaps that was it. She . . . she understands me.' He stared at Langham as if working out whether to tell him something.

292

At last he said, 'She's the only person who really understands me, Langham. Understands how . . . how weak I am.' He laughed. 'Are you surprised that I'd admit that? It bucks my . . . my usual arrogance, doesn't it? The fact that I can admit it, own up to the fact that I'm a failure . . . Perhaps that's why Renata took to me, because she's strong and pitied me. She gave me something which no woman has ever been able to give me before . . .'

'Love?'

Gabriel shook his head sadly. 'No, Langham. She gave me her understanding, her sympathy. She saw how weak I was and she didn't hate me for it.'

'And,' Langham asked, 'how do you feel about her?'

Gabriel considered the question. 'Do you mean, do I love her? Do you know something, Langham, I'm not sure that I've ever been able to . . . to love anyone in my life. Oh, I feel something for her. I need . . . I mean, I *needed* her. I craved her understanding, I suppose, her sympathy.' He stopped suddenly and Langham saw that the poet was weeping. 'And then she told me she was dying.'

The silence stretched. Langham murmured, 'I'm sorry.'

Gabriel drew a long breath. 'I suppose it was this news which, indirectly, made me kill Vermeulen.'

Langham stared at the poet. 'You?'

'He really was despicable, you know? His taunts, his jibes at my work, my poetry . . . at

293

me. He never missed the chance to ridicule me and my reliance on my father for handouts. Christ, how I hated the man!'

'That's no reason to kill anyone, Gabriel.'

'No? I'd like to see how you would have dealt with him, with his constant criticism, his going behind my back and persuading my father to cut me off. That's right, Langham, he thought me a parasite . . . a parasite, leaching off the old man. And all the while he was bleeding my father dry.'

'But he wasn't, Gabriel. The reason he was here was to retrieve whatever valuables were in the plane.'

The poet ignored him. 'And then . . . then his constant taunting of Renata . . . even when he found out she was ill. Even then he didn't stop his jibes. That's the kind of man he was – sly, snide, underhand . . .'

Langham took a step closer to the poet. 'So he had to die? You came back from Inverness and attempted to shoot Vermeulen on the pontoon.'

Gabriel smiled. 'I never was much of a shot.'

'You were very lucky you didn't end up killing your father.'

Anger flared in the poet's eyes. 'But I didn't make the same mistake the second time around!'

'And when it came to getting rid of the professor?'

Gabriel sighed. 'He saw me discarding the film . . .'

'And he, too, had to die.'

'The odd thing was that it wasn't difficult. I

mean, it wasn't *morally* difficult. It's strange how one justifies one's actions, isn't it? I felt I was justified in killing Vermeulen – and in an act of self-preservation, as the professor was at the end of his long life anyway . . .' He shrugged.

'And when you decided that I had to die?' Langham said. 'Did you have any moral qualms then, Gabriel?'

The poet looked away. 'The odd thing was that I think, subconsciously, I wanted to miss you . . .'

Gabriel turned and looked over the battlements. Langham took a step closer, careful not to alarm the poet.

He looked back at Langham. 'But if you think you can stop me . . .'

'Gabriel!'

'As if I'd meekly come with you and face the gallows . . .'

He turned towards the battlements and attempted to scale the crenellation; he swayed, lifting one foot on to the stonework. Langham dived, crying out, and managed to snatch a handful of the young man's shirt. Gabriel lashed out, missing Langham but sending himself into a spin. He came up against the wall, falling forward into a notch between two stone blocks. He leaned forward, tipping himself through the gap, and Langham dived again and grabbed Gabriel's arm, hauling him away from the wall. He struggled with the poet, aware of his bovine strength as they grappled on the icy walkway.

Gabriel overcame Langham, pushed him away and dived towards the battlements. He slipped, crying out, fell full length and hit his head against the wall. He lay very still, sprawling in the light of the moon. On all fours, panting, Langham made his way towards the poet and felt for a pulse.

He was alive, but out for the count.

Langham smiled to himself at the irony that even this, a final, suicidal gesture on the part of the poet, had resulted in abject failure.

He climbed to his feet as the door from the tower opened and Ryland appeared, followed by Maria.

The detective said, 'I've locked Vermeulen back in the dungeon.' He looked across at the unconscious poet. 'Gabriel, right?'

Langham told him of the poet's admission and his attempt to launch himself from the battlements. 'The other guests?' he asked.

'They've returned to their rooms,' Ryland said. 'Mrs F is showing Charles to his room.'

The major appeared in the doorway, paused and stared from Langham to his son.

Langham said to Ryland, 'Give me a hand to get Gabriel down the staircase and to his room, would you, Ralph?'

The major said, 'What was the young fool doing up here, Langham?'

'I don't know . . . He was drunk, confused. I wonder if you could show Maria to my room, Major?' He squeezed Maria's hand and murmured, 'I won't be long.'

As Maria and the major made their way from the walkway and down the staircase, Langham and Ryland manhandled Gabriel upright. Grunting with the effort, they managed to half carry, half

296

drag the poet across to the doorway and down the stairs.

At the bottom, Ryland took his shoulders, Langham his legs, and they carried him along the corridor and up the staircase to his room. They dropped him on the bed and Langham examined the gash on his forehead.

'He'll live,' he said. 'I wonder if you could stay with him, Ralph?' He hesitated. 'I'll be back shortly to fill you in, OK?'

'My pleasure,' Ryland said, drawing is revolver. 'And if he comes round and gets bolshy, I'll threaten him with this.'

Langham made his way down the stairs to the Stewart room.

Renata Káldor was alone at the far end of the room, seated in a high-backed armchair beside the fire. She had laid her book aside and was staring into the flames, and looked up as Langham appeared at the doorway. He hesitated, then crossed to her, drew up an armchair and positioned it before the fire.

He lodged his elbows on his knees and steepled his hands as if in prayer, his thumbs to his lips as he regarded the woman.

'I'm intrigued,' he said at last.

Renata regarded him, her gaze icy. 'About what, Mr Langham?'

'About your . . . your relationship with Gabriel.'

She smiled, but it lacked the warmth usually associated with the expression. 'I take it you had a little tête-à-tête with him up on the battlements,' she said, 'before he passed out?'

'That's right, and he told me all about you and him, Renata.'

'He did? And what did he say?'

'He told me about why he was attracted to you. He admired your strength, your independence. He said you understood him.' He paused, considering his next words. 'But what I don't understand, Renata, is *your* relationship with *him*. I mean, what do you see in the poet that attracted you? You saw through his arrogance, his bravado. You knew him for what he was – shallow, conceited, egotistical . . . and weak.'

She withdrew a cigarette from its gold case with her elegant fingers, fitted it into its holder, lit the cigarette and inhaled. She blew a plume of smoke towards the fire and said, almost dreamily, 'What do I see in Gabriel . . .?'

He held up a hand, 'Let me hazard a guess,' he said. 'Tell me if I'm wrong, but you thought you could use him?'

She stared at him. 'How much do you know, Langham? How much have you worked out?'

'I . . . I think I know pretty much what happened here over the course of the past week, Renata. But I'd like to hear your side of the story.'

She smiled glacially. 'For all your bluff, northern mannerisms, Langham, you are really quite perceptive.'

'So I'm right? You planned to use him to kill . . .?'

She interrupted. 'You're right. I did think I could use him; indeed, I planned to.'

'But you realized that he wasn't quite up to the job?'

298

'Again, Langham, you show surprising psychological insight.' She paused, drew on her cigarette
and went on, 'I planned to use him, but . . . Well,
two things occurred. I realized that although I
had Gabriel in the palm of my hand, he really
was too weak to do what I wanted him to do –
and at the same time I was diagnosed with
leukaemia and given a year to live. And, do you
know something, Langham – that diagnosis gave
me the strength, the anger, to do what I had to
do . . .'

He nodded. That was all he wanted to hear. He
said, 'Were you aboard the plane, Renata, or did
you hear about it later and buy your way into the
project?'

She regarded him and was silent for a time
before saying, 'I was aboard the plane, Langham.
I was in from the start.' She smiled, though the
expression was more of a sneer. 'In fact, it was
my project from the very start.'

'The spiriting of the valuables from Germany . . .?'

'I sourced the gold and other valuables; I
ensured that the Gestapo were ambushed before
they could take the gold from Amsterdam to
Berlin. I hired Patrick Vermeulen and Kurt Dreyer
and I made contact with a pilot who could be
bought.'

'And you headed for Britain?'

'I had contacts in London, people I trusted who
could ensure our safety. We made for Scotland
so as to avoid detection.'

'And the plane came down in the loch. You
were lucky to survive.'

She closed her eyes briefly, reliving the

incident. 'The pilot drowned. I managed to swim ashore with Patrick and Dreyer.'

'Who killed the farmer?' Langham asked.

'That was Dreyer.'

'And the gold sat at the bottom of the loch for more than ten years before you told Hans Vermeulen about the wreck?'

'We tried to locate the plane,' she said, 'but it was impossible without expert help. So, yes, Patrick enlisted his brother.'

'A four-way split, between the Vermeulens, Dreyer and yourself. But you got greedy. You wanted more than a quarter of the gold and you killed Hans for his share.'

Anger flared in her pale green eyes. 'It wasn't like that at all, Langham! They were going to cut me out, Hans and Patrick. And . . .' She stopped, swallowed, then went on: 'I thought I loved him, Langham. I'd gone through a lot with Patrick. I loved him, I truly did. And then he betrayed me, planned to divide the gold and leave me with nothing.'

'How—?' he began.

'Six months ago, here at the castle. Hans was here for the first of the exploratory dives. I overheard them, purely by chance. I picked up the phone in my room to make a call out and overheard Hans speaking with someone. The conversation was almost over, but I pieced enough of it together to work out what Hans and Patrick were planning. Can you imagine how I felt? Can you? To be betrayed by someone you loved . . .'

'And it was then that you thought you'd use Gabriel?'

'Briefly, yes, that did occur to me.' She laughed without humour. 'But I soon realized that Gabriel was not the kind of person who could kill like that. Oh, I have no doubt he might kill someone on the spur of the moment, impulsively, but not with malice aforethought. Anyway,' she blew a plume of smoke, 'by then I was fuelled by rage. I had planned for so long to salvage the valuables, but it was no longer about the money. I was dying. What did wealth mean to me, Langham?'

'So, motivated by rage at what Hans and Patrick were planning, you decided to kill Hans. You tried to shoot him on the pontoon and failed, but succeeded in clubbing him to death.'

Her expression was distant as she focused, perhaps, on a more successful outcome to her plan. 'And I planned to kill Patrick, too. I would have gladly killed him, and Dreyer, once they had retrieved the gold.'

'Killing becomes easy when you've done it once, yes?'

'If you mean Hardwick, then yes – it *was* easy. I was in the Stewart room early this morning. I'd unlocked the window and was about to throw the film into the loch. Professor Hardwick entered the room, then turned and hurried off. I wasn't really sure at first if he realized what I was doing, but I followed him upstairs and saw him knocking on your door like a frightened rabbit . . .'

'So you killed poor old Hardwick then tried to shoot me.'

She smiled. 'One does what one must, Mr Langham.'

He sat back and stared at the woman, admiring her poise *in extremis*.

He shook his head. 'Human beings never cease to amaze me, Renata.'

'Do you mean how could I, a woman, wealthy, successful . . . how could I plan and carry out two murders?'

'No . . . I was thinking of Gabriel, actually. I was trying to work out why he would willingly take the blame for the murders.'

Her eyes widened. 'He would?'

'Up on the battlements he tried to make me believe that he'd killed Vermeulen and the professor. He would gladly have taken the blame to save you, even though you were dying.' He stared at her. 'And when he'd made his admission, he tried to throw himself off the battlements.'

'But you didn't believe him.'

He smiled. 'Oh, for a minute or two I did. Then I thought about it. Like you I realized that, psychologically, he wasn't the type to kill in that way, with malice aforethought, as you said. And I realized, then, that he was attempting to protect someone, and that person could only be you. But why?'

Renata smiled and said, 'Because he was weak, Langham, and pathetically grateful to me. Until he met me he'd lived a lie – the strong, ego-driven male, irresistible to a certain passive type of subjugated woman . . . But I could see through his façade, see the child beneath all the arrogance.' She tipped her head and regarded him. 'I was the first person to make him understand himself, you see, make him see that he was living a lie. I tried to help him, suggested a psychiatrist friend of mine – and he was so grateful to me.'

'And yet, at the same time, he wanted to kill himself . . .'

She tipped her hand. 'He is a little . . . unbalanced, I think, and when drunk is prone to the odd melodramatic gesture.'

Langham leaned forward. 'Did he work out for himself that it was you who killed Vermeulen and . . .' He stopped as she was shaking her head.

'I told him, Langham. I was honest with him and told him all about the plane, the valuables, and Patrick and Hans's planned betrayal. This was after I'd killed Hans.'

'And his reaction?'

'Amazement, disbelief . . . until I explained my motivations. And then he understood . . . and proceeded to drink himself silly over the next few days.' She paused, staring into the fire, then turned to Langham and began: 'It's . . .'

'Yes?'

'I was about to say that it's touching that he should wish to protect me like that, but his concern was misplaced. I am strong, Langham. I can face whatever fate throws at me.' She smiled at him. 'I have come to terms with the fact of my mortality, and the thought of facing the judiciary for what I have done holds no fear at all for me.'

Langham looked up. Across the room, the major was standing by the door, ashen-faced. He wondered how long he'd been standing there.

Langham nodded his farewell to Renata, stood and moved to the old man.

'I heard everything,' the major murmured. 'If you'd give me a few minutes alone with . . .' He gestured across the room to Renata.

Langham nodded. 'Of course.'

He moved to the door, then paused and looked back. The major sat down and stared in silence at the Hungarian, who reached out a tentative hand and gripped the major's, as if in sudden need.

Epilogue

Spring had come to the Highlands and the gorse was in bloom.

A greater contrast to the snows of December Langham could not imagine; the April sky was cloudless and the sun beat down on the silver waters of the loch cradled in the rolling green moorland.

Langham stood with Maria in the small crowd on the pontoon, awaiting the signal for the Dornier to be winched from its watery grave.

When the invitation had arrived from the major to stay at the castle for the culmination of the salvage operation, Langham had been in two minds whether to accept. Maria had decided for him: 'I think it will be a good idea, Donald! We will "lay the ghost" of the events of last December, no?'

Now he squeezed Maria's hand, turned and walked to the edge of the pontoon and stared across at the rearing battlements of the castle. There, on the paving slabs just fifteen yards from where he stood, Renata Káldor had thrown herself to her death.

Maria joined him, murmuring, 'You couldn't have done anything to save her, Donald. She would have found a way to take her life, one way or the other.'

The major had never told Langham what had passed between him and Renata that evening.

305

At ten o'clock, just after the major had bade her goodnight, Renata had taken herself up to the battlements and succeeded in doing what Gabriel, hours earlier, had failed to do.

'I wonder if I should have stayed with Renata and the major,' Langham said. 'But it seemed important at the time that I should leave them together.'

'And so it was, Donald.' She squeezed his hand. 'Her fate was sealed, whatever you did.'

He smiled at her and nodded to acknowledge her common sense. 'You're right.'

She tugged at his hand. 'Come on, we're missing all the fun.'

She pulled him back across the deck to join the onlookers. Ralph Ryland was dancing this way and that, snapping the proceedings with the box Brownie that Annie had given him for Christmas. Charles Elder beamed at them, eating a duck drumstick from the veritable banquet Mr and Mrs F had laid out on a trestle table.

Ulrich Meyer stood to one side, making meticulous notes as the engineer gave the signal for the winch to begin lifting the plane.

Langham considered Gabriel Gordon and said to Maria, 'I wonder how Gabriel's getting on?'

She smiled. 'Probably having a whale of a time in Paris. Living the bohemian life on the Left Bank, writing his melancholic poetry and drinking himself silly in the company of fellow artists and chorus girls.'

'It's significant that the major hasn't once mentioned him,' he said. He and Maria knew of the poet's whereabouts only because Mrs F had told them on their arrival.

Press photographers and reporters crowded the pontoon, along with a posse of curious locals. A knot of officials from the British and Dutch governments stood apart from the other observers; in pinstriped suits and bowler hats they resembled a jury of Puritans about to pass judgement on the general air of festivity. At their feet, and guarded by two uniformed policemen, stood half-a-dozen black metal boxes that divers had retrieved from the Dornier an hour earlier. The haul amounted to fifty gold ingots and jewellery and diamonds worth, a government official had estimated, approximately half a million pounds.

'And apparently I'm in for a small cut,' the major had announced, 'which should allow me to finish restoring the southern wing of the castle.'

The chief engineer made a series of hand signals to the crane's operator in his cab and the crane, straddling the picture-frame shape of the pontoon, took the strain. The engine growled and metal squealed. The dozen chains depending from its boom tautened and lifted free of the loch, dripping beads of silver water.

Langham looked around for the major, wondering where the old man was as – just below the surface of the loch – the cruciform shape of the German plane came slowly into sight.

'Where's the major?' he wondered aloud.

'I saw him hurry back to the castle a few minutes ago,' Maria said, 'summoned by Mrs F.'

Ryland looked up from snapping the plane and nodded towards the castle. 'Here he comes now.'

Charles Elder lowered his drumstick and said, 'And he looks more than a little preoccupied, I'd say.'

'Hope it wasn't bad news,' Langham said.

The old man limped across the gangway and joined them. 'Sorry about that – called to the phone.' He scratched his head as he stared at the small group. 'You'll never guess . . . That was Elspeth. I told you she's been in London since Christmas. Well . . .' He paused.

Maria said, biting her lip as if in fear of dire tidings, 'Yes?'

The old man laughed. 'Well,' he said again, bemused, 'the gal's going to get herself hitched. Met a young buck who works for the Foreign Office. Head over heels. Marriage in autumn. Wants to come up tomorrow and show me the fella . . . Well, blow me down!'

Charles declared, 'I think we should raise a glass to the couple!'

They took glasses from a tray on the table – meant to toast the successful completion of the salvage operation – and drank to the health of Elspeth and her beau.

An exclamation went up from the crowd. Langham turned his attention to the loch as the hulk of the Dornier broke the surface and sat, bobbing, as a cataract of water cascaded from its fuselage. The dread sigil of the Third Reich, the swastika, could just be made out on the tail fin, faded with the years.

Charles said, 'Does anyone know what became of the Dutch thugs, by any chance?'

The major tore his gaze from the dripping

Dornier. 'Heard from the police in London just last night,' he said. 'They wanted Patrick Vermeulen for a couple of bank robberies – and they did a deal with the blighter. He shopped his chum Dreyer for the murder of Fergus Bruce back in 'forty-five, in return for a reduced sentence. No honour amongst thieves, hm?'

The chief engineer raised his hands and called for silence. 'I think that now the major would like to say a few words. Major Gordon . . .'

The major stepped forward, harrumphing in the limelight, and cleared his throat. 'I've lived for this day for the past year or more,' he began, 'and despite certain . . . certain tragic events of late, the successful conclusion of the operation fills me heart with joy. I'd like to thank so many people that it's hard to know where to begin . . .'

Langham gazed at Maria, radiant in the sunlight, as she smiled across at the major.

'Enjoying yourself?' he asked.

She kissed him. 'Of course, my darling.'

Ryland raised his camera and called out, 'One for the album!'